Songbird

Raymond Bruce

THE SONGBIRD

Published by Redux Publishing

ISBN: 979-8-9929326-2-1

DEDICATION

To Christy

The Songbird

Raymond Bruce

A small songbird, the wren is typically active and inquisitive. Wrens are fiercely protective of their nests and territory.

PROLOGUE

This ain't where it started
This ain't where it ends
Just a stop in between
And a pint with some friends

The quatrain, wood-burned onto a piece of reclaimed driftwood, hangs above the rear exit of the Eastside Taproom. Tony's daughter gave it to him for the 20th anniversary of the day he opened his bar.

The Taproom has now been closed since the weekend Brody Todd disappeared.

With a bit of imagination, detectives were able to loosely reconstruct that Friday evening. It took imagination because security footage was limited and so was sobriety as the bar neared closing time.

This is what happened.

Anyone walking up the alley behind the Taproom will pass through the spill of light from the Taproom's exterior lamp.

The parking garage across that alley is better lit; the cold fluorescents showcase the structure's deterioration. The flaking yellow stripes. The spalling concrete.

Only a half-dozen vehicles occupy that lot at just past midnight, although it's busier during the day with the government offices located along Carter.

Brody Todd's truck is parked about six spaces deep, two tires overlapping a handicap spot.

With the rusted fenders and the cracked windshield, the white Ford doesn't look like it belongs to someone who works at a dealership.

But Brody did buy the truck from Boeckman Motors once upon a time.

Once upon a time. The theme of his life.

A few other patrons have parked in the lot, as well, but the weekend scene in this neighborhood has been dying for years. Just two blocks down from Eastside, the pool hall closed at midnight.

Otherwise, the storefronts have been dark all evening, and the streets remain mostly empty.

Two cameras typically survey the lower floor of the garage. When the Mariston police request the footage in the coming days, they'll find that the cameras haven't recorded anything for two weeks.

If the devices were functional, detectives would probably match all but one of the vehicles to the patrons of the Taproom.

Nobody inside Tony's bar arrived in the gray Camry parked nose-out at the far end of the garage.

Surveillance elsewhere in the neighborhood recorded the Camry approaching the garage approximately an hour earlier.

While that footage didn't catch the license plate or the driver, a vehicle matching the description was reported stolen the morning after Todd's disappearance.

It was found abandoned days later.

Back through the garage, country music comes muffled from in the bar. Through the rear entrance and past the restrooms, a short hallway opens into intentionally dim lighting.

Six customers remain, and Jason Aldean sings to them about small-town justice.

INTERVIEW OF ANTHONY HARDIN (excerpt)

For clarity, unnecessary words like "um" and "ah" have been omitted from the following transcript.

Detective Wren: So, you had just four customers that night? Around the time that Todd left?
Anthony Hardin: Five, if you count Brody.
Detective Casey: Slow all night?
Anthony Hardin: Everything's moved to downtown now after the revitalization shit. That's where the kids go, at least. Maybe I should put $17 bourbon shots on the menu. Don't know where they get the money.

The Eastside is Brody's style. It's where he and his buddies got tanked years ago, and the taps do the trick just as well now. The Taproom stays open until 1:00, the latest allowed by the city.

Brody stares into his mug, thinking about the couple who'd walked away from his best shot at a commission all week.

But the husband wanted to play hardball, claiming to have found the same make and model cheaper in St. Louis. Probably so. The gateway dealerships played the volume game.

But Boeckman Motors is a hometown business. When Brody started with the dealership, loyalty meant something. People traded with Boeckman then because "Big Vince" sponsored ball teams and college scholarships.

"Bet he didn't think …" Brody's elbow slips on the bar as he hunches over his mug. "Bet he …" He loses his train of thought.

Nate thumbs through his phone. The two men are a contrast. Nate seems like he can eat anything without putting on a pound, whereas Brody had just picked up some new trousers for work and found he'd expanded to a size 40. Even then, he only managed to squeeze into a brand with a "flex fit" waistband.

"Probably be back tomorrow." Nate says without much conviction as he looks up from his phone and scans the bar, realizing how empty it has become. "He's just trying to make you sweat, man."

And Brody is sweating it, though he tries not to let on. There was no commission today or yesterday to pay for tonight's beer.

He'd sold a Malibu on Tuesday—no warranty, no backend. The week was bleeding out.

"Yeah, I'll see them again." But Brody isn't hopeful.

"Hey, I gots to go," Nate says, patting Brody on the back and tossing cash on the bar.

Brody turns slightly on his stool, surveying the place. A couple of guys rack up their last game at one of the two tables up front. Brody doesn't know them, but he *thinks* he knows the mousy guy feeding dollars into the bar top slots.

And he wishes he knew the brunette between that guy and himself. She looks to be in her early 40s and is half-watching baseball highlights on the screen over the taps. The Redbirds continued their losing streak earlier on Friday.

The woman is nursing her second Amaretto sour.

Detective Wren: The guy at the slots?
Anthony Hardin: Didn't know him. Drank vodka tonics and fed dollars into the machine for a couple hours. Been here before, but like I said, I don't know him.

Detective Wren: The two guys at the pool table?
Anthony Hardin: Them neither. Maybe Quinton, one of 'em.
Detective Wren: Ever thought of investing in more cameras? Crime's up on your side of town.
Anthony Hardin: Why bother? Retirement sounds easier. The east side is dead. Punks run the neighborhood, like you say. And, hell, with Todd gone now, I lost damned near a fifth of my customer base.
Detective Casey: Just saying, dude, cameras would have been helpful.

"I'll get the next of whatever she's having," Brody says to Tony, who glances at the brunette with a wry smile.

She ignores the offer. Brody shrugs.

Tony wanders over with a rag in one hand and wipes down the bar where Nate had been sitting. "Don't worry about it, Brode-man. She's holding out for a rich old guy with a bad heart."

The woman at the bar smirks and shows Tony her middle finger without even a glance in their direction.

"I'll take her drink, then," Brody says, pushing the empty mug toward Tony.

"Brody," he says flatly, "you're on number four, and last time you went for five, I had to replace a picture frame you knocked off the wall on the way to the toilet."

Brody smirks. "I was redirecting the Feng Shui."

Tony doesn't smile back. "Your buddy left. Need me to call a ride?"

"Yeah … call the president of the People's Republic of the United States of Chinerica." Brody attempts to climb off his stool, but stumbles backward into a table. "Tell him I need Air Force One and a security detail."

Tony doesn't answer. He sees the stumble and detects the slur.

Brody knows he is fine to drive home. Just a little buzzed.

"Which is it, Brody? Am I calling a taxi or Samantha?"

At the mention of Brody's wife, the bartender's sister shakes her head.

But Brody isn't a cheat.

He just doesn't look forward to going home on a Friday night with the same … *expectations* … as he might have earlier in the marriage.

"I'll get my own damned ride." He pats his pockets before realizing that his phone is on the bar in front of him.

Opening the McDonald's app, Brody tries to order a double cheeseburger for the ride home. A little food will offset the alcohol. But the app reminds him that the closest location closed at midnight.

"There," he says, closing the app. "My driver, Ramesh, will be here in five."

Dropping a wad of bills on the counter, Brody grabs his jacket from the stool.

"Later," he says to no one in particular.

Tony doesn't respond.

Detective Wren: Did you think he actually called for a ride?

Anthony Hardin: Maybe he did. Maybe that's who did him in, right? You check out the driver?

Detective Casey: The Uber never happened, bro. He was impaired, and you let him walk out, right? And he tried to drive.

Anthony Hardin: Like I said, I'm done with it all. Tired of the shit. Tired of guys like Brody Todd.

Brody fumbles and drops his keys outside the Taproom, nearly falling as he shifts to pick them up. The bar music is muffled by the closed door, and the warm night air absorbs every sound in the world but a fluorescent hum. As he nears his truck, Brody's heavy steps echo in the garage.

Just before pulling himself up and into his truck, Brody pisses against the garage wall. He notices, as he stands there, that his tire is wearing unevenly on the outside edge. He'll have to replace them soon.

Big Vince no longer lets the sales team borrow the inventory like in the early days. If he could hit a good streak, Brody wanted to upgrade to something that doesn't have a growing set of rust tumors and a hair-trigger engine light.

Inside the truck, Brody backs up in a wide arc several feet before he hears and feels the rear of his truck scrape a pillar.

"Dammit."

He pulls forward without noticing the gray sedan exiting from a spot deep in the garage. The vehicle's headlights remain dark as Brody crawls through the garage exit.

Both vehicles disappear down the road as, back in the Taproom, Tony announces last call.

Brody turns left and heads west on Monroe. The car follows. It'll be a few miles away from the Taproom before the low-pressure light appears on his dash and he pulls over to check it.

Because the Eastside Taproom is not where the bad stuff started.

And it won't be where it ends.

CHAPTER 1

My phone buzzed just past 6:45, and I knocked it off the nightstand trying to find it with my eyes still glued shut from exhaustion.

This was about two hours earlier than I would have preferred to crawl out of bed. Most mornings, I was up before five while Henry slept. Enough time to run, shower, dress, and caffeinate.

Yet, despite enough Excedrin to bump the company's stock, I was working with barely four hours of sleep, my night punctuated every half-hour by a throbbing skull and bladder.

Besides sleeping in, I'd hoped to use the day to catch up on laundry, and I'd also promised Henry we'd go out for his birthday lunch after I picked him up from the friend's house where he'd spent the night.

But Henry's gift from Mom was likely to be a gift-wrapped box of disappointment.

Because when I saw the call was from Roy Hollis, my lieutenant, I knew my plans were shattered.

"What's up?" I shifted into a sitting position on the mattress. The change to vertical made the headache worse.

"Wren, it's Roy." Hollis had a habit of stating the obvious. "Hope you were looking for something productive to do today."

My top, bra, and shoes from last night were on the floor next to my bed. I had fallen asleep on top of my bedding, dressed in jeans and a Dead Sara t-shirt. Did I like the band? Yes. Did I buy the t-shirt to be ironic?

Also yes.

From my seated position, I made the mistake of glancing at the dresser mirror. My eyes were puffy and a little red. I'd straightened my hair for Ed, but hours of tossing and turning had left me with tangles of brown.

"Body in a church parking lot," Hollis continued. "I don't think he's here for the praise and worship. It's another mutilation. Got officers securing the scene."

Another mutilation. It took me a moment—the cylinders weren't all firing yet.

"A connection to the El Rincón body?"

"Maybe. You'll see."

About a week ago, we'd found a guy, dead and nude, outside a Mexican restaurant on the east side of town. James Woodhouse—Jimmy to his friends and family.

Two women had spotted the late Mr. Woodhouse on a greenway bench alongside the El Rincón parking lot. From a distance, the corpse might have passed for a morning jogger taking a break. Since the body had also been stripped of all clothing, they kept their distance. Otherwise, they would have noticed the burn marks covering his face and body.

The case was still hot, no pun intended. Okay … intended just a little.

But a week later, we still had no solid leads.

Hollis said that this morning's John Doe had been found in the parking lot of the Second Baptist Church on Dunklin and Ash. The first cops on the scene arrived just in time to put up a cordon before the choir began arriving for the 7:00 service.

"Jesus," I muttered.

"I suspect that's what Pastor Campbell said," Hollis replied. "But probably not as reverentially as you."

"I'm told I'm pretty reverential." My phone clamped between my shoulder and ear, I dug through my closet, tossing items on the bed.

In the background of the call, I heard the quick yelp of an emergency vehicle. Hollis shouted to someone on the scene, telling them to keep another someone "over there and out of the way."

"Casey's already here," Hollis said.

"Hey, Wren," Detective Casey said from somewhere nearby.

"But you're heading up the investigation," Hollis finished.

As a sergeant and senior detective, I was also overseeing the Woodhouse murder.

"I guess I'm late to the party. How long have you been there?"

"Check your phone log. I tried you twice already."

"Yeah, okay. Give me a few. Coffee, clothes. Have we ID'd the body?"

"Possibly a guy named Brody Todd. Wife reported him missing early Saturday morning—around 1:45—when he never came home from the bar and wouldn't answer his cell."

"Yeah, that was on my radar." I tossed a blouse and slacks on the bed. My shoes were scattered on the closet floor. Ed was the neat one. One of the Chelseas I was searching for was in the actual caddy. The other boot was missing and none of its friends were talking.

"The corpse resembles photos of Todd," Hollis continued, "though I don't think the head is shaped exactly the way it was the last time he took a selfie."

I finally found the other boot. It was behind an unopened box containing a jewelry rack that Ed bought me last Christmas.

The background noise from Hollis's end filled a short pause, and I thought of the crowd that would have gathered by now.

"The Woodhouse body was unclothed."

"This one, too," Hollis said, anticipating my concern. "But the responding officers blocked most of the view with their vehicles and put up a tarp."

"Tarp is good."

Hollis finished. "Also, there's … another similarity with last week. Shit, this crowd is growing." And then to someone on the scene, "No! Don't touch that!"

"Take care of things there," I said. "I'm on my way."

"Yeah, okay. See you in a bit."

Hollis forgot to disconnect the call, and I listened to about fifteen seconds of cursing and yelling before ending it, myself.

Over the years, the rank of lieutenant had become mostly a desk job in our precinct. Nearing retirement, Hollis was getting too old (in cop years) and cranky to manage rookies and gawkers at a crime scene.

I needed to rescue him.

Tossing my phone on the bed, I ran to turn on the shower and made a quick run to the kitchen to start the Keurig.

Two water glasses sat upside down on a towel, where they'd dried overnight.

Ed.

He'd declined another drink and (to my disappointment) the offer to stay over, but we'd chatted on the couch for a bit. Kissed a bit. Beyond that, I don't remember how I got from the living room to the bedroom.

Dashing back down the hall and through the bedroom, I pulled my hair into a ponytail. I didn't have time to dry or style it. The bottle of Excedrin was still open near the bathroom sink. I popped three more and stepped into the shower.

Turning the knob further to the left, I leaned into the spray, hoping the hot water would massage the headache away. I then switched it to cold to shock myself alert. As I lathered, scrubbed, and rinsed, I tried to process the limited information from Hollis's call.

Both bodies appeared to have been staged in relatively public locations.

El Rincón is a Mexican restaurant on the west side of town. Anyone using the trail there would have seen Woodhouse's body. And this morning, another corpse had been found in a parking lot that should have been filled for worship by now. How many families have arrived, kids in tow, only to find police tape and death?

As I stepped out of the shower a few minutes later, it hit me again that more than just *my* day had been ruined.

I allowed myself one or two choice words—nothing Pastor Campbell would have condoned—as I grabbed my phone to text Ed. I tapped the dictation icon while I toweled off.

Hey, I need you to pick up Henry this morning. Call me when you wake up. All hands on deck.

My nautical reference was, I acknowledged, a euphemism. I wanted to avoid exacerbating an ongoing conflict between me and Ed. Our date last night felt good. For the evening, I had been able to put aside thoughts of the El Rincón case.

This had been the first nice evening we'd had together since Ed moved out in May and into this phase called *separation.* Maybe we were on the road back to normal, he and I and Henry.

No problem, Ed responded. A few dancing bubbles appeared as he continued his response.

Then, a pause. I didn't like pauses.

Finally, *He can give me a hand washing the car and all the Sunday stuff.*

All the Sunday stuff.

Ed didn't mean for that last text to sting. Despite the interruption to our marriage, he remained supportive and approachable. But it was tough to think of them spending Henry's birthday together doing domestic things while I worked a crime scene.

Did Henry already think of the condo as *Dad's place*?

I don't know if his suggestion of a trial separation was meant as a wake-up call to me or if this was just the shallow end of a deeper swim.

All hands on deck meant that I wouldn't be available for Henry's birthday lunch. Maybe supper instead. Maybe tomorrow. Ed knew how it worked.

Sadly, Henry did, too.

CHAPTER 2

The 2000 blocks of Ash were almost all commercial. The Mariston Second Baptist Church sat between a mattress store to the right and an insurance company to the left.

Most of the businesses closed over the weekend. The few exceptions included the church and a chromy diner near the intersection. They shared the same Sunday morning crowd.

I parked across the street. Two news crews had already arrived and claimed the lot at the insurance building. To avoid them, I approached from the other direction.

By now, someone from the CSU would have snapped photos of the gathered crowd and started scouting for potential witnesses. The onlookers largely reflected the congregation of a church in a low-income, mostly-black neighborhood.

Generally, the gawkers were respectful and kept their distance. A handful of kids had gathered for the show, most in shorts and t-shirts.

Thankfully, the responding officers had arrived early enough to block off the alley adjacent to the parking lot, giving us plenty of room to work.

Looping the badge cord around my neck, I ducked under the tape, signed the scene log, and approached Hollis, who handed me a Styrofoam cup. The black stuff inside was still steaming.

"Thanks," I muttered, scanning the scene.

"Happy Sunday."

"It's Henry's birthday. We were planning on lunch together with Ed. So, yeah, happy Sunday."

Hollis didn't respond. He knew I wasn't complaining, but he also knew Ed and I were struggling. Hollis got divorced just over a decade-and-a-half ago. That would have put him about my age at the time.

Note to self: don't pick Hollis for a life coach.

"I'm hoping we had a chance to walk the perimeter before the crowd arrived?" I scanned the parking lot, assessing the activity.

"Yeah, and Casey did a 360 of the scene."

Hollis looks like a seasoned cop whether you spot him at the hardware store or riding the Whirl-a-Wheel at the county fair. The permanent furrow in his brows. The white-gray fuzz over his espresso cheeks.

I'm hoping that the stress and long hours haven't aged me too much. I *think* I can still put on some makeup and a short dress and pull off a seven.

A Mariston seven, at least.

Fun fact: the Lieutenant also has a glass eye. He lost his left one during a struggle with a meth head earlier in his career. A couple of days after I got promoted to detective under him, I found the eye sitting on my desk, positioned to stare me down when I returned from lunch.

Next to it, a note: *I've got my eye on you!*

Hollis owns another artificial eye with the iris missing—just a black-dot pupil floating in a milky white pond of creepy. He bought it off a discount site and sometimes pops it in to spice up interrogations and Halloween.

At the rear steps to the church, I spot Casey in an Oxford and loosened tie. He's talking with one of our worker bees.

Detective Pete Casey's been with the force for six years. He's tireless and thorough.

Casey also happens to hold the record for pull-ups at the precinct gym. He looks great in a shirt like that, those biceps visibly sculpted through the tight sleeves. It's the kind of physique that someone not nearly as professional as me would notice at a crime scene.

He spots my arrival and sums up the morning with a quick raise of those Zachary Quinto eyebrows.

Here we go again, he says in that one gesture.

Returning to his conversation with a uniformed cop, Casey waves his hand at the apartments behind the parking lot.

I quickly peek through a gap in the tarp.

The signs of blunt trauma are obvious. The morning's shower, caffeine, and pills had reduced the throb in my head to a dull pulse. One look at the corpse reminded me that my headache could have been worse.

"Pastor find the body?"

Hollis shook his head. "Volunteer."

The hand with the coffee cup indicated an elderly black man standing against the yellow tape. The guy was thin, hunched, and old enough to have attended Sunday services back when Jesus was preaching.

"Name's Albert," Hollis continued. "Arrived early to unlock doors, turn on lights. Said he didn't touch anything. Said he knew it was murder."

"You think?" I considered the victim's bean bag head. "We should hire Albert with a gift of intuition like that."

Another news crew arrived and parked close to where a perky blonde and her cameraman had already set up. I recognized her from the Woodhouse crime scene. She spotted me spotting her and her eyes lit up. When she stepped up to the tape, I turned away and pretended to be deaf as she called out my name.

A CSU tech was nearby, a camera around her neck. I gave her a quick nod.

"Did you get overheads?"

"Not yet. Drone's in my trunk."

Glancing over my shoulder, I saw a mother holding her toddler. Several teenage boys pushed against the tape.

"Maybe leave the drone," I told her. "We don't need to attract more neighborhood kids. Find the pastor and have him get you access up there." I indicated a window on the second floor. "I want to get moving on this so we can clear the scene."

While several crime scene photos would have been taken by now, there was work to do before we could examine the corpse without sabotaging admissibility.

"Okay," I said with a sigh, pushing a tarp aside. "Let's see what we've got here."

Hollis followed me in.

As the lieutenant had shared over the phone, the corpse was naked. I guesstimated that about 250 lumpy pounds of him had been left on display for us today. Todd obviously enjoyed his carbs, beer, and deep-fried balls of butter.

"Whoever moved this guy probably needed Motrin this morning." I circled the body to internalize as much as I could of the *in-situ* condition.

As there was no visible trace of blood on the asphalt, this was likely just the dump site.

"Too bad he left the body so neatly placed inside the lines," Hollis said. "Otherwise, we could bust him for double parking, too."

I glanced at my lieutenant and blinked twice. "You know what double parking is, right?"

"Yes, Wren, I know what double parking is. It was a joke."

"I mean, it's Traffic Cop 101, Roy." I crouched down next to the corpse.

"I should have let you sleep."

Bad joke aside, Hollis was correct that the body had been placed neatly within the lines of one of the spaces. Had the killer staged it this way? Possibly. Everything looked deliberate.

One of the deceased's arms extended above his head, the other bent along his side. The legs were in running position. It would have resembled a cliché chalk outline except that his legs each had an additional bend below the knee. The tibiae had been shattered. Flashbacks of nasty encounters with coffee tables was enough to make me wince.

By the looks of it, the beating had continued even past death. But this wasn't the most intriguing detail.

And in addition to the brutal contusions, a section of skin had been removed from the victim's back.

Hollis saw me studying the marking. "That's the similarity to Woodhouse I mentioned on the phone."

"Yeah, I see it. But it's—"

For a brief moment, everything stopped inside the tape as someone in the crowd belted out the first lines of a gospel song.

When peace, like a river, attendeth my way …

Soon, several others joined in.

It is well, it is well with my soul …

"I hope they don't do a collection," I said. "I'm broke."

A box of latex gloves sat on the ground next to the body. I plucked two. It was time to get to work.

The tarp flapped behind me. Casey joined us and squatted next to me.

"Morning, Traviesa." Casey often used this ambiguously flirty nickname for me. Despite three years of high school Spanish, I'd had to Google the word the first time he'd used it.

Troublemaker.

"Rough night?" he asked.

"Not as rough as this guy. Assuming it's Todd, do we know much about him?"

"It's definitely Todd. Middle-aged. Lower-middle income. Wife. Two kids."

Our victim fit a similar demographic to the El Rincón victim.

There had also been a section of skin missing from Woodhouse's body. A thin, rectangular piece of flesh had been stripped from overtop his spinal region, approximately a foot from top to bottom. As with this body, Woodhouse's epidermal layer had been removed post-mortem. There was no evidence of the blood-spill that would have resulted had the heart still been pumping.

Since the removal of flesh hadn't been torture, I assumed the killer had kept the skin as a souvenir. I had resisted entertaining the inevitable images that came from years of horror films–the killer at home, wearing his mother's underwear and a mask of dehydrated skin.

The missing strip of flesh wasn't large enough for a mask, anyway. But it would make a cute coin purse or some fun wristbands.

But now, it was obvious what Hollis had implied over the phone. The strip that had been removed from Woodhouse's body had been a message to us.

Though we didn't realize it at the time, it was the number 1.

A large 3 had been carved into this corpse with precise lines and angles, like the digital number on a microwave. Let's call this font *psychopath sans*.

Was last week's victim the *first* in a series? It seemed that could be the case.

Two flies landed and began exploring the wound. I shooed them away, careful not to touch the body.

"Coffee wake you up enough that you can guess my first question when I saw that?" Casey asked.

"If this guy is number three," I said without looking up from the corpse. "Then where's the second body?"

CHAPTER 3

Henry was slumped against the car door and breathing deeply by the time we turned off 7th and headed north toward home. Shirtless and shoeless, he'd repurposed his travel bag as a pillow. A still-moist swim towel served as a blanket over his lap.

It was evening. The sun floated just over the horizon ahead of me as I drove west toward an orange-pink sky.

We rode in silence, the radio off and the air on low.

Henry breathed deep and slow.

I glanced at him frequently in my rearview mirror, still shaken by an afternoon trip to the Todd household.

Our family liaison officer arranged a visit with Samantha Todd for early evening.

The house matched what I had learned about Todd's life. Clover choked the flower beds, and the siding begged for a power wash. Though it was June, Christmas lights drooped from the gutters.

Sam Todd wore jeans and an oversized shirt when Casey and I came to the door. Her hair was pulled into a ponytail and she wasn't wearing make-up. The little guy she held tried to show me his plastic truck while we talked on the doorstep. He had no idea.

Todd's widow struggled to push all of the words out of her mouth, clutching her son's head close to her chest to muffle the conversation. She wanted to know what we knew, and we wanted to know what she knew, but this wasn't the time or place. We'd give her a day or two to process the news before a more thorough sit-down.

I generally compartmentalize well, but I was struggling, even if I had conditioned myself not to reveal it.

It was the kid I couldn't stop thinking about.

Not the toddler on her hip. Another boy—nine or ten years old—half-hidden behind the hallway wall, watching his mom fall apart. Watching me biting my lip and giving silence its moment before saying all the things you say when you have a badge and you're standing on the doorstep of a newly-widowed mother.

An older woman, probably the kids' grandma, appeared inside by the boy. She pulled him back into another room, but not before I'd caught his eyes. For a second, I saw Henry looking back at me from around that corner. Not crying. Just soaking in my words so they could crawl into his brain and rewire everything he believed about life and people and hope.

No one prepares you for that. There's no page in a handbook and no day of cop school that explains how to look back at a child that age and not think about what your words just stole from him.

How much am I screwing up my own son? What dysfunctions manifest in a boy when his mom's soul carries the weight of a town's sins?

At a stoplight, I reached back and found one of Henry's knees, grasping it softly, not to wake him. Just to connect with my now nine-year-old little guy. With a quick glance over my shoulder, I took a mental picture of his sleeping face, the dark hair curls pasted against his forehead.

His shoulders, nose, and back were sunburn pink.

Because *of course* Ed's condo has a community pool.

Ed isn't being competitive. The pool just came with the rent. I believe him when he says he wants to keep working on us. The date last night—it had felt like things were healing.

Until Ed looked at his watch.

"Sometimes you need to step outside of something to see it clearly. To diagnose it," he'd said back in May, the night the word *separation* became a part of our working vocabulary.

It felt, though, that it was me, not the marriage, that was the thing being diagnosed.

We were on the patio then, the door closed and Henry asleep. Ursa Major lumbered across the sky. The almost full moon was a spotlight on my crisis.

Ed, being Ed, tried to rationalize. I remember staring at the brick of our house as he stumbled through some stupid analogy about being an architect and being separated from the emotions when he designed a home.

Objectivity, he said at one point.

Perspective, he said at another.

"You need space ..." He said to me, as if this split was a gift to me. Except, after a pause, this part followed: "... to figure out how I fit in."

Ed's architect brain knew how to fit things in. A nook over here. A powder room over there. He felt, it seemed, as if he were something extra in my life right now that I'd found storage for under the stairs.

There are moments—this being one of them--when I wonder if either of us understands what is really going on. Occasional dates. Late-night, sometimes-sobby phone calls. Are these attempts to reconcile or just interludes in our journey of dissolution?

"Do you still love me?" I'd finally asked him, not making eye contact. It was the only thing I remember saying after he asked if we could talk. I couldn't look him in the eyes, but instead watched a moth struggling in a spider web as I waited for the answer.

"Of course, I love you," he'd said. Saying this broke him. He lowered his head, swallowed hard, and then wiped his eyes. "And I'm trying to make sure we can both say that a decade from now."

When I picked up Henry this evening, I noticed with a small knot in my gut that Ed wasn't wearing his ring anymore. Were we still separated, I wondered, or had the next terrible step begun?

In the house that Ed and I own together, some of his clothes still hang in our walk-in closet. Many of his past projects remain in his home office—floor plans and schematics for houses and commercial spaces.

It's the place with our family pictures on the wall, not just propped on tables, like in his condo.

It's the place where Henry's birthday measurements climb the garage wall. Four feet and two inches last year. Tonight, we'll measure him again. Just he and I.

As we tossed wet clothes into my backseat, Ed apologized for Henry's sunburn, promising that they had used sunblock, which must have washed off. In front of us both, Henry asked if he could come over and go swimming again this week. He'd met some other boys his age.

I allowed myself the drive home for self-pity. But only that. Mariston had its first serial killer in … forever?

Tomorrow will be an early morning for me. But I wanted my son home with me tonight, on his birthday. The intensity of my job was about to increase substantially, so we might not see each other much over the next several days.

But while Henry was old enough that we often trusted him to stay home alone, I didn't feel good about it right now. Sensing my conflict, Ed volunteered that during my shifts he could relocate his home office back to our house …

our house

… for as long as I needed.

If I worked late, he assured me, he'd throw a pillow on the couch and stay the night.

Maybe it was guilt. Maybe it was mercy.

Probably it was pity.

Regardless, I had a set of murders to solve. While we didn't have confirmation of a serial pattern, the nature of the victims' death and post-mortem mutilation suggested something more sinister than two isolated murders.

The next several days would be exhausting as we conducted interviews and scrutinized footage.

But, for now, I needed to get back to my home and my son and decompress.

Our house at the end of the cul-de-sac butted up against several acres of conservation land. While the two-story craftsman had been built in the 70s, Ed had designed the expansions. In our eight years there as a family, we'd expanded the kitchen and living room.

Rolling to a quiet stop in the garage, I killed the engine and twisted to glance at Henry, who remained asleep. I brushed hair from his forehead.

"Hey, Bubba." I squeezed his knee again. "We're home, Hankster."

"Time for ice cream cake?" he asked, eyes still closed while he slapped the towel off himself.

"You got it. Ice cream for the birthday boy."

At the mention of food, I realized the hunger I'd been suppressing. I'd been going since just past dawn and hadn't had more than a couple of protein bars and a cheeseburger.

I'd hoped for us to eat the birthday cake this afternoon as a family-complete.

But Ed had already had his time with Henry.

I immediately hated myself for that moment of spite.

With my arms full of boy clothes, I used an elbow to close the garage door to everything that threatened to steal from my time from Henry.

Tomorrow would be another long day of digesting the crime scene documentation and area video surveillance. But tonight, I'm celebrating nine years of being the mother of the most amazing little guy in the world.

CHAPTER 4

He'd been monitoring the news, of course.

"... another gruesome murder ..." The blonde on Channel 17 nodded her head as she spoke. She stood alongside the lot of the Dunklin Street Second Baptist Church.

The reporter hoped this was a reel-worthy opportunity, he realized. She'd send the clips of these broadcasts with her resume when she applied for jobs in St. Louis or Kansas City.

And, by then, the score would have been settled and his motive known well beyond Mariston.

Because there was more work to be done, following a pattern that only he understood at this time.

"Police will not comment on whether there is a connection to last week's discovery of a victim found along the greenway trail," the reporter said. She knew how to suggest a narrative without asserting it.

> *of course a connection but cops too blind to see it now did they notice that brodytodd number three maybe another body would help them and that would be soon enough*

The Walker leaned forward on his couch, watching the cops bumble around the crime scene behind the reporter. One of the reasons he'd left the bodies in such public places was to make sure that it wasn't only from the badges that the media got their information.

Not only would it take some of the control away from the detectives, but it would build up a public frenzy that would tax the valuable time and resources that the cops would need to study the murders.

"The killer appears to be *numbering* his victims, according to witnesses," the blonde continued. "Police have yet to officially confirm this information, but an unidentified source connected to the investigation confirms that markings on the victim's body do resemble one-digit numbers."

> *show the number newsgirl but of course she cant didnt show jimmywoodhouse either but he knew they knew but there were things they didnt know not yet*

Probably someone above her head in the studio had made the decision to minimize the graphic details and the speculation about another body.

But he could see in her eyes that she wanted to show what he had done. She knew her viewers were hungry for the truth that the police were trying to hide.

He hadn't killed Todd or Woodhouse for the attention, but he was surprised how much he enjoyed the celebrity. Soon they would give him a nickname like in the movies. *The Numbers Killer*, maybe.

But he liked to think of himself simply as *The Walker*, a name he might reveal later. It invoked horror films with lunatics trudging through the woods. It implied his deliberate and calm approach to subduing his victims.

Yes.

The Walker.

but there was another reason for the walker that they will find out and that brodytodd and jimmywoodhouse now knew didnt they after he really hammered it in and burned it into their thoughts had burned it in good do you remember me jimmywoodhouse do you jimmywoodhouse

He'd recorded the evening news from all three of the local stations, but this blonde was his favorite. She understood that he had a story to tell.

"The victim matches the description of a recent missing person," she said.

"While police did not offer comment on other leads, sources claim a white Ford truck, possibly belonging to the victim, was found abandoned alongside Rte. 4008 early Saturday morning.

The Walker remembered being concerned when he'd seen exactly how drunk Todd appeared to be as he stumbled from the bar and almost face dove onto the alley. Then, Todd had nearly backed his vehicle into a concrete pillar.

Todd dying from an accident on the way home would have been a disappointing turn of events. But once out of the parking garage, Todd's truck had navigated the empty streets with a wavy precision that kept him mostly in the right lanes.

About halfway along the route to his house, though, Todd must have noticed the tire-pressure light come on. His truck edged toward the shoulder. Though not quite making it all the way off the road, the truck had come to a stop.

Following close behind, The Walker had also pulled over—a concerned motorist helping out his fellow man.

When Todd climbed from his truck and began inspecting his tires, The Walker had stepped out of his own vehicle and approached.

By then, Todd had located the problem tire and leaned over, using his phone's flashlight to look for a hole.

> *do you need a hand there buddy looks like you picked up a nail or something can i give you a ride big lug brodytodd get you home easypeasyskullsqueezy*

Walker had worn a low-level disguise—ball cap, glasses, and a pasted mustache—and he tried to deepen his voice.

> *do you recognize me friend we go back a ways dont we but no brodytodd dont recognize because drunk brodytodd kept cursing and spitting damn tires damned truck damned wife damned life*

"Too late for that," The Walker had said as Todd began searching for the jack. "Cops are out tonight, and you don't look fit to drive, buddy."

Eventually, Todd relented and agreed to park his truck on a nearby gravel drive.

Todd had followed him back to the Camry and climbed into the passenger seat as The Walker returned to the driver's side.

"Here, you look like you need to hydrate," The Walker said. Twisting the cap off the bottle, he offered to Todd. "It'll hold off the hangover."

> *drink it better for both of us if you guzzle it down brodytodd thirsty brodytodd toadybodd now eartug go to sleep old friend*

Thankfully, Todd took the bottle and emptied it in a quick succession of swallows. The drug shouldn't have worked as quickly as it did, but the alcohol contributed to the effort.

Brody Todd was unconscious before they were a mile out from the abandoned truck.

The irony of modern media's obsession with violence was that newscasters, blending solemnity and urgency, provided him with more information about the investigation than the other way around. The coverage was a one-way mirror by which he could observe the floundering of his main adversary.

Sergeant Sara Wren.

The name appeared at the bottom of the screen during the report.

"We're dedicating 100% of our resources to this investigation." The detective read from a script that had no doubt been prepared by the department's communications team. It was meant to sound optimistic, but non-committal.

"We're hopeful," the detective continued, "that with the cooperation of the public, we'll soon be able to move forward and identify potential suspects."

This and other clips from the statement had appeared on various media broadcasts. Even though the detective was years from retirement, the weight of her job could be seen in her eyes.

Despite her small package, Detective Wren exerted her authority and her command over the situation through her tone and her direct eye contact with the camera. She would glance quickly at her script and then repeat the words with conviction.

She had a face for the camera, too. Hardened, but attractive. The bonus was the little Cindy Crawford freckle. The Walker knew he would enjoy watching Wren's public resolve deteriorate over the coming weeks as her team struggled to make meaningful progress.

hello songbird smallbutloud but soon singing a different song

One of the evening broadcasts played brief interviews from witnesses to the scene.

"What happened to that man ..." began one elderly black woman, tears welling in her eyes as she looked away for a moment and struggled for composure. "And to leave him there by our *church* for the children to see ... The devil's in this thing. The devil's in this thing *deep*."

The Walker considered it a bonus to know there were children at the scene. That he'd sewn evil into their day and nightmares into their sleep.

He hadn't chosen the church for that reason, but it had to be *that* location where they found Todd's body. That specific church. Eventually, the songbird would realize that.

Eventually.

On his timeline, not hers.

CHAPTER 5

What had we missed with the Woodhouse murder? Throughout Monday's grind, this was the question I kept asking myself.

I'd been up, showered and dressed since 4:00. There was a limit to what I could do at the kitchen table with my laptop, but I'd needed to wait for Ed to arrive before I could leave Henry. When I checked on him this morning, he was still asleep, his new Xbox controller snuggled against his body like a plush toy.

Ed hugged me when he arrived. No kiss (and still no ring), but he knew the weight I was carrying. He and I had talked about the case after Henry fell asleep the night before. This was the biggest thing I'd handled since receiving a detective's badge, and I'd be lying if I said I wasn't intimidated.

"Got time for breakfast? Eggs?" Ed asked. He saw my open laptop and no empty plates on the table. He knew I tended to neglect myself when work got heavy.

"Over easy, please."

Ed glanced at me over his shoulder. "Not scrambled?"

"Changing things up. Midlife crisis. Don't forget the cheese."

As I packed my computer and a few scattered documents, I watched him flip, salt, and pepper. Ed wore a polo and dress slacks. Even though he now did most of his work from home, he still insisted on showering and dressing for "the office." It was a way of psychologically transitioning himself to work mode within his living space.

"How are you feeling about things?" he asked as he ran a block of sharp cheddar against the grinder and sprinkled it over my eggs. "This seems like a tough one."

"It's a tough one," I agreed, grabbing my mug from under the Keurig. "It doesn't help that the media cuts our feet out from under us. I've decided I hate Stacey Southern."

"Who's Stacey Southern?"

"The blonde chick with Channel 17 news. She leaked information we didn't want leaked."

I told Ed how we'd tried to keep some details confidential, such as the numeric mutilation on the two corpses.

Now that information was public, I imagined nicknames the media might conceive. *The Auditer*?

Or, I hope not, *The Count.* We'd be on the lookout for an autistic vampire.

"I suspect she flirted the information out of Albert," I said as Ed used his spatula to guide the eggs from the cast iron onto my plate. "He's the volunteer who found the body."

Ed has started letting his hair grow out some. It was from him that Henry got his dark curls, but Ed had kept a pretty tight haircut for the last decade or so. I don't know if it was bachelor neglect or a subtle reinvention of himself, but I felt conflicted.

Ed's hair, along with his dark eyes, were crush material when we met two decades ago, and they were doing their work on me again. But then I remembered that this was my *estranged* husband serving up my eggs over easy.

I sprinkled hot sauce and shoveled my breakfast down at the counter.

"I'll get this," he said, taking the plate from me at the sink. "Anything you need done today?"

I swallowed back snark, my default reaction to nearly any question when I'm stressed or upset. Ed was trying, I realized. But was I?

"Towels are in the dryer, if you want to fold them," I said. "And you can switch the whites over."

"Towels and whites, got it."

For just a moment, my legs didn't work. Ed sat back against the counter, holding my dirty plate.

"You're going to crack this," he said.

"Yeah." I turned to leave. "Text me when Henry's up."

By six a.m., I was at my desk. There was little other activity in the bullpen, but I kept my door shut to cut out the background noise.

Casey arrived shortly after me. He rapped hello on my window as he passed.

Paper copies of the initial medical exam and the crime scene analysis sat beside my scrawled notepad.

Although I'd gone over the Woodhouse files twice last night, I forced myself to start fresh. No assumptions or shortcuts.

I already had a small team running Brody Todd's social, financial, and phone data through every filter we had. Detective Adrian Witt, our digital forensics expert, headed that search.

Now that we knew the dorsal markings were numbers, we were cross-referencing with our investigation of the El Rincón body, looking for common patterns.

But, as of yet, we hadn't found any helpful leads with the first body.

In addition to the intended shock value, the nude bodies helped the killer reduce the risk that his DNA had been left with the victim, and even if we had found something, it was unlikely that we'd have results back from the lab for a while.

At least the numbers gave us the beginnings of a pattern. The problem is that patterns don't typically catch killers. Mistakes do.

If some psycho is numbering his victims, he's trying to communicate with us in some way, but we'd need some kind of a rosetta-stone breakthrough to understand the message.

Still troubled by the idea that we'd possibly missed a second body, I asked Casey to review any other fatalities over the last two weeks, looking for similarities.

It was possible that the carved numbers were a red herring, suggestive of a message, but nothing that would betray the killer's identity.

The 3 did look as if it had been practiced or traced, which could possibly give us some information about the killer's background. I was anxious to get the ME's full report back and compare it to the report on Woodhouse.

From the start, the obvious brutality of Woodhouses's death had rattled us even before we realized he was part of a serial pattern.

When we'd arrived at the El Rincón scene over a week ago, we found that Woodhouse's arms had been propped on the bench to which he'd been secured with a nylon cord. His eyes were open and glassy.

It might have appeared to a distant observer as if he were just lounging and enjoying the sunrise.

The examiner noted second- and third-degree burns across the torso, arms, and face. These weren't flame injuries—no smoke in the airway, no blistering from open fire.

A state fire marshal's consultant reviewed the photos and confirmed what we suspected: these were contact burns, localized and precise.

The ligature marks told the rest of the story. At some point before the staging, his wrists had been tied so tightly that rope fibers had embedded into the skin. Residue from tape around his hands suggested that he had been forced to hold something extremely hot.

When the ME summarized it in a preliminary report, the words were clinical but devastating: "Thermal injury to palmar surfaces with concurrent tendon contraction and severe dermal fusion suggests the decedent was unable to release the heated object voluntarily. Duration of contact cannot be determined precisely, but likely several seconds to beyond a minute of exposure to the heated surface."

Whatever Jimmy's hands had been tied to had been removed before he was transferred to the bench. Along with that object, most of the skin from his palms and fingers had pulled away.

The same thing had happened to his lips.

Post-mortem analysis put the time of death somewhere between Saturday evening and early Sunday morning. Rigor had partially resolved by the time patrol arrived, and lividity was fixed in the posterior. The core body temp on recovery was 83°F, and the ambient temperature in the low 50s. That gave us a window of 24 to 30 hours prior to discovery.

Beyond that, we were still playing the waiting game. The official medical examiner's report would take weeks, despite the urgency of the case.

But what was obvious now is that nothing about this was frenzied. Whoever had done this had planned it. Thought it through. Transported Woodhouse. Bound him. Burned him.

Now that we had a second body and the hint of a pattern, I had every reason to believe that this investigation was only going to get deeper and wider, but I had a good team, with Casey as my wingman.

While Casey tended to be a bit crass and impatient, his nose led him, and his gut pushed him to keep digging. I assigned him to head up the ground work, tracking down anyone who knew Woodhouse or Todd well. Coworkers, exes, neighbors.

If either of our victims had enemies, Casey would sniff that out, one way or the other.

The two deceased didn't seem to have a concrete connection. They were roughly the same age and had gone to the same high school, but when Woodhouse and Todd were teens, there was only one high school in Mariston, so that connection was weak.

Born over a decade after either of them, I'd gone to the newly-opened Riverbend High. I was a Riverbend Rocket, *see us soar … step aside and watch us score!*

Unfortunately, Rockets never went past districts in any sport for most of my high school journey. It took several years before the programs matured.

Hollis showed up at the station a little before eight with coffee in one hand and a manila file in the other. His tie and slacks matched, as did his belt and shoes. His look was a little less disheveled than yesterday.

I have a hunch that, since her husband's promotion, Mrs. Hollis laid out his clothes for him during the week.

"You get any sleep last night?" he asked, pulling over a chair from near the door. He picked up some photos of Todd's body and looked through them.

"Four hours. It was a good night."

"Brutal stuff here," he said, studying a photo of Todd's legs.

"Examiner believes that the whatever caused Todd's breaks and bruises was about two-and-a-half inches in diameter. Maybe a bat or large pipe."

"Okay. Anything else? Suspects?"

"Nothing much. Still digging."

"Okay, well, I'm just down the hall." He nodded and used the folder to tap my biceps in a guyish way before stepping into the hall.

I watched him navigate the desks and cubicle to his office.

It seemed obvious that Hollis had something on his mind.

A half hour later, I'd get to meet that *something*.

CHAPTER 6

She was in her early thirties with shoulder-length, flat-ironed hair and librarian eyeglasses. A stack of file folders cradled against her chest, she looked like the teacher's pet ready to turn in her book report before anyone else.

"Wren," Hollis said, "this is Detective Avery Shaw."

"Hello, Detective Avery Shaw," I said, not taking my eyes off Hollis. His silence earlier was because he was worried—rightfully so—that I wouldn't be cool with him bringing someone new into this investigation without consulting with me. I wasn't sure what was up, but whatever it was, I wasn't on board.

Shaw offered her hand, which I shook without standing.

"I've reviewed your work," she said. "Looking forward to collaborating."

I flashed her a quick smile. If it appeared patronizing to her, then I nailed it.

"Collaborating?" I directed the question at Hollis, who shifted a bit. His pupil was dilated, I noticed. The glass one stayed the same size.

"Shaw is out of Springfield and just finished a rotation on the regional narcotics task force Detective Casey was heading up. He recommended her for the team."

Thanks, Casey …

"She mentored with the FBI violent crimes division before exiting the Bureau two years ago," Hollis added. "Seemed like a good fit to assist you directly and learn a few things in the process."

"Got it." I knew his flattery was just sugarcoating. "So, Detective Shaw, will you be the Assistant Lead Detective or Assistant to the Lead Detective?"

Shaw smiled at me and then Hollis, trying to read the dynamics. She'd missed my joke, obviously not a fan of *The Office*.

"Happy to help however you need, Detective Wren," Avery perked, straightening her posture. Her thin frame was a whisper of presence next to Hollis's out-of-shape linebacker physique.

I enjoyed the moment of awkward silence, as neither Hollis or our new pet seemed to know what to say.

Finally, after glancing at me, then Hollis, and then me again, Shaw continued, "I did start sketching a linkage analysis model based on both victim profiles and staging elements. The patterns in body positioning suggest expressive symbolism, and I think we might be dealing with a developing signature. I've got a preliminary matrix in my notes if you want to take a look."

She offered the folders. I ignored them. She set them gently beside my case files, as if they might collapse the desk.

"Detective Shaw, do you mind if I have a brief word with Lieutenant Hollis?"

"Absolutely," she said. "I'll …" She looked at the files again, perhaps worried that they might sit there, unopened until the sun burned out. Then she nodded and excused herself.

Hollis shut the door behind her. When he turned, his jaw tightened. Yes, he was my superior, but he knew I felt blindsided.

"I don't have time to babysit, Lieutenant."

"She's self-sufficient, Wren. Just take what's useful, She's a fresh set of eyes."

"I feel undermined, here. You didn't consult me on this. You're the boss, but …"

He started to answer, but caught himself. A moment of silence. I was right that he shouldn't have sprung Shaw on me the way he had.

Then, "*You* are who I want running this investigation. You've got a good team, but …"

"You think I'll stretch thin."

"I think this is bigger than we suspect. Some extra help now keeps this under our control." He pulled over a chair from the corner and took a seat next to me. "And I can't have you burning out."

Hollis was being diplomatic. He didn't have to say it—I wasn't going to be home much in the coming weeks. He knew about my domestic mess.

He explained that Shaw had formerly been assigned to a multiple-county, interagency narcotics task force, which was being downsized. While Casey had taken credit for scouting her, Hollis confided an ulterior motive for accepting the transfer.

"Wren, you're going to nail this. But something about these two murders tells me we're going to get state level attention. We're also undersized since Berger and Zimmerman retired."

Hollis had a point. Counting him, we typically had eight detectives on the force. Casey was with me on this case, with Detective Witt helping as needed. Two of our guys were assigned to narcotics. While we had three applications for the vacant spots, this case couldn't wait until we'd made selections and completed training.

"If we can use Shaw as your gofer, you and Casey will have room to work."

"Hollis …"

"Wren …"

"*Hollis …*"

I wasn't crazy about the idea of a tag-a-long, but we needed to resolve this one quickly.

It continued to haunt us that the numbering suggested another body somewhere in Mariston. At any moment we could get the 911 call that had us taping up another crime scene while our leads grew colder for Woodhouse and Todd.

Shaw and I spent most of the morning reviewing what we had. She was fast and efficient. She logged everything, labeled conversations, and cross-referenced timestamps.

I briefed her on the details from CSU and the medical examiner's early report. Todd's cause of death was obvious with multiple blunt-force impacts to the skull and chest. What stood out was the timeline.

Based on stomach contents, core temperature, lividity, and early-stage insect activity—fly strike, specifically—the ME estimated time of death was somewhere between 10 p.m. and midnight on Saturday.

The killer kept Todd alive for most of a day after he left the Eastside Taproom. Maybe longer.

"No sign of blood spill." Shaw was skimming through the CSU report.

"Right. Nothing at Rte. 4008 either. The church was a dump site."

"Same as Woodhouse." As she looked over the files, I noticed Shaw using her thumbs to pop the knuckles on each finger in succession.

"Yep. Same as Woodhouse."

"Big guys, both of them," she said, after a pause. "A lot to move around."

She was right, of course. The two men would have been a haul, each of them over 200 pounds of dead weight. My new pet detective was trying to piece together a profile, but I couldn't shake the question of location.

If both bodies were a challenge to move, why had they been staged in such public locations rather than dropped somewhere in the woods out of city limits?

There was a significance to the Second Baptist Church and El Rincón.

Toxicology confirmed high blood alcohol and flunitrazepam in Todd. No injection site, no residue. Just traces in his stomach, meaning he likely consumed it.

That lined up with what we suspected. The truck was found abandoned just off Rte. 4008. No struggle, just a flat tire from an obvious sabotage. CSU recovered a modified spring pin from the tire tread. The pin, which had been ground to a sharp point, lay in a bag on my desk.

Area cameras had detected a gray Camry approaching the Taproom earlier Friday evening. It didn't appear to belong to any of the Taproom patrons, but the vehicle did match one that a business camera caught following Todd just after midnight.

A few years ago, the city secured a grant for license plate reading cameras. Using the plate number or even a general description of the car, we had limited tracking ability through several sections of the city. Todd's license plate number and a description of the Camry allowed Detective Witt to track both vehicles for several blocks before he lost them.

Not only were there no LPR cameras during the last few miles, but for privacy reasons, the software only allows rear footage of the vehicles. We couldn't get an image of the driver.

We did, however, catch the plate number. It was the one reported missing earlier.

As six p.m. neared, I needed to get home. I was taking advantage of Ed and had to show him I could balance the demands of this case and motherhood, too. There'd probably be late nights in the days ahead, so I was banking on a few early evenings home to buy some grace.

Shaw checked in on me after a quick trip to both of our recent body dumpsites. Even though we'd cleared the scenes, she'd wanted to see the two locations for herself.

"I'm heading." I gestured to a stack of files on the corner of my desk. "But I'm bringing homework with me."

Shaw nodded. "I'm taking some things home, too. I want to look over the staging pictures and notes, and tomorrow I'd like to request access to look around in the ViCAP database."

In my time as a cop in Mariston, we'd never worked a case where it was even a consideration to cross-reference the FBI's Violent Criminal Apprehension Program, but her instinct was probably correct.

"And there are some useful profiling taxonomies that we should consider."

"We already have Witt as a resource for ViCAP," I told her. "but enjoy your taxonomies."

I sensed immediately that my impatience had shown. In truth, Shaw had actually been tolerable today. "Look, just get some rest tonight. I appreciate your help. Welcome to the team."

Shaw smiled.

"I'll be in between six and seven tomorrow," I told her, and she said I could expect the same from her.

Shaw paused outside the door, and a moment of silence suggested she had something else on her mind.

"Shaw, is something wrong that I should know about?"

She exhaled and clenched the side of her mouth.

"When I came back to the office …" Her head cocked. "Detective Wren … do you know why there's an eyeball on my desk?"

CHAPTER 7

Late Tuesday morning, our communications team fielded two phone calls about a dead body along the Missouri River bank. At the time, I was revisiting the spot where Todd's truck had been located on a county road.

It was a fifteen-minute drive across town to the river, even with my lights clearing the road ahead of me, but if this was our missing body, I wanted to beat the crowd and the media to the location.

The body had been found at a homeless encampment half a mile down from the Hwy 40 bridge. A narrow gravel road took me to the water's edge, cedar branches scratching against my Durango as it crawled down the slope.

From where the path ended at a crumbly boat ramp, I abandoned my vehicle among several others and hoofed it to where the body had been found.

A half-dozen uniforms stood guard around the body. First glance told me that the body most likely had no connection to our case. There were no signs of aggression or the type of staging we'd seen with Todd and Woodhouse.

It was tough to make a generalization on the age of the deceased, as his body from the shoulders up had been submerged in water for at least a day. But the remains of a riverbank fire and a scatter of hypodermics and other paraphernalia suggested overdose.

I stayed long enough to tentatively rule out homicide and then walked back to figure out how to get my vehicle turned around amidst the cluster of official vehicles.

It was in my early twenties that I decided to become a cop. At the time, I was pursuing a four-year degree as a sociology major. The professor of one of my intro classes allowed a police ride-along as one of the options for a class assignment.

The night I'd chosen was cold and rainy. There wasn't much action. We came across an opened bay door at an auto shop and pulled someone over for a bad headlight. But, toward the end of the evening, I met Ronni, a homeless woman living in the woods near the tennis courts. She wore a tied scarf over her shaved head and a too-big coat.

She and I were roughly the same age.

Despite her ruined skin and disappearing teeth, I could see the girl Ronni had been before she'd signed her life over to meth.

My ride-along-partner knew Ronni by name from previous encounters. He was familiar with many of the homeless in the area, pointing them out like a scavenger hunt as we'd driven through the night. Ronni's parents now took care of her only daughter, he told me, and they had full legal custody of her.

After we completed a loop of the area and exited through the way we'd entered, I spotted Ronni several yards away, sitting alone on a park bench and staring over a creek.

The encounter haunted me long after that night. *This* is what I wanted to do. Young and inexperienced in life, I was under the impression I could help people like Ronni most directly with a badge. I could encounter life at its rawest.

By the next semester, I'd changed my major to criminal justice, with a minor in psychology. Completing that, I applied to the police academy.

I'm glad I wear a badge. I'm good at what I do. But it's not the job I thought it would be in my twenties.

I hadn't helped the man at the river. Nor had I helped Todd or Woodhouse.

Most of my job is reacting to the harm already done.

As my physiology de-escalated from the drive to the river, I realized that a strange type of anticipation had been coursing through my nerves. If we had found another body—particularly one with the block-letter 2 carved beneath the shoulder blades—it would possibly have confirmed the pattern.

After the excitement of that morning, the rest of the week was a blur of caffeine and case notes.

By Thursday morning, the boards in our squad room looked like a conspiracy theorist's den. The walls were covered with stringed maps, timelines, pinned photos with half-legible scribbles. My desk had two distinct piles: leads on the right and long shots on the left. Unfortunately, the stack on the left continued to grow.

Casey's team had been running nonstop interviews, including coworkers, neighbors, and former teammates.

"A couple of high school friends remembered the two of them hanging out," he shared. "Beer parties on somebody's uncle's back forty."

"Nothing recently?"

"Different social and business circles as far as I can tell. Woodhouse hadn't even bought either of his last two cars from Boeckman Motors. He likes the foreign models."

The high school angle felt like the plot of a teen horror movie, but it was the only connection we had so far. At just over 50,000 residents, Mariston wasn't a metropolis. Long-ago grudges can run deep when they don't get swallowed up in the daily hustle.

"Any enemies? Unsettled debts?"

"Found a lady who claimed Todd stiffed them on a used car for her boy."

"What about the Rodeman lead?"

The closest we'd found to a person of interest was a boy named Vincent Rodeman. He and Todd each got suspended for three days their freshman year for fighting in the locker room after PE. Todd had stolen panties, pink shorts, feminine products, and a bra from his sister's bedroom and switched them out for Vince's school clothes.

"Nothing there? That seems like how Norman Bates would have gotten started."

"Rodeman recalled that another JV athlete had pocketed the panties during the fight, and the pink undergarment became an unofficial traveling trophy for best play during the remainder of the season."

"Well, that's creepy," I said. "But nothing else?"

"Nada en absoluto," Casey responded. His complexion and conversational style contained hints of his mixed ethnicity. As with his nickname for me, *Traviesa*, I noticed he mostly only threw in Spanish in conversation with me.

I suspected flirting, but Casey flirted with everyone.

Right?

As far as any other connection between the two victims, Todd and Woodhouse seemed to have a relationship that fluctuated over the last few decades, trending toward acquaintances in recent years.

Members of the same graduating class, both men played football through all four years of high school. But Jimmy wore a catcher's mitt in the spring, while Brody threw things for the track team. Brody also wrestled heavy weight through his junior year, but left the team following an injury.

A scouring of yearbooks, the school newspaper, and other documents from that time placed the two men together on several occasions, along with a larger group of friends, many of whom still lived in or around Mariston.

After high school, Woodhouse went to a state college and eventually secured his MBA. Todd accepted a modest track scholarship at a small college up north, majoring in business. He dropped out after his freshman year and started selling cars.

By Wednesday, Shaw had used senior yearbook photos, which she enlarged as much as the original resolution and quality would allow. From this, she began sorting their classmates for interviews and deeper dives. She had them categorized every which way, including occupations, social circles, and criminal histories.

"How many of Todd's classmates were into goat yoga," I asked.

With a couple taps on her keyboard, Shaw brought up a spreadsheet of YMCA memberships from the common graduating class.

"I don't have it sorted out by fitness programs yet," she said, clenching both thumbs in a fist to pop the knuckles. "But I could have that within the hour."

"Please do," I told her. "We'll want to interview the goats."

Shaw nodded and then realized I was joking and smiled.

"I'm serious about the goats," I said, walking off.

Shaw continued to buzz in and around my office with all the charm of a sweat bee. She worked on matrices and continued coding interviews.

I got regular and often unnecessary updates, and I made a note to buy a sheet of gold stars on my way home.

Regular low-level crimes continued in Mariston, but the squad room pulsed with a frenetic energy driven by the Todd and Woodhouse murders.

Hollis was studying a large map of Mariston, the pins indicating the locations of the bodies and other relevant locations. The operations team was keeping busy logging half-baked leads.

As I scanned the room, my head throbbed from sleepless nights, feeling the weight of the teams' eyes on me. A town expecting answers I didn't have yet.

When Chief Hilke took the job two years ago, he'd undertaken a major renovation throughout the station. Most of the carpet and some wood paneling had been pulled out and the lighting upgraded throughout the building.

Among the improvements was the large glass cubicle around our intel team. That's where I found Witt, who had been deep in the data on his three wide, curved screens.

In his early thirties, Witt had the physique and complexion of a man who spent most of his time plugged in. I suspected Witt had worse sleep hygiene than I did. A Lego set recreation of an imperial star destroyer was perched on his desk in a frozen trajectory toward his cubicle neighbor's head.

Because he comes with a background in cybercrimes from his eight years in the Navy, I'd assigned Witt to look into phone dumps, bank records, and social media.

Other than a suspicious Reddit post and a burner account liking victim-adjacent content, Witt hadn't found anything he could trace to a real person—yet.

His contact with the feds found a shallow ViCAP connection from a decade ago. It was still in Missouri, but several counties away. The perp had been arrested and convicted on solid DNA and electronic evidence.

"Todd has just shy of 200 friends on his Facebook account," Witt said without turning when he sensed my presence behind him. He kept a plastic tin of nicotine pouches next to his keyboard and popped one between sentences. "About six people regularly like his political rants. Of which he averaged two or three posts a day."

"Well, he wasn't selling a lot of cars. He had to do something with his time."

"Some gambling sites, as well."

Even before online gambling had become legal in Missouri, Witt told me, Todd had accessed the sites through VPNs. However, we were coming up empty on any connections to his debt.

"Woodhouse has been inactive on Facebook for the last year." Witt sipped his Mountain Dew. "Mostly kept to LinkedIn and X. No red flags other than I think he's a closet Olivia Rodrigo fan."

"That checks out." Woodhouse, now divorced, had been dating a woman in her late twenties. "Let's keep digging. Let me know."

With Witt striking out on any leads in the virtual realm, I was hoping we'd make some progress now that Samantha Todd had finally agreed to come in for a proper interview. We'd previously reconnected with Woodhouse's ex, but the two of them had been estranged for long enough that she had very little to say about any recent events in his life.

Our hope was that Brody's widow would give us something to leverage moving forward.

CHAPTER 8

Casey joined me for a conversation with Samantha Todd early Thursday afternoon.

I'd have brought Shaw along, but I was afraid she would start cleaning out the garage or alphabetizing the spice rack.

We arrived at the Todd residence a bit after 1:00, choosing to meet the widow Todd in a comfortable setting so that she'd open up a bit more.

"Something changed in him when Woody died," Samantha said. *Woody*, of course, was James Woodhouse, the first victim. Samantha explained that he and Brody weren't really close anymore, but that his old classmate's death resonated with her husband.

We talked in the living room. Sam Todd was on the couch, a framed cross-stitch on the wall above her. Casey and I faced her in matching chairs we'd pulled in from the dinette.

Sam had dressed in jeans and a buttoned blouse for our visit. She wore make-up and had her hair back in a ponytail. While not a complete makeover, she'd obviously wanted to present herself as a more composed woman than we'd met at the front door days earlier.

Her oldest boy, the one who had caused me the guilt trip on Sunday afternoon, was staying with a friend.

Sam had kept her toddler home for the conversation. He'd found a plastic hammer and was banging it against the bookshelf. He also smelled in need of a diaper change. I quietly suggested to Casey that he take care of it, but he declined.

"He was crankier and started going to bed earlier, though I'd stay up until past midnight watching TV here on the couch." Sam fidgeted with her wedding ring as we talked.

"Do you think he was worried?" Casey asked. "That he had reason to believe his life was in danger?"

We all paused for a moment when something thudded by the bookshelf. Little Isaac Todd had given up on whatever he was trying to fix with the hammer and began pulling knickknacks and books off the lower shelves, letting them fall to the hardwood.

"Mrs. Todd," Casey said, drawing focus back to our discussion. He leaned in, and his voice softened. "Do you think Brody knew what might have happened to Jimmy? That he had some reason to be concerned?"

Detective Casey was an asset in these situations. He'd shown up in a buttoned shirt and slacks, but not a tie or jacket. He brought a certain grace to conversations like this. With a different crowd—a rougher one—he'd switch from the living Ken Doll persona he'd taken on this afternoon and would have worn short sleeves, exposing the extensive tattoos on his arm.

Casey had done undercover work before being promoted to detective. He knew how to match the context of a situation and build trust with just about anyone, from junkie to executive.

"I don't think it was that," she said, the last two words trailing off. "Are you suggesting he was hiding something?"

He was hiding his debt, right? That's what I wanted to say, as we suspected that Sam Todd had previously been in the dark about what her husband owed.

But interviewing grieving survivors is a delicate tight-rope walk.

"We're just trying to help get justice for your husband, Mrs. Todd," I said. "It seems he owed some money. Do you think he was under pressure from anyone?"

Sensing I was hungry, little Todd wandered over and offered me a slobbery fist full of the cereal balls his mom had placed out for a snack. Normally, I'd have said yes, but I'd had a big lunch.

"Brody and I …" She started to tear up and plucked a tissue from the box on the table between us. "We haven't been talking much for a while. Except to argue. A lot of those guys … things worked out better for them than they did for me and Brody."

Our deep dive into the couple's background indicated that the Todds had struggled with finances for years.

"I'd started an evening job," Sam answered. "Sunday through Thursday, cleaning at the bank."

She explained that she knew Brody had struggled with gambling in the past, both at the boats and online. They'd gone to counseling for it and she didn't realize until too late he had fallen off the wagon again.

Unfortunately, by that point Brody had lost a good enough chunk of their modest savings that catching up had become a Sisyphean task.

It was no consolidation for Samantha Todd that her husband's life insurance had paid off most of their lingering debts. It was a small policy, already spent with the kids still young.

"Jimmy had the type of life Brody was chasing, and I think he blamed me for never getting there. But he wasn't moving cars like he used to."

Isaac had moved on from the lower shelves and was stretching for a set of ceramic angel figurines. His diaper sagged like a bag of marbles between his support leg and the one propped on the second shelf.

Sam stood and scooped him up. When we'd met on her doorstep earlier in the week, I hadn't appreciated what a tall woman she was. Along with the height and girth they'd get from their dad, the two boys would probably be giants.

When Sam returned to the couch, Casey indicated a framed photo on the coffee table. "Mrs. Todd," he said, reaching an open hand toward it. "May I?"

Sam handed Casey the photo, which he turned so we both could see it. Brody Todd held his youngest son, the older boy leaning against him and clutching the type of large souvenir cup you'd buy at a theme park. They were dressed for splashes, speed, and sun.

"When they found Woody's body ..." She held the squirming two-year-old in her lap. He was pushing to escape her grip and return to his destruction. "When that happened, I think Brody realized how short it all was. Life, I mean. And his chance to make something of himself."

Overall, we talked for just over an hour. In that time, we'd jotted down the name of an uninsured handyman roofer they'd taken to small claims court over a persistent leak. Sam also mentioned a neighbor with whom they'd clashed with over property lines and fencing.

We left with pages of notes, but the gambling problem was still the best lead we had.

"I didn't want to say anything to you during the interview," I said as we headed back to the station, "but …"

Casey was playing with his phone and looked up to meet my glance.

"It smelled like someone shit their pants in there. Was that you?"

Before he could respond, my phone buzzed. It was Samantha Todd.

"This is Wren," I said.

"Detective?"

"This is Detective Sara Wren, yes. Mrs. Todd?" I quickly pulled the phone away and thumbed the speaker icon.

"I thought of one more thing just after you left. I don't know if it's anything, but …"

"Everything's important right now, Mrs. Todd. What did you remember?"

"A couple weeks before he was … before he died, Brody got something in the mail. There wasn't no return address."

Casey and I exchanged glances. This was *something*.

"He never told me what was in the envelope," she said. "But it upset him. A lot."

I ended the call and tried to process what I'd just learned. Samantha didn't know what he'd done with the envelope or its contents, but she promised to look through the bedroom and anywhere else that he might have kept it.

Casey took the next turn without signaling. "If we're lucky, maybe it's still in the house."

"If we're lucky," I echoed.

CHAPTER 9

"Forgive me, Father, for I have sinned."

His sigh was audible from the other side of the confessional.

"This is my first confession."

A pause. Then, "Okay, sure. Let's hear it."

"When I was a girl, my little brother always peed on the toilet ring and never cleaned it."

"Sara ..."

"He wouldn't stop, even after Mom and Dad got onto him. So I'd wipe it. With his pillow."

"*Stop.* I've plugged my ears. No absolution."

"And I'd return the pillow, all uriny, to his bed. I don't think he ever figured it out."

Our parents hadn't practiced any faith when we were kids. During college, Wes's girlfriend pulled him into a Newman Center community, and he started attending regularly with her. The girlfriend didn't stick, but the faith did. A few years into his post-college job working for the state, Wes changed course and entered the seminary.

Today, my brother is Fr. Wes Brandt, pastor of St. George parish in Regensburg, a small rural community thirty miles down Highway 48.

"Sara," Wes said from his side of the confessional screen. "Tell me you didn't cut in front of penitent sinners just to annoy me."

"There's no line, Wes," I told him. "I'm your last customer. Anyway, about that forgiveness thing I'm supposed to get. Does it come in the jumbo size?"

"Did you really wipe urine with my pillow case?"

"Sure. But just once or … thirty-seven times."

"I think that's the unforgivable sin."

"Hmm, is it? In that case, let's cut out of here and get lunch."

I'd never been in a confession booth before. The kneeler and the lattice window—I wonder if this set up would work in the interrogation room.

The door opened behind me. Wes wore his priest garb, black with a white collar. He had our dad's height and retreating hairline, the latter supplemented by a thick beard.

"I've got noon Mass," Wes whispered. "Stick around. It's a half-hour."

"I'll make a few calls outside. Things are crazy."

"Yeah, I've been following the news."

Two older ladies, both dressed as if they'd just finished a walk, entered through the main doors. Wes smiled and waved. They returned the wave but withheld the smiles as they attempted to interpret the scene before them—their priest talking to an armed woman. I'd left my blazer in the car, but not my shoulder holster.

"Besides," I said to Wes, "the flames might distract you if I stay in here during the Mass." One of the ladies overheard me and glanced back as they entered a pew. I gave a friendly wave.

Shaking his head, Wes headed toward the front of the nave.

"Hey," I whisper-shouted, "aren't you supposed to give me some kind of penance?"

"Say the Miranda Warning thirty-five times."

Ugh.

As I snuck out one of the side doors and Wes headed toward the altar, I caught sight of a mother attempting to direct her kids' attention back toward the altar. I suspect they were hoping for the flames.

At Hollis's insistence, I'd taken the rest of the day off after wrapping up paperwork and running a morning tactical. He, and probably the rest of the team, could tell I was getting cranky and frustrated, despite the fact that we'd had a possible lead if Samantha Todd could find the envelope Brody had received.

During a brief conversation with my lieutenant, I read between the lines and suspected he was getting pressure from our chief, who might be getting pressure from higher up. Hollis didn't need me hitting a wall with two unresolved, high-profile murders.

Either way, I'd worked last night and started the day early today, which was only possible since Ed had stayed over.

He'd crashed on the couch, of course.

Before I'd left the station, I'd learned that a gray Camry, most likely the one used to abduct Brody Todd, had been found abandoned outside city limits late Thursday night. The plates were from another vehicle, but the VIN matched that of one reported missing a couple of weeks ago.

Using the LPR system, we ran the plates and traced the car along the same route as Todd had taken. The time stamps put the mystery driver several yards back, assuming both cars were traveling close to the speed limit.

As with Todd's vehicle, the Camry escaped the video trail well before the county road.

After Mass, Wes and I met at a café on Main street. It was one of four restaurants open in the small German settlement town where Wes oversaw a St. George parish and elementary school.

"Governor Roark issued a statement to the press supporting us," I told Wes as I squeezed a lemon into my iced tea.

"Yeah, I caught last night's news." Wes had given up soda during a health kick last winter. As he spoke, he poured a third packet of sugar into his tea. The two of us sat in the vinyl benches of a booth against the front window. Regensburg traffic passed either way at the frequency of a faucet drip.

"But if we don't make headway soon, we'll have pressure on us to expand the team." I stared at the menu. All the dishes were named with punny country music references. The Philly Nelson Cheesesteak. The Loretta Limburger on Rye. "If the patrol gets involved, I'll just be a gopher on their task force."

I was overblowing the scenario. Missouri had a mutual aid statute that allowed cooperation among law enforcement agencies without overriding jurisdiction. But as this case became more crowded, the lines of authority would blur.

Our conversation paused as bosomy Suzette came to take our order.

"We'll both take the corn chowder." Wes closed his menu and sat it within her reach. "And I gotta go with the Johnny Cash-ew Chicken Wrap."

"And you, darling?"

"Um … I'll do the blackened tilapia," I said.

"Come again, sweetie?"

You've got to be kidding me. "I'll take the … *Clint* Blackened Tilapia, please."

"Sandwiches in just two shakes, Hon," Suzette said, patting Wes's shoulder. They love him here, especially at the elementary school. He's putting on weight because of the old ladies and their casseroles.

"We're moving too slow," I said.

As if on that cue, my phone buzzed.

Wes noticed it, too and gestured for me to check it. It annoyed him when work interfered with personal life, but he understood how big this case was.

I tapped open my messaging app while Suzette delivered our chowder.

The text was from Shaw. We'd finally received a preliminary coroner's assessment, though it didn't reveal anything we hadn't already suspected. The official report probably wouldn't arrive for weeks, as the toxicology and histology results would take time.

Too much time.

I didn't say what popped into my mind at that moment, which was that I didn't want to have a conversation with another widow.

"You feel like you're failing?"

I shrugged and scooped up a spoonful of chowder. It was delicious. For a brief second, I wondered if I should quit police work, move to Regensburg, and just eat chowder every day at this café.

"So, fingers crossed …" Behind Wes, our waitress was cleaning up after the previous customers, stacking their empty plates quickly and noisily.

I considered Wes's annoying ability to read my mind. I *did* feel like we were failing. We needed some kind of a break soon. Maybe we'd find a strand of hair at a crime scene or, from the found Camry, a suggestion of the last radio station accessed. I'm not sure if it mattered if our killer was a country or hip-hop type of guy, but I cringed at the thought of his victims being forced to listen to that sexy tractor song.

I suspect, though, that the killer had been careful and thorough. So far, the most we'd figured out from the Camry is that someone, most likely the original owner, enjoyed gummy bears and salt and vinegar chips. There was a stash of both in the console. Other than that, the interior of the car had been wiped and vacuumed thoroughly.

The sandwiches came.

I sipped more soup.

"How are things with Ed," Wes asked.

"About as promising as the case. The romance? Just as cold as the bodies."

I managed to break down the situation without actually breaking down. I'm not really into talking things out, but Wes and I lugged around the same baggage. Mom and Dad split before either of us got to high school. And life was pretty messy before that. Literally messy. Dad was a compulsive hoarder.

"If I make an observation," Wes said, pushing aside his empty bowl, "would you prefer I say it like a priest or a little brother?"

That was tough. A reflection on Mary and Martha or wisdom from the urine monster?

"The priest version."

"You need forgiveness."

"Okay, the little brother version."

"You need forgiveness."

"Well, that was a …"

"From yourself, Sara. When you're not at work, you're thinking about work. When you're not at home, you're thinking about home. Is the problem that Ed can't cope with you being pulled in two directions or that you can't?"

That's why I can't move to Regensburg. I forgot. Wes has the annoying habit of saying the uncomfortably true.

On the half-hour drive home after lunch, I reflected on Wes's advice just long enough to conclude I didn't want to reflect on his advice. Instead, I made a couple of calls and checked up on progress. Nothing more with the car, and Sam Todd hadn't reached out about a discovered envelope.

Ed and I sat and chatted for a bit when I got to the house. He'd knocked out work earlier in the day and then taken Henry to his dentist appointment (no cavities) and to buy some grip tape for his bat. Henry's baseball team had a scrimmage on Saturday afternoon. I'd invited Wes to come, as well.

The conversation with Ed was nice, but short. It wasn't about *us* or work. Just chatting. Ed had just secured a contract to design a building expansion for an insulation factory. He still did not have his ring on, but I resisted asking about it. I *did*, however, make sure my left hand was visible as we chatted.

When he left, it felt as if his exit had sucked half of the oxygen out of our house. Maybe I was hoping he'd suggest we go out for dinner. Maybe I should have suggested it.

I'd been the one to ask Ed out when we first met during our college years. It hadn't been a set-up, but mutual friends had invited each of us to a blues festival. Ed and I had parked our lawn chairs next to each other because we were the only two in our group who didn't have a default person to hold hands with.

When he learned I was a criminal justice major, Ed shared his scandalous criminal history. He and some friends had once been briefly detained for rearranging a church marquee during Homecoming. When the police lights flashed behind them, the three boys were an exclamation mark away from changing NO BUNGEE CORDS NEEDED—WE ENCOURAGE LEAPS OF FAITH! to WILDCATS EAT POO!

Luckily the cop was a former running back for the Mariston Bulldogs and they got off easy.

A few drinks into that long-ago evening, I told Ed I needed to do a case study on a reformed criminal. I asked if he wanted to grab a bite to eat in the near future so I could hear more about his checkered past.

Two weeks later, we had our second date. Three years after that, he proposed.

Single again for now, I had Henry help me with pizzas and salad after Ed left. But when grabbing a large bowl from one of the lower cabinets, I noticed something.

"Did your dad fix this?" The previously-crooked cabinet door was now straight. Henry had bent a hinge by leaning on the door weeks ago.

He nodded. "And some other stuff."

Of course, he did. This was, after all, his house, too. Even if our separation became more permanent, Ed had a vested interest in keeping things in shape.

During dinner, Henry told me that Ed had also fixed the stuck screen door to the deck, replaced some light bulbs, and weeded around the shrubs out front.

It wasn't until after Henry fell asleep on the living room couch that evening that I noticed one more of Ed's projects from today.

I'd decided to let Henry sleep on the couch, pulling a blanket over him before turning off the lights and heading down the hall. In my bedroom, I kicked my shoes into the closet while brushing. That's when I noticed the jewelry organizer.

It had still been in the shipping box this morning. It was a simple wall-mounted design with hooks and small drawers. I'd asked for it as a birthday gift back in August, but we didn't get it hung right away.

Then we started fighting again, and it still didn't get hung.

And then we separated in early May, and it stayed in that box, shoved out of the way between the wall and a low-hanging row of winter tops.

Its only purpose seemed to be to hide my shoes.

Ed hadn't just mounted the organizer. He'd gone through the trouble of half-filling it with my favorite jewelry.

Because he knew my favorite jewelry.

My heart was pounding and breaking at the same time. I wanted to quit my job, call Ed and offer my body to him in some nasty way if he drove over tonight.

At one point, while brushing, I picked up my phone, considered it for a moment, and then tossed it on my mattress.

Then, I spit out my toothpaste, crawled into bed, and cried myself to sleep.

CHAPTER 10

He'd never been to the little town of Regensburg before. He'd never eaten at the restaurant on Main. But his biggest fan—Detective Sara Wren—chose to eat there, so maybe he should give it a try sometime.

Watching from the market parking lot across the street, he enjoyed anonymity. For anyone who spotted his car from the restaurant, the windshield would be just a reflection of the midday sun.

But it didn't seem that Songbird was at her best today. After all, he had followed her here for nearly thirty minutes on the highway, trailing just close enough to track her progress over the Missouri hills. He'd followed her into Regensburg and to this restaurant.

Regensburg. Walker knew the name, borrowed from a German town from which many of the original residents had immigrated.

ich beobachte dich singvogel

I am watching you, Songbird!

His father had spoken some German. The Walker learned it in the army during his time stationed in Böblingen as a Marine.

He remembered, as a child, his father's campfire tale of the *Wiedergänger*, or the one who walks again. The creature, his dad had told him under the summer moon, returned from the dead seeking vengeance.

The one who walks again.

Another layer to the name he had chosen for himself.

Like his father, The Walker picked up the German language easily enough. Besides the memorization of words, learning a language was just the act of recognizing and creating patterns.

He was good at patterns.

The inside of his car began to heat up, and The Walker opened the driver and passenger windows to allow a breeze through.

> *so nice to take a break while children cry because daddy cant come home songbird how many bodies so far eins, zwei … and will you still have time for pie after drei, vier, fünf?*

The strawberry-rhubarb pie advertised sounded delicious, though. On the café window, the restaurant's resident artist had painted a cartoonish slice.

The window art obstructed his view some, as did the sun in his eyes, but he could see well enough to track their progress through the front doors and to a booth in the corner. His imagination took him into the restaurant. He imagined the chrome napkin dispensers, the jukebox, the sassy waitress like on the television shows he'd once watched with his dad.

> *Kiss my grits!*

Not knowing the German word for grits, he spoke it into his phone and asked for a translation.

"Küss meine Grütze," he said out loud.

Who was this priest to her? He'd tracked her to the parish and continued past it, circling back a mile down the road. He'd found a place to pull over and watch until she exited the church doors, her phone pressed to her face.

Ten minutes and then twenty minutes and then thirty.

Finally, a few parishioners ambled out through the heavy wooden doors. By then, she was sitting against the trunk of her car, still on her phone.

And then the priest had exited. He gave Songbird a quick hug, and drove back in the direction of Mariston.

A friend? Maybe. Or a brother? A partner in scandal?

The trip to the café didn't answer that question for him, but The Walker was confident he would find an answer.

> *because i know where you nest songbird will send you a picture of the prettyhouseprettygrass in the sunshine and prettyboy playing outside even autograph it for you my biggestfan*

He knew she had a husband. Or maybe *had* a husband. Possibly a once-upon-a-time husband who sometimes paid visits to the house.

There was time to learn more about the husband and the priest. And more about Songbird.

But not today.

He hated leaving so soon, before Songbird and the priest finished lunch.

But he had someone waiting for him in the basement. It would be rude to neglect him much longer.

Turning the ignition key, the Walker shifted into reverse and backed out of his spot. As he turned out of the small lot and slipped easily into the slow Regensburg traffic, he kept his radio turned off, entertaining himself instead with a German lullaby he remembered singing to his own son.

Mein liebes Kind, pass besser auf,
Fritz Haarmann sucht nach dir.
Er wird dich aufschlitzen,
dein Blut verspritzen
zum stillen der hungrigen Gier

"My dear songbird," The Walker whispered, translating and modifying the song as he drove back toward Mariston, "Better watch out. The Wiedergänger is looking for you. He will slit you open. He will splash the blood around to satisfy his hungry greed."

CHAPTER 11

By Monday morning, it was back to work.

On top of the two known homicides, we'd received a missing person call late Sunday evening.

Normally, for a town the size of Mariston, we could expect to receive one or two calls like this a week. People generally turn up. Often, it is simply a miscommunication among family members.

Especially now, with the media coverage of the Todd and Woodhouse murders, we could expect our call center to be busier than typical.

But I had a bad feeling about this one.

At 48-years-old, J. T. Russell was the same age, within a few months of our recent victims. His wife, who made the call, said Russell had been scheduled for a two-day sales trip to Illinois. She'd received a couple of texts from his phone claiming he was extending the trip and staying with a college buddy in Collinsville.

Collinsville was just across the Mississippi from St. Louis. Ed and I took Henry there last year to see the Cahokia Mounds and place token bets at the horse races.

Russell never made it to his appointment. He also hasn't answered his phone or responded to recent texts.

I had a hunch that things were about to ramp up.

At least Ed and I had a nice time over the weekend. Wes joined us for Henry's Saturday ball game, trading his priest black for shorts and sandals. The cloverleaf ballpark was packed. A few yards from our bleachers, a teenage boy in a parks and rec t-shirt flipped patties on a propane griddle.

Sitting between my brother and Ed, I was happy to be the main ingredient in that sandwich of normalcy as we watched Henry and the Mariston Sparks take on the Wildcats.

It was mandated-water break hot outside, which was how youth baseball worked in Missouri. Cold and wet the first half of the season. Two days of spring. Then scorchers.

Typical clueless mom, I'd bought him a bag of sunflower seeds because *real* baseball players liked sunflower seeds. And then I saw the sign on the dugout. *No Sunflower Seeds.*

Henry generally played right field. When the team was ahead by several runs, the coach would sometimes shift him to second.

"Uh … yeah …" Ed said at one point. "Maybe we should work on pop flies." This, after Henry misjudged a ball's arch in his corner of the outfield. He backtracked, scooped, and threw, but the batter slid into second. The guy on second rounded third and trotted to home plate.

"That's all right, number 22!" Wes shouted. "Let's go Sparks! Neuter those Wildcats!"

Several fans glanced. I elbowed. Wes shut up.

I hope I bruised him.

There probably weren't any D-1 scholarships in Henry's future. But I still loved my little guy in his baseball uniform, the back of his shirttail perpetually untucked. The faint grass stains on his knees had won the battle against bleach. If blood and fingerprints were as impossible to remove as grass stains and the red smears of infield dirt, my day job would be a lot easier.

Henry walked his first up-to-bat and struck out during the second time through the lineup. Then, he got a hit.

He got a hit.

It was a sloppy, hesitant swing, the ground ball hopping between short and third. Wes stood and began yelling, and I grabbed his t-shirt and pulled him back onto the bleachers.

Though there were two outs, the short stop tried to throw to the catcher to stop the scoring runner, rather than get the easy out on first.

Henry stood at the plate for a second, as stunned as we were. Then he ran, holding the bat far too long down the baseline. I cheered. Ed and Wes cheered. Everyone cheered for my son on that hot Saturday afternoon.

Henry got on base, and the catcher bobbled the out. The Sparks won by a run.

As the teams lined up for fist bumps, I leaned over to Ed.

"By the way, thanks for hanging the jewelry rack." I took his hand.

He smiled and squeezed my hand. "Sorry it took so long."

The investigation had continued, of course, over the weekend. Two deaths don't make a pattern, but all the signs were there that the killer intended to leave us another victim. The staging. The dermal numbers.

I tried to put myself into the mind of the killer. Besides whatever sick perversion drove him, what was the connection between the two victims?

Casey, Shaw, and I continued to contact associates, friends, and family of the deceased, but our progress was exhaustingly slow. We had worked through anyone we could locate from their senior yearbook, prioritizing those who've remained in the area.

With no solid leads, we were basically speed dating our way through dozens of names, hoping for something that might help us refine our search.

It was the same set of questions over and over.

Do you know anyone who would want to hurt either of these men?

Have you received any strange phone calls or emails? Anything in the mail?

How did the victims act the last time you saw them?

The first victim, Jimmy Woodhouse was in a supervisory role in municipal utilities, overseeing water, sewer, and electrical services. Pushing fifty and twice divorced, "Woody" had been dating his receptionist.

Detective Shaw had been with me during the interview with Macey Sidner, Woodhouse's 28-year-old midlife crisis.

We'd interviewed her before, of course, when her boyfriend's body had been found, but now we were looking for a pattern with Todd's death.

Despite her default social awkwardness, Shaw surprised me by making a connection with Ms. Sidner, who wasn't thrilled to be sitting with us again.

Part of Chief Hilke's revamp of the station was to create a softer interview room for victims and witnesses. If we wanted to intimidate someone, there was another room for that. There, the fluorescents were bright and the walls were white cinderblock.

But the room where we met with Sidner could have been the reception section for a wellness center. Comfortable seating, plants, and a Rothko print that made me thirsty for a tequila sunrise.

The ambiance was lost on Macey Sidner, who was waiting stiffly on the couch when we entered. A bottle of water sat unopened on a side table near her.

As we dragged chairs to sit across from her, Sidner tugged at the sleeves of her shirt like they were a security blanket. Her eyes darted between the two of us, landing mostly on Shaw.

I wasn't surprised.

Shaw naturally came across as harmless and gently curious. Her smile muscles worked better than mine. She was starting to grow on me a bit. Maybe I should stop being a bitch to her all the time.

"Thanks for coming in," Shaw said, her tone warm but professional. "We know this isn't easy."

Sidner gave a slight nod. "I just don't want to get dragged into a bunch of shit." She had a cute face—a red-head with contact-enhanced blue eyes. Faint acne scars, but the eyes won.

"We're just trying to understand what Jimmy was going through before he died," Shaw said. "We realize this is tough for you."

"We already talked. I don't know what else to tell you."

"Another body, so new questions," I said.

Shaw gave me a glance. My irritation with our slow progress had shown.

"You knew him well," Shaw said, attempting to reset the tone. "Probably better than anyone, lately. We're just looking for connections. Anything to help us find this person before he hurts someone else."

"Jimmy was *different* for a while before …" Sidner glanced at the floor and then the ceiling. "I thought he was angry at me for … something."

The way she said it. *Something* she wouldn't do in bed, I wondered. *Something* they'd fought about?

Her soft voice and mousiness didn't seem a fit for what we'd learned about Jimmy's more boisterous and loud presence. When he wasn't working, he practically lived at the Mariston country club, which he couldn't afford, according to his financial records.

"I know he got some money from when his dad died," Sidner said. "He didn't like to talk about money, but I think all of that is gone now."

She was right. Woodhouse wouldn't have told his girlfriend, but he was barely making the minimum payment on two credit cards and had received shut-off warnings on his utilities on and off during the last year.

As with Brody Todd, my mind went to a possible creditor. But to my knowledge, Mariston didn't have any sharks who operated with the type of vengeance inflicted on these two bodies.

"You said that the last few days he was acting different." My mind went to Todd's wife mentioning the envelope that Brody had received weeks before his murder. "What do you mean by *different*?"

"We'd go out, but I could tell his mind was somewhere else. He'd get annoyed easily."

"This was, what? Close to when he disappeared?"

"No, before that. This was weeks before then. It seemed like he snapped out of it eventually, and then …"

"Right. Ms. Sidner, you don't remember anything about Jimmy getting some strange mail in the weeks leading up to his death, do you?"

"Something in the mail?" She shook her head, and her expression was genuine. "No, not that I know of. Like a threat?"

I shrugged. "Anything." My phone buzzed, but I ignored it.

We had, of course, gotten a subpoena to search Jimmy's home after his body was found. Though his two adult children were cooperative, nothing had turned up. But, at the time, we hadn't known what we were looking for.

"The restaurant near where we found him …" Detective Shaw leaned in as she transitioned to another thread, "Did the two of you eat there often? El Rincón on Eastland Drive?"

Sidner indicated that they may have eaten before, but that Jimmy's favorite restaurant was an Italian place on the west side of town. They ate there once a month, at least.

As Shaw continued the conversation, I explored that question in my mind. Why had the killer staged the body at that location? Everything about the way we found Woodhouse and Todd suggested the bodies had been very deliberately staged.

There were still details about the crime scene that I'm sure we were missing, I was sure of it. For instance, why did the killer utilize two unthinkable, but very different, methods of torture? Was there some symbolism that we weren't tracking?

Were we spending too much time looking for similarities, when we should have been thinking about the differences?

While Woodhouse's body had been found along a recreation trail, it hadn't simply been dumped on or alongside the path. He had actually been propped in a sitting position on the bench. Todd, on the other hand, had been left splayed on the pavement of a church that he never attended and where he would have stood out like … well, like a pasty white guy within a predominantly black congregation.

Brody and his family didn't attend anywhere on weekends, according to Samantha Todd. And Jimmy Woodhouse wasn't a jogger.

Why *those* locations?

Why *those* forms of torture?

Shaw continued the interview while I went on autopilot, chasing those questions down the rabbit hole until I felt my phone again and took a quick glance to make sure it wasn't urgent.

It was.

The first text was from Detective Casey: *New body. Old Stage Rd bridge over Wagner Crk.*

Russell, I thought, remembering the missing person call from last night.

The second text, fifteen minutes later, was also from Casey: *Another guy missing. Wife just called in.*

As I processed that second text, my phone buzzed again. But this one from Hollis: *What the hell is going on?*

He read my mind.

CHAPTER 12

The truss bridge over Wagner Creek was colored by rust. Rot ate into the wooden planks—several of them had been replaced in the last few years.

The temperature had been in the mid-nineties for the last week, and the humidity was heavy. I was sweating before I'd even arrived. This was despite the forest of red cedars, hickory, and oak towering over the road and creek.

Wagner Creek trickled beneath the bridge. The exposed bank on either side of the water measured the days since our last good rain.

By the time Shaw and I ducked under the cordon, Detective Casey had finished up a conversation with an officer and joined us. Casey had previously asked for the day off, but Hollis had called him in. His eyes were puffy, and he hadn't shaved. He winked nonetheless.

"Afternoon, Traviesa."

Sheesh, Casey, give it a rest

Then, he smiled at Shaw. "And you, Chiquita."

Shaw straightened her glasses and tried (unsuccessfully) to suppress a smile.

Wait, what? … *Chiquita??*

How does Shaw get *ita*?

"Late night?" I asked, moving past the pettiness since I'm apparently the *mature* one. Casey, still single, enjoyed his nights out, and I suspect he did well with his bad boy ink and bad boy stories of his time undercover.

"Hung out with my big bro. Cigars and bourbon. Too much of both."

"Hungover?" I asked.

"Observant. You should be a detective?"

"Thought about it, but the hours are murder."

"Hmm. That's the best you got?"

"Ugh … thought about it, but I look terrible in a fedora?"

"Yeah, let's just figure out this murder."

"Good call. And, for the record, I look sexy in a fedora."

"I've already imagined it," he whispered.

I tried (unsuccessfully) not to look as flustered as Shaw had. I really need Ed back home.

Casey nodded at a guy in a baseball cap sitting on the tailgate of his pickup. "Guy over there … Kip Stanning. Owns a farm about ten miles down the road. Came across the body on his way into town."

I placed Stanning in the mid-thirties. He had a thick beard and a too-dark tan. Probably spent most afternoons out on a tractor, growing corn and melanoma.

"Our guy was headed into town to buy some PVC," Casey explained. "A leak under his daughter's bathroom."

Stanning noticed me noticing him, took a sip of his coffee, and turned his gaze to the ground. Maybe his kids like to drive the side-by-side down this gravel road. Maybe Kip Stanning was imagining one of them having found the body parts first.

"I've sent some cars out to check with the neighbors," Casey continued. "See if anyone had surveillance cameras that might have caught the traffic along the road."

"Let's send the guy back home to his family. We can circle back later if we have any other questions."

Farmer Kip wasn't much use to us hanging around if we could establish his alibi or rule him out with a few basic screening questions:

Have you ever had your mother taxidermized?

What are your lampshades made of?

Is your dog a good conversationalist?

Wagner bridge had once supported train travel before the route was decommissioned. With the tracks removed, the gravel road mostly served the few farms that had been dissected by the route decades ago. The road stretched for miles in either direction, passing under limestone bluffs and stretching over the tributaries that fed the Missouri river. Had the route been converted for recreation, like the Katy Trail, a biker or jogger might have found the body earlier.

Someone, probably Casey, had already completed an initial canvas of the area and left tented number tags next to possible evidence. There was a dark stain on the road just where it reached the bridge. A lidless McDonald's cup lay in the weeds near the creek.

Two officers parted to give us access as we stepped onto the bridge.

"Where's the rest of him?" Shaw asked.

Casey lifted the hand with the coffee cup and pointed at the far end of the bridge, where more of our uniformed team bumbled around, trying to look busy absent further direction from one of us.

Just in front of where we stood, two legs had been propped against the steel framed railing of the bridge. It looked as if our victim had been hanging out there, enjoying the morning chatter of the squirrels, when something sliced through and took away everything from the knees upward.

"The rest of him is down there." Casey gestured to the far side of the bridge. "Can't get through by vehicle without running over it."

"Is this Russell?"

"I think so." Casey gave me the run-down on Jesse "J. T." Russell, an HVAC install account manager for a four-state territory. After repeating much of what I already knew from Mrs. Russell's missing person report, Casey shared that the couple had two kids, one in college and one at home.

The trio of us walked toward the bridge, Chiquita trailing me and Casey.

"I called Hollis on the way over," I said. "He's going to check on Russell's wife while we manage things here. What do we know about this afternoon's call?"

"Curtis Riedel," Shaw said. "He fits the demographic."

I crouched down to look more closely at the severed limbs, attempting to ignore the sour-sweet staleness of decomposition.

The site of amputation showed jagged, irregular tissue damage. Slippage had begun near the point of amputation, suggesting that the legs were removed a few days ago.

"But at least he didn't ruin the shoes," Casey offered.

While blood had dried and darkened on his upper calves, it hadn't dripped down to ruin his newish running shoes or socks, which overlapped the dried crimson stain on his skin.

Had the killer put the shoes and socks *back* onto the removed legs?

"I mean, they're nice shoes." I stood and stared down the length of the bridge to the huddle of officers around the rest of the victim.

I'm not a pathologist, but I've been around enough death to recognize what I was looking at. The legs were bruised deep purple along the backs where the blood had settled into fixed lividity. The rest of the skin was pale, almost gray.

Slipping on a pair of latex gloves, I gave one of the calves a squeeze, confirming my assumption about the body's state of decomposition. It yielded to my gentle press.

"What does that tell us, Shaw?"

"Along with the odor," she answered without missing a beat, "we're probably past secondary flaccidity and entering the early stages of putrefaction and autolysis."

"So …?"

"So, he's been dead for at least a day, but probably longer."

I waited to see if she'd catch the assumption she'd made.

"Well," Shaw added. "At least this part of him had been. We'll have to see what the rest of him looks like."

"Right."

Given the ragged amputation, our victim had most likely been conscious and struggling against the work of a tool that hadn't been designed for the operating room. I suspected that the pathologist who examined the body later would see a shock response in the nearby tissue.

"Stanning found the torso first," Casey said as we began across. "He'd driven right past the legs and didn't notice them until he reversed back off the bridge."

Even though Hollis had ended our call abruptly, he'd suggested a strong connection to the Todd and Woodhouse bodies.

"When I cross this bridge," I said to Casey, "I'm going to find the rest of the body facedown, right?"

"Yep."

"And a number carved into the back, right?"

"That's right."

"And—let me guess—that number will be … hmmm … four?"

"Nope."

I looked at Casey. He raised his eyebrows.

"Five?"

Casey shook his head.

"Eighteen," he said. "A one and an eight on either side of his spine."

Either there were fifteen more bodies scattered around Mariston, or our narrative had just been shattered.

CHAPTER 13

The torso was cold and clammy, and a faint green tinge crept up from the lower abdomen. There was no strong smell yet, though the victim had obviously been dead for several hours.

My hunch was correct—he'd been kept alive during the removal of his legs. The point of amputation was a charred mess of cauterization below the greenish-black marbling of early decomposition.

Todd had been beaten to death and Woodhouse scarred by heat. Now this victim, dismembered.

The different locations.

And the numbering. One, three, and eighteen …

"He's sending a message," Casey said.

"Text would have been easier."

His pattern was a message, but possibly one we're not supposed to figure out. He may be communicating an intent, assuming we break the code. Or he might just be playing a game.

"The conditions of the bodies hint at narcissism." Shaw seemed emboldened by her earlier analysis of the severed legs. "The killer is operating with a sense of self-importance and preoccupation with power. Arrogance and exploitation. Classic power/control type on the Holmes and —"

"Shit." Both Shaw and Casey turned to follow my gaze back across the bridge. Southern from KMMO 17 had arrived, the first of the media to this scene. As her camera man set up to capture the scene, Southern had already spotted Stanning and appeared to be talking him into an interview.

"Let's get a team to scour the surrounding area at least fifty yards out in each direction," I told Casey. I didn't think we would find anything, but assumptions are the key ingredients in failure for detectives.

Walking back over the length of the bridge, I looked for tire tracks or footprints. Since it hadn't rained in recent weeks, anyone who walked onto the bridge rails from the rural road might have marked their steps with gravel dust.

Unfortunately, that included Kip Stanning and the responding officers. There were footprints everywhere, but most were distressed beyond readability by the aging wood planks.

Something splashed in the water beneath me, drawing my attention back below the bridge. The creek was maybe twenty feet across at this location. At best, during this dry spell, it could be traversed by kayak or canoe.

Why this location? Why the bridge? Why the split locations of the split body?

Gravel crackled behind me. Hollis pulled his Explorer into the shade and walked past Southern. She reached out, as if to catch his attention, but Hollis had a phone pressed to his ear and walked past without regarding her.

"That was Roark's office." Hollis informed me that the governor was now *suggesting* we let the feds have a more active role in the investigation.

I didn't have a response. We were striking out on this case. I was failing.

"How'd it go with Mrs. Russell?" I asked.

"Highly self-medicated and emotionally unresponsive. Said the last time she'd seen J.T. was Wednesday morning. They'd gone out the night before for his birthday."

"Happy birthday, J. T."

"*And many more* ..." Hollis muttered, looking around to take in the activity.

We were interrupted, then, by a young officer, who jogged over to our location.

"Detective Wren," he said, giving a glance at Lt. Hollis to acknowledge his rank. "We may have found a tire track."

The officer led us off the bridge, near to where Stanning had parked. A small V-shaped stretch of tracks, imprinted in the mud alongside the road, marked where a vehicle had pulled off the gravel momentarily.

"Someone turned around here," Hollis observed.

"Yeah," I said as Hollis' phone rang. He stepped away to take the call.

The track wasn't deep, as the ground was too hard. It might be tough to make a cast, but the tread mark in the loose dirt had decent definition. "Probably the rear driver's-side tire," I said to whoever was listening, but more just to force my focus on speculation. "Backed up enough to cut to the right and double-back."

I spotted the photographer from CSU and waved her over.

"Let's get some measurements of these." I snapped my own photo. The tracks weren't much, but if they belonged to the killer, it was a slip. Maybe he was getting comfortable and overly confident.

Phone still in hand, Hollis returned. "We may have found Curtis Riedel."

"Alive?"

A small shake of the head. "The body is at the Community Center down on Ventura."

It was a two-for-one deal today. Just what we needed.

"No positive ID just yet," Hollis said as the two of us walked over to his car. "The Center's closed on Mondays, so the body could have been there all day without anyone finding it."

We'd be working until past Henry's bedtime. I needed to call Ed.

"And, since I know you're about to ask, we don't know if there's a marking. He'd been left face-up."

"Casey's got a handle on things here," I said. "Are you free to stick around with him while Shaw and I head in that direction?"

Hollis waved me on, and Shaw followed as I started back toward the car.

"Detective Wren," I heard behind me. It was Southern. "Detective Wren, is it true that another body was just located?"

"You know how it works," I told her without making eye contact. "You can reach the communications office for any official updates."

"Has the department made progress on identifying suspects?" she asked as we walked away. Then, "Will the state patrol or federal agents be involved now that we have two more bodies?"

This was turning into a shitshow.

We drove in silence for several minutes with only the chatter of the two-way radio and the drum of gravel under my tires. The road was long and straight over where the Missouri River, in its younger and wider days, had leveled the hills.

Then …

"Wait!" Shaw pulled out her phone and tapped it with her thumb.

"What is it?"

"Today's the 21st."

"All day long, so?"

"Hollis said Russell and his family had gone out for his birthday Saturday night."

"So, Monday, Sunday, Saturday …"

"The number on his back was 18. His birthday was—"

"Also 18." Though it seemed a stretch, I saw where Shaw's theory was headed as she unlocked her phone and began tapping at the screen frantically.

I accelerated off the gravel and onto the paved road that would take us to the highway that intersected town.

"Shaw, are you suggesting the deaths have something to do with their birthdays?"

"Hold on," she said, still tapping the phone screen. "So, yeah. I *knew* it. May 1."

"Woodhouse?"

"Yes."

My job was to notice details, and sometimes those small bits of information sat on a shelf in the back of my head until the right moment came along. How had I not noticed this?

"And Todd, it's August 3 or September 3, right?"

"I don't know the day, but he's Virgo." I remembered this because Ed's birthday was also in early September.

"He's calling attention to their birthdays," Shaw said.

I wanted her to be correct. We needed some kind of a break.

"Anyway, I'd put money on what we'll find when we flip Riedel's body," Shaw said. "25."

Shaw was one step ahead of me with her notes. Since Curtis Riedel had been reported missing, she'd already pieced together a profile on him. "He's also a July birthday."

"Shaw," I said, "I'm not convinced here."

She didn't answer.

"But look, when we get back to the station, start searching for any other cases matching this pattern. Check NCIC and MULES."

The National Crime Information Center would help with a broader search for crimes matching our pattern, and Shaw would default to that with her work on the interagency task force. But I had a hunch this killer was local, and the Missouri Uniform Law Enforcement System might help refine the search.

There was still much work to do at Wagner Creek while the responding officers secured the crime scene at the Mariston community center, but I felt a surge of hope. The tire track wasn't much, but it might help us verify a match to the crime scene if we identified a suspect and vehicle.

And now, we might have made the first step toward solving our killer's riddle.

CHAPTER 14

Screams come in different types and qualities.

Like wine.

To him, one bottle often tasted like the next. Sometimes dry, sometimes sweet, and sometimes acidic. But he knew enough to understand that complexity came from subtle things: the soil, the fermentation, the aging.

The Walker knew these things, but recognized that his taste was not refined enough to discern the difference between a $9 bottle of wine and one that cost hundreds.

He was not a connoisseur of wines, but of screams in their many varieties.

Just as an uncultured palate might confuse one vintage for another … there was a sophistication that preceded one's ability to truly relish the nuances and cultivation of a good scream.

Of course, most people knew the experience of screams of delight and excitement—children running through a sprinkler or playfighting with a pet dog. A parent watching their child hit a double during a tight ball game.

These screams and their superficial high were like the small bottles of wine found on a gas station shelf, two sections down from the motor oil. They were of the lowest quality.

But he remembered his first exposure to the finer things that could be squeezed from the vocal cords. It was the yelps of pain that poured out from the neighbor's cockapoo (*hey puppypuppygoodboy*) decades ago, when The Walker decided to peel back the skin and see what it looked like underneath.

Just as mixing grapes produced unique flavors of wine, The Walker liked to create unique screams, letting them rise from a complexity of emotions within the victim.

> *how does that feel brodytodd those legs feel good now brodytodd that feel hot to you jimmywoodhouse let me know if that feels toohot what are you saying i can't hear you can you say that louder eartug*

Sudden, often wordless screams of panic blended with the half-born cries of anticipation and finished well with screams of terror.

His next two victims had been plucked with care—J. T. Russell, the traveling HVAC rep whose work trips kept him out of town for days at a time, and Curtis Riedel, a flooring contractor known to vanish into solo jobs without a word.

With a few forged details, a burner phone, and an empty farmhouse to serve as bait, the Walker had lured each man separately. Russell was convinced he was meeting a new client near Columbia; Riedel believed he was quoting a hardwood refinish on a rural property. They came alone. They always came alone. And with Russell's phone—unlocked under duress—The Walker had even managed to keep his wife from worrying—just a few short, reassuring texts. Enough time to begin the real work.

J. T. Russell had offered such rich and deep screams from the chair in The Walker's basement where he had been tied since the previous night.

As The Walker tightened the tourniquet around his left thigh, the reciprocating saw rested on a nearby table.

hello jt are you awekenow hi wake up buddy old friend i texted your wife and let her know all is good all is in order just hanging out with a buddy which is true isnt it be home soon love you honeybunches

The Walker prepared methodically, testing the toothed blade's bite on a 2x4.

He had applied a heavy dose of the local anesthetic lidocaine to just above where he would remove the lower part of J. T.'s leg. He had craved not the screams of pain with this procedure, but the more refined cries of panic and anticipation. Such sounds came from the visceral reaction to seeing one's body parts removed as casually as automobile parts.

tell me if that hurtsnow friend dont want you to be uncomfortable down here that chair okay for you do you need anything before i start just give me the sign

When he was a boy, The Walker remembered, he'd join his dad and two uncles at his grandfather's house for butchering. Once in the spring for beef and sometime before Thanksgiving for pork. He remembered from then the trick of sticking the blade of the saw through a garbage bag to keep the blood and pieces of flesh from splattering over the arms and the body of the saw.

A blade designed for metal worked best for bone. As he placed the teethed edge just inches below J. T.'s left knee, the screaming began. With one quick squeeze and release of the trigger, the blade ate through the skin and scored the bone underneath.

The Walker paused for a moment to watch the blood stream down from the incision.

Finally, he lifted the blade back to the initial cut. This time, when he squeezed the trigger, he did not let go.

The Walker wanted to keep his friend from passing out and missing out on their time together. In addition to the anesthetic, The Walker kept a hypodermic of epinephrine and a bottle of ammonia on the table to help J. T. stay awake and alert.

There was pain, of course, even with the numbing drugs, but these screams had been different than Brody Todd's or Jimmy Woodhouse's. Panic and desperation. Russell had strained against the twine and zip ties that held him to the chair. He cried. The crotch of his pants darkened.

> *oopsie how embarrassing but no worries just us oldfriends down here wont tell nobody at all*

Just as one might sniff a fine wine, or hold it in one's mouth for a moment, aerating it over the taste buds with a pursed-lip inhale, The Walker closed his eyes. Savored the sound.

After removing the legs, The Walker replaced the socks and running shoes he had removed. They were too nice to stain during the procedure. Russell had probably bought them hoping that evening walks would help him shed a few pounds before his next class reunion.

> *Noproblemthere jt isthere i helped you lose those pounds justnow didnt i*

The next day, The Walker had been more patient. He'd waited in the shadows as Curtis Riedel stirred awake in the brown dining room chair near the stairs to the basement.

The light was dim there but sufficient for Curtis to see across the room. When Riedel's eyes locked on his old classmate, he'd spied both legs propped in Russell's lap like souvenirs.

Riedel had then realized the items on the small table next to his chair were meant for him, in particular a box knife and a drill.

From a dark corner, The Walker had been waiting for that moment when his new basement friend would realize his present situation. That moment when he could again sip from the intoxicatingly long and high-pitched screams of terror. The pleading. The sad negotiation.

Yes, The Walker had enjoyed the inebriation of many types of screams, but there was one vintage he had not yet tasted.

Screams of grief.

He knew that such screams had probably poured from the throat of Brody Todd's widow.

But *imagining* the hollow, broken sound of these cries of grief was not enough.

The detective wanted so badly to meet him. To get his autograph, maybe. The Walker thought it would be good to invite her to his basement sometime soon.

> *so confident arent you songbirdwren coming to get me i better watch out*

There, she would witness new blood shed, only not her own.

The Walker imagined he might even purchase a small sampling of cheeses to enjoy when the time came. What paired well with a full-bodied cry of grief?

Maybe a nice cheddar, he supposed.

Aged … like his patience.

CHAPTER 15

"These incidents are being treated with the utmost seriousness, and our approach involves meticulous investigation." Chief Hilke's hands clasped the podium. His tone was measured, but firm. "We are coordinating with regional and federal partners with a focus on community safety."

We held the press conference on Tuesday morning in the precinct courtyard. The station's brick exterior served as our backdrop, including the state and national flags flopping in the afternoon breeze. The commons space on the lower level of our station could double as a media room, but Hilke preferred the outdoor location. It suggested transparency and accessibility.

Chief assured the gathered crowd of mostly reporters that cases of this magnitude were not unprecedented. The chief was a good fit for his leadership position. He towered over many of the officers, he'd mastered the piercing stare, and he spoke with a measured cadence.

He'd be a tough act to follow. But, apparently, that was the plan, as I was up next.

Another shift under Hilke's leadership was his emphasis on female leadership in the department.

Under our previous chief, either he or our director of communication would have handled any critical press conferences. But preceding Hilke's promotion, KMMO had spotlighted the department in a series of sensationalized reports.

Claims of a male bias in municipal staffing included a mention that our station's swat team had never included a female officer.

True, but only because it's tough as hell to meet the standards. Several female officers have applied, including me. I fell 17 seconds short in the time trials, tripping twice while lugging sandbags up several flights of stairs. In my defense, those sandbags might consider keto.

"But let me assure you …" Hilke emphasized his next line with pause as he made eye contact with several of the cameras surrounding. "I have complete confidence in my team, led by Detective Sara Wren, to lead the work forward."

That last line might have been meant more for me than the cameras. Hilke had called me and Hollis into his office yesterday evening after I returned from the Community Center. He'd told us that with the case getting state-level attention, he was going to accept some "low-level" assistance from the feds. It was still my case, he assured me. This was just a *resource.*

"Now," Hilke continued with a brief glance to his side where I stood, "I'm going to hand this conversation over to Detective Wren to update you on the investigation." The chief stepped aside and, with a gentle hand on my back, ushered me toward the microphone.

Stepping up to the podium, I flattened my prepared notes and adjusted the microphone downward. There was over a foot of difference between my height and the chief's.

"Thank you, Chief Hilke, and good morning. Thank you all for coming."

As I recapped activity in the case over the last few days, I spotted Ed and Wes deep in the crowd. While they came to support me, it made me more nervous to see them among the reporters.

"We are working to determine a connection between these previous cases and the recent deaths of James Woodhouse and Brody Todd. At this time, we cannot confirm a single perpetrator across all four cases."

I recognized several of the reporters, some of them veterans with the local stations and the *Mariston Gazette*. My favorite newscaster, Stacey Southern, had arrived early and secured a spot up front. She gave me a little wave when I first spotted her.

Hey, bestie!

"We've identified patterns in the way these men were targeted, and we believe the targets were selected deliberately.

"All the same, we encourage the public to remain vigilant. Be aware of your surroundings, especially after sundown or in isolated locations."

My motherly instinct underscored this last paragraph. Henry had a YMCA day camp throughout the week, and while I trusted the camp officials, I'd met with the directors of the program late last week to review their procedures and supervision practices.

"Trust your instincts. Remain calm. Stay alert. If you or someone you know believes they may have information—no matter how minor it may seem—we urge you to contact the department's tip line.

"To the families of the victims, our hearts are with you." I made sure to make direct eye contact with Sullivan's camera. "You deserve justice, and we are committed to seeing that delivered."

With my next line, I suspected Chief Hilke might regret inviting me to the microphone. I went off script.

"To the person responsible: You want to be noticed. I promise you, we're watching. And we're closer than you think."

As I concluded the update, I glanced at Ed and Wes. Wes gave me a thumbs up close to his chest. Ed wore a supportive smile. I wanted to join them, but I'd be swarmed by the media.

Plus, we had work to do. Shaw had prepared a presentation based on her profiling, and Witt had located surveillance video from near the community center.

At just past 3:15 a.m. Monday, security footage caught a black crossover passing near where Curtis Riedel's body would be found later that day. The vehicle could have been an Equinox or a Tucson or a similar-looking model. With a hatch and collapsible back seat, the small SUV would easily stow a body.

The pawn shop where we'd found the footage was located a block away from the community center. Thirty minutes after the first sighting, the car passed again, heading in the opposite direction. This was enough time for the killer to have staged Riedel's body.

The footage was from very early Monday morning. There was very little illumination other than street lights, especially for the low-resolution camera, meant primarily to survey cars in the parking lot. The license plate wasn't visible from the angle, and street lights put a problematic glare on the driver's side window when the car passed a second time. But it *appeared* that a white male was driving the vehicle.

As with the Camry from Todd's disappearance, our LPR system was able to work off a description of the car, especially since it had been traveling at night, when streets were relatively clear.

Though we successfully tracked it deeper into the city, the system eventually lost the scent. Most of our LPR cameras are clustered near government buildings and in areas with higher crime patterns, so it's far from the perfect network of surveillance that we needed now.

If this were a television show, Witt would have already used some powerful AI program to enhance the image to crystal-clarity. We'd be able to zoom in and determine if the driver needed to invest in a nose hair trimmer. We'd be able to isolate the reflection in his eyes to see what radio station he preferred.

But with the actual software available to law enforcement, no amount of noise reduction, enhancing, or deblurring was going to give us a clear description of the driver. It couldn't reconstruct a license plate from a few pixels captured at a tricky angle.

Casey had knocked on a few doors in the largely-Hispanic neighborhood near the community center, but nobody indicated being familiar with a vehicle matching that description.

However, we had a tire track from the Wagner Creek scene, and we had a short list of possible makes and models. Maybe, with the next break, we'd be able to triangulate our information and zero in on a useful lead.

Following the press conference, we gathered in the briefing room for Shaw's presentation. In addition to the key members of my team, we had a guest. Special Agent Victor Hale, on loan from the FBI field office, sat quietly off to the side.

Creases in Hale's forehead and a few gray strands suggested he was in his 40s, but his slim frame in the dark suit made him look like a teenager headed to Homecoming.

All he needed was the corsage and a half-ounce of Axe body spray.

Hale *did* maintain a better mustache than most high school kids, though. But just barely.

After the agent arrived this morning, our only exchange was brief. He gave his name and then studied our office.

As Shaw continued her presentation, Hale studied the room. It seemed he was trying to get the measure of this local crew.

"I'm estimating the perpetrator is in his late 30s to early 50s," Shaw continued, glancing excessively at me. I tried to support her with occasional nods. "He is physically strong enough to subdue and move grown men."

As Shaw continued, I tried to hide my yawn. I've been neck deep in the case since early this morning. Last night, after a quick run home to check in, I'd returned to the station and worked past midnight.

I'm sure that, when I did the press conference for the local news this morning, Stacey Southern used the latest ultra-high-def cameras to catch the bags under my eyes. I was operating on fewer than three hours of sleep on a single-mattress bed in the station crash room.

I was tired and cranky.

"He's organized. That's the biggest thing." Shaw advanced to a slide that displayed all four of the discovered bodies. "The level of planning, the disposal sites, the precision—these aren't rage-kills and there's no evidence of sexual contact with the victims. He's trying to demonstrate his control over them and this entire situation."

Estimates suggest Curtis Riedel died more recently than J. T. Russell. Riedel got to keep both of his legs, but his trade-off wasn't any better.

The medical examiner was still working with the corpse, but upon arriving at the body, I counted over twenty wounds just on the front side. A drill bit had chewed through his lower jaw, leaving a ragged circle of torn enamel and bone dust that still clung to his lips. Several fingers and toes had small holes through the nails.

Shaw should add it to her profile that our guy is a fan of home improvement shows.

Shaw tapped her pen. "We're dealing with someone who's ritualistic and theatrical."

I glanced at Hale and caught his smirk. I don't have a lot of confidence in behavior profiles, myself. It seems like they always produce the same results, that the perp is a young man, white, with a low-level job. He has difficulties maintaining relationships, and harbors lots of anger, especially toward women."

But for Hale to drive into Mariston just to smirk at *any* member of my team …

I wanted to tase the guy.

"The torture methods are distinct and escalated," Shaw continued, flipping through photos of the victims. "But they're not sadistic in the way some serial offenders are. He's not deriving pleasure from blood and guts. He's staging a message. The number carvings, the posing, and the locations are symbolic. And he wants us to see it. The wounds aren't frenzied—they're precise."

I disagreed. He *is* deriving pleasure. But I kept my mouth shut. Agent Hale showed no reaction, and I felt he was analyzing Shaw more so than the case.

So I was on her side here.

"He likely lives alone and has access to a space where he won't be interrupted," she continued. "He's forensically aware and possibly has a background in something like maintenance, logistics, or even medicine. He's comfortable with tools and pain, but not sloppy about it."

She looked up. "If I had to guess, there's a trauma history here. Something from childhood or adolescence—something that curdled into fixation. These aren't just killings. They're reenactments. He's replaying something."

"Nice job," I whispered to Shaw as we walked past each other following her presentation. But I could tell she was still deflated from a setback when her theory was debunked at the community center.

When we were finally able to roll Riedel's body yesterday afternoon, his back was marked with the same subcutaneous numbering as the three previous victims.

Only, it turns out, the killer had not marked Riedel's body with Shaw's prediction of 25, but with the non-calendrical number 43.

I'm not a fan of perpetrator nicknames, as I feel like they glorify the bad guy. But the 'Birthday Killer,' as some of the officers dubbed him after Shaw's theory, had thrown us another curveball.

CHAPTER 16

Tuesday night, Ed, Wes, and I went to Henry's game. The three of us munched on popcorn and cheeseburgers as Henry's team, the Sparks, took on the Rebels in the recreation-league playoff game.

Though the June heat pressed upon us, a cool breeze had moved in. It was likely a harbinger of the storm that was darkening the sky far to our west.

Henry started in right and batted deep in the lineup. He'd reached base twice—once on a walk and once after a fastball into his calf. The Sparks held a two-run lead going into the final inning.

I sat by Ed, my hand next to him on the bleachers, my pinkie tickling his thigh. At one point he noticed it, smiled at me, and took my hand in his.

Several times during the game, I had to shush my brother, and at one point, the umpire did it for me when Wes asked him if his strike zone was still bound by the four dimensions of space and time.

"You're going to get us ejected."

"The ball was literally above that kids nose! He would have needed a step-ladder to hit it."

"I mean, he's right." Ed shrugged. He wore a jersey that the coaches had conspired with the moms to make for a previous game on Father's Day. HENRY'S DAD, it read on the back.

Ed is a notoriously mellow sports fan. He'd run cross country and swung a tennis racket in high school, two sports where the parents rarely showed up buzzed and ready to argue calls.

As the game wound down, my restless mind kept revisiting the case. For the last three innings, there was *something* nagging me from the case.

All the victims were middle-aged men from Mariston who appeared to know each other casually. Their bodies had all been staged in public with grotesque signs of the torture they'd endured before the mercy of death.

There had to be a connection.

Sam Todd had still not located the envelope Brody received, which I hoped would be a key to unlocking our next development.

Movement on the field pulled my attention back to the game. The Sparks had returned to the dugout for their at-bat. They were five batters deep with two outs.

"Henry's probably not going to bat again," I said to Ed.

"Not likely. He's had a good season. Soccer in the fall?"

"Unfortunately, yes." Henry would play recreation league soccer, as well, so his games would take place on Saturday mornings on the floodplain fields. It was a ridiculously windy experience, and I always underestimated how cold and dewy it would be.

My phone buzzed. The text was from Hollis. Stacey Southern from KMMO had called Chief Hilke, pressing for further commentary. She was preparing a report for the 6:00 broadcast. Hollis said that Chief was frustrated with the call and the slant of the questions.

Awesome. Just what we needed.

The batter swung at the next pitch, low and outside. Strike three. He smacked his bat on the ground and sulked back to the dug-out.

Henry and his teammates jogged out to defend their lead in the last inning. With a score this tight, Coach wasn't going to pull him in to second base this inning.

I'd played short stop on my high school softball team, and our team won state my junior year. None of my athleticism got mixed into Henry's DNA.

The temperature had dropped several degrees as the storm approached. A napkin tumbled past. I wished I'd worn jeans.

My phone buzzed again. This time it was Shaw.

Got time later? She asked.

At a game, I responded. *What's up?*

Just want to connect. Not urgent

Ed heard my sigh and put his hand on my knee. "Everything good?"

"Yeah," I said. "Work stuff."

He smiled. "Okay." Then a wink. "I feel like we're near a win here. Just gotta hold 'em."

Wes had stepped away and was pacing back behind the bleachers, keeping his mouth under control as the Sparks tried to secure their first victory in weeks. Occasionally, he'd offer commentary to fans on the back bench, who typically responded with a glance or polite nod.

I'm good for a call in fifteen, I typed.

Something happened on the infield, and I saw runners advance.

Can I come by? Shaw wrote.

My house???

Whatever she wanted could surely wait until tomorrow morning at the station. I wasn't sure I wanted Shaw—or anyone associated with the case—around during one of the rare and brief moments when I could be home.

Yeah. That okay? Shaw responded.

Sure … but won't be home for a bit. I'll text

We'd probably catch a bite to eat after the game, and Shaw had said there was nothing urgent.

Among the half-leads we had, the numbers were still running through my head. Shaw had been wrong on her birthday theory, but I couldn't shake the feeling that she had been close to figuring out the real connection.

1, 3, 18, 43.

They'd appeared in sequential order. Three were tied to birthdays. Was that beyond coincidence? Something was dancing right in front of us.

The phone buzzed again, but as I looked down to see Shaw's response, the Sparks crowd got loud. I looked up in time to see one of the Rebels running from third and sliding into home. Their fan section lit up next as the lead narrowed to one run.

"Nice catch, Hank!" Wes shouted from behind us. He ran up to the fence. "Two down, one to go for the win! Let's go, Sparks!"

Ed nudged me. "What about that!" he said, but his smile faltered when he saw my phone open on my lap and, no doubt, a mixture of confusion and regret in my eyes.

His eyebrows furrowed for just a moment.

But long enough.

And then Ed smiled, patted my knee, and attempted to rescue me from the moment.

"Pretty good catch, wasn't it?"

My heart stopped. What had I missed?

I quickly scanned the field and spotted Henry in right field, punching into his glove and ready for the next batter.

"Snagged a deep line drive," Ed said, giving me a quick scratch on the back. He saw that I was beating myself up for having missed the play. "Definitely a reason for ice cream after."

I nodded, closed out the group chat, and stared into right field, willing another pop fly in Henry's direction so I could see him catch it this time.

I hate myself.

CHAPTER 17

After finishing his early morning work at Wagner Creek and the community center early Monday morning, The Walker decided to dedicate the next few days to getting to know Detective Wren better.

The detective maintained a low profile on social media, but she was a public figure. After less than an hour online, he had located several useful pieces of information, including pictures of her and her husband at a fundraising event.

Ed Wren had a robust social media presence, which he mostly used for professional networking and for displaying houses and professional buildings he had designed.

There were, though, pictures of their son—Henry, according to a few posts.

The family on a beach, the pier in the background.

The boy and his baseball team posing with trophies.

In one picture, possibly a costume party, the detective is dressed like a lobster. Her husband, an octopus. The boy is dressed as a starfish.

> *hahahahahaha funfamily lobstercop and starfishboy the strong arm of the claw haha*

With a few minutes of tapping on his keyboard, The Walker located the husband's business in public records and also the family's address. Street view allowed him to visit the home from the laptop in his dining room.

The two-story house sat near the end of a cul-de-sac. The Walker wondered if the architect husband had designed the two-story house. Tan board siding complemented the cream brick. Dark brown trim matched the woodwork on the gabled front porch.

In a more congested neighborhood, The Walker might have been able to stake out the location from the road, but the larger lots only allowed a dozen houses up and down the road. All of them had attached garages, so very few cars were parked along the street.

Fortunately, the cul-de-sac backed up to a section of wooded conservation land, and later that day, The Walker was able to find a location in the brush nearby. A pair of hunting binoculars allowed him a good view of the Wren family home from the privacy and the shade of the conservation area's untamed flora.

On Tuesday morning, he noticed that before Wren left in the morning, her husband *arrived.* Did he not live here any longer? Architects didn't work night shifts, after all.

His suspicion was further heightened when, rather than entering the house, the husband knocked on the door. The Songbird answered. Separated? Divorced?

He would have to do more online research that evening.

The detective, dressed for work, stood at the front door and talked with her husband for a couple of minutes.

At one point, the songbird turned back into the house and appeared to speak to someone inside.

> *was that the cutelittleboy or maybe a new man to replace octopushusband*

Wren did a motion with her hand that seemed to indicate that whomever she spoke to should hurry up, and a couple of minutes later, Henry appeared at the door. He wore summer clothes and a backpack.

The Walker made a mental note to research opportunities for summer school and area camps.

Before her husband and son left, Wren pulled a tube from a pouch on the boy's backpack and rubbed its contents on his face, neck, and arms. The Walker took a moment to study the husband's car, memorizing the license plate.

After mom, dad, and son had left for the day, The Walker used the surrounding conservation area to survey the rear of the house.

> *could try the door and go inside but better not now maybe sometimesoon to stop by for a visit maybe stop by the bedroom and say hey songbirdwren just in the neighborhood wanna come downstairs and get coffee bring cutelittleboy with you if you want and we can tug ears and all have fun since octopusman is not here and we can talk about that tough case and those poor men*

On Tuesday morning, he learned that the boy attended a camp at Singer Lake. The several acres of water were surrounded by wooded areas, a disc golf course, and other recreational sites.

The camp had been the most likely of the summer activities he had found online the night before. Wren's son didn't look dressed for sports.

It took him several minutes to navigate the conservation area, back to where he had parked. From there, he drove to Singer Lake and eased through the parking lot, scanning for the husband's car.

Bingo.

Spotting the white Highlander, The Walker backed into a spot and waited. While Detective Wren might have had the instinctual awareness to notice that she was being trailed, the husband seemed clueless. The Walker held back several yards, just close enough to track the vehicle.

From the lake park onto another street and another, one vehicle tracked the other. Both eventually took a ramp onto the highway and exited into downtown Mariston.

Maybe the architect husband kept an office outside the home, as well, The Walker speculated as he pulled up two cars behind the target at a red light. But after two more intersections, the Highlander signaled left mid-block, indicating an exit into a public parking lot. Across the street was the Mariston Municipal Center and, next to it, the police headquarters.

what is going on here looks interesting and cameras and news this looks interesting for sure

A small crowd had already gathered. News vans in the parking lot suggested that a press event was about to take place.

After the husband turned into the lot, The Walker and the vehicle in front of him accelerated past. He made three left turns at the next intersection, however, and parked in a metered spot along the road nearly a block away from the station.

After exiting his vehicle, The Walker put his phone to his ear and pretended to be distracted by a conversation as he descended the hill and approached the station.

The Songbird was standing by the lectern, chatting with another officer nearby as the reporters and camera crews prepared for someone to approach the microphone.

What a lucky day!

He repressed a chuckle as he thought about how frustrated the police must be. He'd cleaned his last borrowed car spotless, wiping meticulously everywhere he might have touched, even to the point of using a nail file to shove disinfectant wipes into tight spaces.

But, in just two days, The Walker had learned so much about Detective Wren. Where she lived. Where she sent her son to camp. The names of her son and husband … or maybe he was an *ex*-husband.

And now, he would push the irony even further, crossing the street to listen in to a press briefing. Just a curious pedestrian killing time before returning to the drudgery of the office.

As the detective finished her conversation and approached the microphone, The Walker noticed that, in a survey of the gathered crowd, Wren's glance passed over him without a pause. Dressed in a Polo and slacks, he would have passed for one of the thousands who worked in the downtown area.

After a few words from the police chief, the detective approached the microphone.

"Good morning," the songbird said, glancing at her script. "We are working to determine a connection between …"

Hearing Wren's words, he felt like a playwright watching his lines performed on stage for the first time. While he did not write her speech, his actions had shaped it.

"We've identified patterns in the way these victims have been targeted." Wren paused to give this line emphasis, glanced at her notes, and continued, "And we believe these victims were selected deliberately."

> *yes they were have you not figured that out for sure detective but really just a noisy songbird*

The Walker suspected—no, *knew*—that the team of detectives and their worker bees were scrambling to decipher his pattern, despite the many clues he had left.

Soon, he'd reveal his motive. But, by then, the narrative will have changed.

Scanning the crowd, The Walker spotted the husband Ed near the back of the crowd.

And … he wasn't alone.

The priest had come, too.

Fr. Wes Brandt.

The Walker had learned the name after accessing the parish website later in the afternoon on the day he spotted him eating with Wren. Brandt, with his black shirt and pants and thick, brown beard, stood out in a crowd of reporters who had dressed for the summer heat.

> *bless me father for i know not what i do or bless me not father for i know what i do*

The Walker had been curious, at first, as to why the detective had driven to the church so far out of Mariston. When she and the priest departed and lunched together at the diner, he realized that the intent of the meeting was something other than confession, though he suspected the detective did need of absolution, given her lack of humility at the microphone.

As if to substantiate his assumption, Wren concluded her comments with a message directly to The Walker.

"I promise you, we're watching," she said. "And we're closer than you think."

> *here i am songbird but i am watching you too and closer than you think i am right here*

When The Walker arrived back home that afternoon, the house felt strangely empty with J. T. and Curtis now delivered to the city.

Soon that would change.

Back online, he began the research he should have done the first time he witnessed Wren and the priest. He found a picture of the two of them together on Brandt's Instagram page, Wren in a bathing suit and Brandt shirtless, but with trunks on. In a boat and on a river, they were making silly faces for the camera and pointing at each other.

He hadn't been able to see it before, when watching them through binoculars or at a distance during the press release. But the family resemblance was undeniable.

If not twins, then close-aged siblings.

> *you and i should spend some timetogether*
> *songbirdwren and talk about things maybebring that*
> *brotherpriest withyou or cutelittleboy or*
> *darlingliveselsewherehusband*

It was about time for them all to get together. He'd happily host them at his house.

CHAPTER 18

The four of us, along with another family from Henry's team, went out for pizza and ice cream after the game. Wes ate most of a pizza by himself. In high school, he'd had the metabolism to do that, but I often have to remind him that he's now in his thirties and no longer on a soccer team.

Geoff and Brooke, the other couple, were friends of ours from Henry's school. When you have a kid, you find that your friends are mostly the parents of your kid's friends.

Following Henry's catch, our pitcher had walked a second runner, who stole second. A bobble at short gave both runners the go-ahead, and the scoring run slid into the plate just as the catcher snagged the left-fielder's impressive throw.

Game over. 7-6. The Rebels won. The season was done. And though I missed Henry's catch, I was able to channel his joy as the four of us ate pizza and shoveled ice cream.

Henry and I headed home in the rain, which fell so heavily that we often had to slow to below the speed limit. Several times, my tires sent up walls of water from the streams of drainage alongside the road.

Henry brought up his catch multiple times during the drive. One of the younger boys in his class, he struggled to keep up with the others physically, especially with so many families red-shirting their kids before kindergarten. Catching that ball in right field was the highlight of his season.

As I pulled into the garage, Henry told me he thought he might need a big barrel bat next year.

I played along while amused that, in his mind, his base hit from an accidental contact would've cleared the fence.

If he'd just had the right bat …

Dropping my purse on the kitchen counter, I sent Henry straight to the shower and bed. He jogged up the stairs, still wearing the rec league participation medal.

Then, I remembered the lingering request from Shaw.

Home, but wiped out, I typed. *Maybe tomorrow?*

A few response bubbles popped up, danced around, and then disappeared and didn't return.

The phone would let me know when Shaw responded.

The onslaught of rain continued outside my bedroom walls as I kicked my shoes into the closet and changed into something I could fall asleep in. After brushing and washing my face, I wanted to collapse on the mattress. Despite the respite of a ball game and dinner with friends, my tank was empty.

But my evening wasn't finished.

As much as I wanted to avoid perseverating over the case at the moment, I needed to watch the KMMO report.

On so many days over the last week, Ed had been home with us. It felt like he should be with me on the couch now. Preparing to sleep there, maybe.

But *with me* nonetheless.

The house seemed larger and emptier. Even though I knew Henry was preparing for bed upstairs, it felt as though he was with Ed somewhere else.

And Wes was with them, too, as was the family we had eaten with. Everyone except me, alone on a couch in a house a world away.

Just me … and Stacey Southern.

Once I found the earlier broadcast, I forwarded through general news and the weather. The urgent graphics and bumper track transitioned to Southern standing in front of the Mariston community center.

"Good evening." Southern nodded gently toward the camera. No smile tonight. "Mariston police continue to struggle in their search for the individual behind four violent murders in the last three weeks. Recently, the department has requested help from the FBI."

"Bitch," I muttered. It was the nicest of the words that came to mind at the moment.

Lightning flashed outside the patio door. The house vibrated and the lights flickered.

It looked like Southern—whatever kind of a last name that was—had her hair done up for the special report. Cascading waves of blonde fluttered in the breeze.

"Running the investigation, Detective Sara Wren updated the public in front of the Mariston police station yesterday. We were there."

"Of course, you were there," I hissed. "You're the news, and it was a press briefing. Why do you even have to say that part?"

In the video of me addressing the press, my hair is anything but a display of cascading waves. I'd barely dried it that morning and the wind whipped it in every direction.

"Night, Mom. Love you!" Henry yelled from the top of the stairs.

Pausing the video, I yelled back at him, "Proud of you tonight, Superstar!"

Not long ago, he would have refused to go to bed with a storm like this.

Reluctantly, I returned to the special report.

"If you or someone you know believes they may have information, no matter how minor it might seem," I said in the clip, "we urge you to contact the department's tip line."

That's it.

That was the entirety of what the broadcast included from my public update.

"So, while law enforcement officials plead with the public for assistance," Southern told her viewers, "victims' families struggle to find peace or closure as a killer remains free."

The special report cut to a shot inside the Russell home with Woodhouses's widow Kaitlyn and her two boys sitting together on a sectional couch.

This isn't going to be good.

Shaw and I had visited Kaitlyn yesterday evening. She'd been cooperative, though generally unhelpful. In addition to losing her husband, she'd realized during our conversation that the texts she'd received had been from the killer posing as J. T.

In Southern's report, she sat in a chair next to Kate and asked if the widow had hope that there would be justice for her husband's death.

Wiping back tears and taking a deep breath, Kaitlyn shook her head. "I don't know why they can't find the monster who did this to Jesse."

The boy to Kaitlyn's left, a slimmer and mop-haired version of his father, took his mom's hand. I now felt like the bad guy in this scenario. Russell had only died because we … I … allowed it to happen.

"If they'd found him after the first one or the second one," she said, "My Jesse would be here with us tonight. These boys would have their daddy."

The youngest boy caved and buried his face into his mother's side.

My heart was pounding. My mouth was dry.

I'm sure that Southern had also interviewed the Riedel family and was saving that conversation for the second part of her exposé. We'd talked with Curtis's widow this afternoon. She hadn't been ready for the conversation on Monday after learning that he'd been found dead at the community center.

The report over, I switched to a sitcom and fell against a pile of pillows, inhaling deeply. I held my breath for several seconds and then exhaled with force.

Repeating the controlled pattern, I sought calm and hoped for sleep, though I doubted I'd find either. Given my restless nights I should have gone to bed, but I stayed on the couch, taking comfort in the spot where Ed slept when he stayed over.

As I stared at the TV, my mind circled back to that moment during the game when I'd almost seen a connection.

Instead of chasing sleep, I considered grabbing a notebook and journaling to chase the thoughts down. But exhaustion pressed harder, and the paralysis of indecision kept me from both revelation and rest.

Sleeping pills waited on the nightstand in my room.

Almost rolling off the couch, I started down the hall toward the bedroom.

And that's when I heard the knock at my front door.

CHAPTER 19

My gun was in the nightstand. I instinctively wanted to grab it, my nerves on edge with the level of evil we had been dealing with.

Calm down, Sara …

Instead, I pulled out my phone to access the doorbell cam. But as my thumb dropped to tap it, I saw three unread text messages from Shaw. I'd set the phone to do-not-disturb during pizza—an attempt to redeem myself from the earlier mom failure. I'd never switched the settings back and had missed the notifications.

Headed to your house, Shaw had sent a half-hour ago. *Bringing ice cream*

Then, fifteen minutes later: *You there?*

And just now, she'd written, *Hey, sorry. Outside* Here, she inserted a frowny face and lightning and storm clouds emojis. *Can I come in???*

As I walked to the foyer, I debated what I was going to say when I opened the door. If she'd come to my house at nearly ten in the evening to talk about the case, there may be a new body dump site to investigate tomorrow.

Shaw wore a thin rain poncho, rain dotting her glasses. She cradled a quart of ice cream.

"Are you serious right now, Shaw?"

"I saw the news broadcast," she said over the drone of the heavy rain. "And it's been a rough week." She lifted the quart toward me as a peace offering. "So …"

"You know I want to shoot your tires out so you have to walk home in this rain, right?"

"I know." She moved her fingers so I could see the label. "Salted chocolate caramel. Your favorite, right?"

"Who's the spy?"

She mockingly zipped her lips.

"Let's narrow it down to a small group. Does his name rhyme with Detective Feet Facey?"

Shaw shrugged, a dimple betraying her secret.

"You're allergic to dairy."

"And eggs. This would literally kill me."

Shaw is allergic to everything.

"Were your plans to just watch me eat ice cream? Because … not weird at all."

"I'm not allergic to wine, and I brought that, too."

"Shaw, I'm not going to drink wine and eat ice cream with you at 10:00 on a Tuesday night."

She made a face and looked even more pitiful now. I eyed the dark, the rain, and the sad figure on my doorstep. Then, I reconsidered the ice cream and stepped out of the way.

"I'll get you a towel."

She smiled and did a funny shrug with her shoulders. "Yeah!" She took a step forward.

"Wait," I said. "Get the alcohol first."

Minutes later, I was drinking wine and eating ice cream with Shaw at 10:00 on a Tuesday night.

Under her poncho, which we left in the foyer, Shaw wore sweats and a tank top, her hair pulled back into a little fountain on the back of her head. I felt like I was in middle school, hanging out with my BFF.

Especially when the subject of boys came up.

"We kissed once," she said, referring to her time on the drug task force with Casey. "A few times making out, and …"

"And?"

"And one time not just making out," she said, looking down, smirking, taking a sip of her wine to let the comment linger. "But just once."

I wanted to suggest this is why Casey recommended her, but I've been beating Shaw down too much, taking my frustrations and self-doubts out on her.

"Shaw, I wish I could say you were wrong about the birthdays," I said. *In vino, veritas.* "Because I feel like there's still something there."

"Hale thinks I'm ridiculous. I can tell." She stared at her glass, holding it between us and slowly swirling the wine.

"Hale's an ass," I said. "A man-child with a suit and a gun."

She shrugged. "But the birthday theory *was* wrong."

"I can't shake the feeling that you're right anyway. Maybe it isn't *the* answer, but I think it's *part of* the answer somehow."

I didn't want to suck our discussion back into the case. That was tomorrow morning's burden. But with her vulnerability under Hale's scrutiny, I felt protective. The annoyer of my annoyer …

Shaw didn't respond. She stood and walked to a family picture across the room. In it, Ed, Henry, and I were standing in coordinated spring colors in front of a barn.

"This is your family," she said, taking the photo from the mantle. "Ed, right?"

"And our son, Henry."

"Hunky guy. Ed, I mean. Things any better?" she asked.

I answered with a shrug.

I'd not invited Shaw into my circle of trust regarding our marital struggle, but I wasn't surprised that she knew. I'm sure everyone knew. Stacey Southern was probably trying to set up an interview with Ed right now for her next exposé.

"Tonight was nice." I told her about the ball game and the pizza. "Maybe if …"

It was back. The intuition that had eluded me during the game. The mercurial connection.

I leaned forward, putting my wine glass on the table.

"Wren?" Shaw returned, sat next to me, and put her hand on my arm. I probably looked like I had turned ill, but the thought was pressing hard now, wanting to be discovered.

1. 3. 18. All birth dates.

"Wren, what's going on?"

"You were right, Shaw. It *is* something with the birthdates, but …"

Something had clicked when Shaw asked about the family photo. Some deep thought was signaling from the dark. I took the frame from Shaw and stood to walk around the table as I considered the photo.

"43, 43. Shaw, what is 43?"

She stood next to me now, trying to scrutinize the photo like it was a stereogram.

Henry. It was something with Henry.

Why was my brain hinting at a connection between my son and this nightmare case?

Henry, my handsome goofball. My undaunted optimist.

Henry, my anchor, my best thing with Ed.

Henry, my …

My awkward little athlete.

Then, I saw it. I saw the pattern.

CHAPTER 20

Late Wednesday morning, we gathered in the briefing room. Agent Hale invited himself when he saw us assembling. Coffee mug in hand, he nodded to the small crowd as he entered, again taking a seat in the corner.

Shaw, Hollis, and Casey sat in the front row with a few other members of the team scattered behind them.

The four of us had met prior to discuss the new theory behind the murders. Adrian Witt arrived five minutes into the briefing and took a seat near the door.

Last night, when Shaw and her bottle of wine had paid me a visit, the elements of the case finally swirled into an image of Henry running from the dug-out to right field.

"Jersey numbers!" I'd shouted, leaving Shaw sitting stunned on the couch as I jogged up the stairs. Henry's uniform lay atop a scatter of baseball gear on his bedroom floor. Back in the living room, I held it up for Shaw to see the large 22 on the back of the shirt. "Maybe the carvings are supposed to resemble jersey numbers."

The Sparks wore white jerseys with red lettering, which now looked disturbingly like the red, block-letters carved into the victim's backs.

When I'd brought Henry's uniform home at the start of the season, I told Shaw, he'd been disappointed to see it was the number 22.

"Know why?"

After a pause, Shaw's eyes had opened in revelation. "Wait, when was your son's birthday?" Shaw had impressed me again by intuiting the answer within seconds.

"June, but not the 22nd," I'd said. "I'd signed him up late and his birthday number—13—had already been taken. He'd used it for previous years and when he played soccer."

"Three of the men had their birthday dates carved into their backs." Shaw's voice had betrayed her excitement at being vindicated in her earlier theory.

"And," I'd agreed, "Maybe Riedel's mom had just late signed him up. Maybe someone else already had his number. Maybe neither of them cared, and he liked another number for some reason. His favorite pro or something."

At the briefing, I reminded the assembled group of Shaw's theory and displayed a picture of Henry's jersey on the monitors to either side of me.

With a click of the presentation remote, I advanced to a picture of Todd's mutilated back.

In our investigation, we learned that only three of the four victims attended the same high school—J. T. went to a private school—and even those three didn't share a common roster for any collegiate sports.

"So, what about before ninth grade?" I asked rhetorically. "Had they been on a youth team together?"

It seemed a stretch to believe this would have anything to do with the murders. But being a detective means training the brain to solve puzzles by piecing together interlocking clues. Seeing motives in the mundane. Clues among clutter.

Yes, there was always a risk of apophenia, a tendency to see patterns in unrelated ideas, but a healthy measure of skepticism can keep this in check.

"Woodhouse attended a parochial school before ninth grade." I clicked to a picture of Hope Lutheran School and followed that with slides of the two public middle schools as I continued. "Russell went to Eisenhower Middle School on the east end, while Todd and Riedel were at Truman on the west side."

Hale had been on his phone since the briefing began, taking only quick glances early in my presentation. But now, his posture had straightened and he was studying my slides.

"But the one thing these men had common," I continued, "was this team."

The next slide pictured several boys in baseball uniforms, half of them kneeling and the others standing behind them on either side of the coaches, one of whom hefted an obnoxiously large trophy.

This, and other pictures in my slideshow were from photos Todd's parents had provided from their collection.

I still remember the look of resignation when the older couple offered these tangible memories of their son to our investigation. If it were me, with pictures of Henry, I know I would feel I was giving away the lingering spirit of him, one ethereal piece at a time.

"I know it's hard to see in this picture," I continued, "but we've confirmed with one of the victim's mothers that *this* is Woodhouse." The next slide zoomed in on one of the boys in the standing row. I'd inserted a red circle around the number 1 on the chest of his jersey.

"Here's Todd." I advanced to a similar picture, this time of a kneeling boy. A green arrow graphic indicated the 3 on his jersey.

Hale was paying attention now.

"Russell." The jersey number in his photo was distorted by the way his shirt folded in the kneeling pose, but it was obviously either 18 or 13.

"Here is Russell pictured with a youth football team." In a zoomed version on the next slide, the 18 was clear on Russell's padded jersey. "He was born on the 18th. He picked it for his jersey for every sport he played."

I noticed Hollis react to this last photo, stepping forward to see the picture more clearly. The lieutenant was a bit older than the victims, but given his size, I suspected he'd also played on the team for Eisenhower Junior High, a feeder for the Mariston public school.

"And here is Riedel." I returned to the baseball group shot again, including a close-up of Riedel's mutilated body. In both images, the number 43 was clear. "The marking on all four men are consistent with the jersey numbers we see in this and other pictures from their junior high teams."

The wine and breakthrough girls' night had ended with a hug and an apology from me for the way I'd treated Shaw over the last week. She had climbed much higher in my list of favorite people.

"Woodhouse isn't pictured with the football team," I continued in the briefing room. "But all four victims played for this traveling baseball team, the Mariston *Thunder*."

I returned to the trophy picture.

"This is the year that the boys won their league championship."

The next photo highlighted two of the four adults in the picture.

"Todd's and Russell's dads helped coach."

According to Coach Todd, the team did well in league and tournament play. Their eight-grade year was the last year that this particular group of boys would play together before high school sorted them differently.

Though we'd already interviewed a few surviving members of the team in our earlier work, we had been basing our earlier questions on adult and high school connections.

Now we needed to revisit those conversations in light of the junior high team. We'd have to hunt down coaches and team parents and try to sniff out whatever was motivating our killer to connect back to this team.

The amount of backtracking that lay before us was overwhelming.

We divided up into interview groups and brainstormed on questions that we needed to keep consistent from one conversation to the next.

"Oh, hold up," I said as we ended the meeting. "The envelope that Sam Todd mentioned Brody getting. That's still a loose end. Maybe nothing, but ask specifically about it when you chat with these guys."

Everyone emptied except for me and Hale. The agent eyed the photo a moment longer. I didn't say anything, waiting for him to make the first move. He finally spoke, voice flat.

"I've seen worse theories."

"That's a really nice compliment, Agent Hale," I said. "Thank you for pouring your heart out."

He wasn't looking at me when he said it—he was still focused on the team photo I'd left displayed on the two monitors. Was he considering the theory or trying to formulate a rebuttal to it?

"You think it's a coincidence?" I tried to repress a smirk, but failed.

"Coincidence and causality are cousins," he said, now turning his attention to me.

I exhaled slowly. "So, you think it's nothing?"

He gave the smallest shake of his head. "I didn't say that." A pause. "I think it's … localized. Tight circle. Personal history. But maybe nothing more."

He walked slowly to the conference room window, glanced out at where Shaw was at Casey's desk, the two of them prepping.

"It's a lot of weight to put on a middle school photo. But …" He glanced at the team roster, still displayed on the monitors.

"Just so we're on the same page," I said, but I knew he wasn't looking to affirm my theory.

Hale turned, finally meeting my eyes. "You've made progress. But the scale of this? The potential for escalation? It might be time to think about our practical limitations."

"Meaning?" I asked, even though I already knew.

He took a sip from his mug. "Meaning if this is the same guy who's already taken four lives, and he's working from a list—then it isn't a question of if. It's a question of *when* we will find one of the men in that picture dead."

I didn't flinch. "Are you suggesting more federal involvement?"

"Are you suggesting you can beat the clock?"

I no longer wanted to tase him. I wanted to do a full body cavity search with a plumber's snake.

"We need this case solved," he continued. "Clean. Fast. Without risking a press conference where you get ambushed on camera by an emotional widow."

There it was. Southern's special report. Hale had probably watched it with a bowl of popcorn and some Skittles.

"Agent Hale, we've been running this investigation with all cylinders firing since the beginning."

"And I'm not suggesting otherwise." He held up a hand. "But I've worked with teams that were too close to a case. Too invested. Missed the larger picture because they were standing inside the frame."

"And you think your team would do better?"

A flicker of something passed across his face. Arrogance? Ambition? Then he checked himself.

"I think …" He flashed a smile. "I *think* that the Mariston crew has laid a solid foundation. Especially today. But this is bigger than you want to admit."

Hale took a few steps toward the door, paused, and turned back.

"Is there something you need to prove, here, Detective Wren?"

I glared at him.

Then Hale gave a tight nod and left the room.

CHAPTER 21

Witt has always been good at patterns, so I pulled him from behind his screens to help now that we had more ground to cover.

Steve Winters was first on our line-up of interviews. In the 8th-grade team photo, he's the tallest and heftiest of the boys in the back row. I saw why he switched to track. He looked, even in that picture, like he could sling a discus across the river.

Winters had agreed to meet us at his house at 1:30. Since we were ready to depart from the station at noon, it gave me and Witt time for a quick detour. In addition to the interviews we had planned for Wednesday afternoon, I wanted to track down the field that Thunder had played on years ago.

Barely visible from the road, the field was tucked behind an Eagles hall. I parked near the admissions hut. Over a decade ago, the Mariston voters approved a substantial upgrade to several of the city's recreational facilities, including the ones where Henry and his team now played.

Private fields like this were used significantly less than in the past. The depth of this outfield was limited by the topography of the area, so it probably only got booked when the other fields were all spoken for.

"You play sports as a kid?" Witt asked as we walked through the entrance gate. It was designed to be locked, but a small chain hung loose through links in the fence with no padlock in sight.

"Softball all four years," I said. "Shortstop. Ran track my freshman year. You?"

"Dad pressured me to wrestle. I did that for two years. Hated every minute of it. Wish they'd had e-sports back then."

The field before us reflected years of neglect. The outfield looked recently mowed, but it had been overtaken by native weeds. Bermuda grass spread like mold across the infield dirt. Trash lay about the spectator area, and a concession window was covered with cardboard.

A half-dozen baseballs lay scattered around the diamond, and I picked up one near where home plate should be located. The ball was heavy and bloated from months of soaking up spring rain water and stiffening in the sun. I imagined it would rattle any batter that took a swing at it in this condition.

Like the waterlogged ball I'd grabbed and the field around me, the photos and trophies celebrating the Thunder roster were relics of the past. What tied our killer to the memories of a team that had played on this field three decades ago?

Tossing the ball a few times into the air, I looked around the infield, trying to imagine a young version of the four dead men. Brody Todd played a lot of second base, his parents had shared, and I pictured him in a defensive crouch as the pitcher wound up.

"I did play baseball until, I think, fourth grade," Witt said.

I tossed him the ball I was holding, catching him off guard. He fumbled the catch, and the ball rolled to where the pitcher's mound would have set.

"That's what happened when they threw balls to me in practice," Witt said. "Coach would make all the boys run anytime anyone did that. They were all probably plotting my death. So … there's a theory."

"That's asshat coaching."

"Right?"

"Something happened, and it might not have anything to do with a game or practice. But something happened with this team. Let's hope someone from the team can shed some light."

A few minutes later, Witt and I were back in the car, heading off to our first interview of the afternoon.

"Ever notice that Casey narrates when he eats?" Witt asked as we navigated to Winters's house. He was playing a game on his phone.

"Narrates?"

"We got barbecue Monday. He's eating burnt ends, and he's talking about the smoke taste and the caramelization."

Witt's thumbs tap, tap, tapped on his phone screen. I should tell him that too much screen time causes ADHD. But anyone who spent much time with Witt would conclude that the damage was done.

But I couldn't complain about the Casey rant. He'd had to listen to me gripe about Agent Hale for the first ten minutes of our drive.

Witt proceeded to tell me how Casey squirted all five barbecue sauces on his plate and described them in detail as he tipped his finger and tasted each of them in turn.

"Good kick," Witt said, deepening his voice to sound like Casey. "Hint of honey. Love the mustard base. KC sauce is overrated."

The more Witt ranted about Casey's bad habits, the more the two of them seemed like an old married couple to me.

"I think this is our place," I said, pulling alongside the curb in front of Steve Winters' house, a modern lodge construction with natural stone accents and wide eaves. The property was located in a section of the county just outside of city limits.

Winters did well in life, as evidenced by the size of the house and the prime lot upon which it sat. This street ran along the edge of a high bluff overlooking the Missouri River.

Winters's family business distributed the credit card machines that siphon off a small percent of every purchase. My addiction to Taco Bell probably paid for his driveway and pool.

The smell of someone's grill met us as we stepped out of the Durango, reminding me that we had skipped lunch today. Witt, who'd been snacking on pretzels in my vehicle, was probably fine, but my stomach growled in response to the hint of charred meat somewhere nearby.

Winters met us at the door. He wore a polo, and his hair was slicked back à la Gordon Gekko. His wife Harper, a trim blonde with beautiful lashes, stood a few feet behind him in the foyer. She offered a nervous smile as her husband stepped out of the way and gestured for us to come in.

The house was all clean lines and comfort—ample lighting, wide-plank oak floors, and a color palette that leaned into warm neutrals with steel and charcoal accents. The open-concept kitchen and living area showcased the backyard through floor-to-ceiling glass.

Portraits of the four Winters kids—two younger identical boys and their older sisters—were framed above the fireplace. They had all worn white turtle necks for the photo shoot. All of them had their dad's porky nose.

"So, am I next?" Steve asked after we'd all found seats. His wife, Harper, froze at that comment as she came from the kitchen with a cup of coffee in each hand. After a beat, she regained her focus and placed the mugs down in front of me and Witt. I noticed a slight tremble in her grip.

"Thank you," I said to Harper. And then to her husband, "I want to assure you, Mr. Winters, we're working hard to make sure that nobody is *next*. And I appreciate you making some time this morning. I know that you had a brief conversation with Detective Casey a couple of weeks ago."

"I carry a gun," he said, "and I've hired security so I can go to bed at night without worrying I'm going to wake up with some psycho cutting my dick off or something."

Harper cringed and put her hand on his leg, a gentle hint to lower the temperature.

"Okay, right, so let's talk," Winters said, his voice sharper and louder than when we'd arrived. "Your department is fumbling around while some crazy out there is whacking my old classmates."

"Teammates," I clarified. When Casey had interviewed Winters, he was one of several we'd connected with from Todd's graduating class. "We have reason to believe these deaths are somehow connected to a baseball team you played on before high school. The team was called Thunder."

"Thunder?" He looked with incredulity at his wife and then back at me and Witt. "You think this has something to do with a junior high travel team from three decades okay? No offense, detective, but seriously?"

I gave him a brief overview of our theory. Since the post-mortem numbering had been leaked to the press earlier, there wasn't any reason to hold back on that detail.

"Right, okay. So, you need to talk to me again. I might be in danger. I might be a suspect. I get it. I don't need a lawyer, do I?"

"Everyone's a suspect, Mr. Winters, but we're just—"

"Hear that, Harp?" he said to his wife. "Looks like you're a suspect, too."

She forced a smile at his joke and patted his arm.

I gave it another go. "We're just here to learn more about this team." I pulled a copy of a team photo from my satchel and handed it to him. "This is you on the top left, right?"

"Um …" He grabbed his glasses and studied the photo. "Yeah, that's me. There's Todd. There's Riedel. And Nick." He poked the photo several times, naming off the roster.

"Your position?"

"Pitched some. Left field mostly."

"Do you remember where the other boys played?" Witt asked.

"Why does that matter?"

"Probably doesn't," I cut in, "but *if* the victims are connected in some way through this team, maybe we can determine some pattern. Anything could matter or none of it could."

"Well, it isn't batting order, that's for sure. Woodhouse was clean-up. Could launch a ball like a Space X rocket."

I noticed Witt scanning the room. His eyes were always moving, taking in the tiny details of the location.

"But, yeah," Winters continued, "you've shipped off most of the infield to the morgue over the last few weeks." He pointed to Jimmy Woodhouse. "Third base. Todd usually played second, and Russell was on short."

"And Riedel?"

"Out deep with me, usually, but we all moved around a little, as needed."

As my coffee grew cold, I worked through our scripted questions. Had he noticed anything out of the ordinary the last few weeks? Anything strange come in the mail? Had much contact with anyone else from the photo?

No to each question.

The sound of rowdiness thudded down through the ceiling of the living room. The pig-nosed twins must be wrestling above us.

"I guess I did have a beer with Wiley the other day. He's scared as shit."

"Nick Wiley?"

"Yeah. He was our starting pitcher most of the time. Coaches called him Wiley Coyote, like the cartoon."

"Sure. Road Runner."

"Right. He was putting a curve on the ball already in fifth grade. Tommy John surgery his junior year."

A loud thud shook the ceiling. Harper looked up. Her husband ignored it.

"Same team in fifth grade?"

"Yeah, I think. Probably most of us."

We chatted for a half-hour. Near the end of our conversation, one of Winters's daughters arrived home. Harper ushered her upstairs.

"It's okay," I said, standing up. "I think we've taken enough of your time. Thank you for the—"

"You better find this asshole," Winters said as he stood. "I can hire a security team, but most of these guys—Nick Wiley—he's got three girls at home and …"

We stood looking at each other for a moment.

"You … you just better find him. This is inexcusable."

I thanked Harper for the coffee, and Witt and I let ourselves out. Across the street, one of Steve's neighbors, an older man in a sunhat, pretended to water his arbor vitae as he studied me and Witt. Two Yorkies fought over a knotted rope in his front yard.

"Well, he was pleasant," Witt said as he buckled and popped in a nicotine pouch.

"Who's next?" I backed out of the drive and started back toward town.

"Padgett."

Witt adjusted the air conditioning. My black SUV had turned into an oven during the conversation with Steve and his wife. So far, June had been a mix of too hot and too wet. The humidity was stifling.

"Where to?" I tapped my voice control to capture Witt's response. He rattled off an address, and my system pulled up the map.

A few miles out, I pulled into a drive-thru and ordered tacos. We ate in the car.

"You know," I said after swallowing the last of my Crunchwrap, "that was a perfect balance of crispy shell and gooey cheese."

Witt didn't take the bait. He was staring out the window, watching the houses pass by.

I tried again, dropping my tone. "This fire sauce is sooo good. It interplays well with the savory seasoning of the ground beef."

"Hmm," Witt said, turning from the window.

I took a quick glance at him as I crumbled up my trash. The look on his face …

He either had some kind of a revelation or he needed to pee.

"So …" Witt's eyes narrowed. "Brody Todd played second base, right?"

"That's right."

Nodding, Witt continued, though with a very hesitant tone, "And his body was found … at a *Second* Baptist Church?"

"What? Seriously?" I took another glance at my interview partner, my eyebrow cocked.

It was a ridiculous theory. Almost as ridiculous as the idea that a killer was targeting a group of men because of the 8th-grade ball team they played on.

"And Riedel played outfield, but probably not left. Winters said that was his spot."

"Okay, right field or—"

"Center. As in—"

This time, I cut him off. "As in the Mariston Community *Center*?"

It was where we found Riedel's body.

"Yeah, coincidence, right?" he responded, but I could tell by the pause that Witt's brain was still churning away.

Wait until Hale gets wind of this theory …

CHAPTER 22

Between interviews, I'd called Shaw and Casey for brief check-ins. From the conversations, now informed by the Thunder connection, some new leads had developed. While this was progress, none of us had so far come across anything earthshattering.

Sometimes the process of doing an investigation felt like opening an infinitely regressing series of Russian nesting dolls.

Besides the victims, all but three members of the team were still alive and also living in or around Mariston. Baxter Cobb, a real estate guy, had died seven years ago in a non-suspicious car accident.

Brett Padget, a pharmaceutical lobbyist, lived on a hobby farm just out of Jefferson City, and Max Crenshaw lived near the mountains in California, where his family moved halfway through his high school journey.

As much as I resented Hale's involvement in the case, I accepted his offer to have a colleague of his interview Crenshaw in person. If there was even a hint that Crenshaw had a lead, we'd dig deeper. Until then, I wanted to double-down on our local investigation.

The reputation of Mariston's law enforcement—and mine in particular—was on the line and in the spotlight. But my team knew the local community, and I felt we were making some progress.

As with all of the players, Padget had experience in several roles on Thunder, but he had mainly crouched behind home plate. Thankfully, he was cooperative and willingly made the drive down from the capital city for a conversation.

I invited Shaw along to talk with Padget while Casey and Witt spent the rest of day revisiting the dump sites, trying to flesh out Witt's expanding theory.

Witt is a sucker for conspiracy theories. The last we chatted, he was still looking for a meaningful way to connect his theory to Woodhouse's body.

"Maybe he was *benched*," Witt had suggested.

"So, Onus Wagner?" Shaw said as we drove to the coffee house where we'd agreed to meet Padget. About an hour ago, Casey had texted us both a picture of the former Pirates shortstop.

"Yeah, Wagner Creek. I mean, okay, but …"

"Russell played short stop for Thunder?"

"That's what people seem to remember," I said, accelerating to catch the tail end of a yellow light. "But …"

"Maybe a stretch."

"Maybe a stretch," I agreed. Or maybe not. It was easy to see how conspiracy theorists got sucked into fantastical narratives, seeing relevance in the mundane.

A few minutes later, we met Padget at a local coffee house—his request—and took the recent break in heat to sit outside, distancing ourselves from other customers. He'd picked up the tab for our orders

"I'd like to say it's nice to be back," Padget said after I thanked him for making the trip in. He wore a blazer over his polo. The years had been kind to him compared to some of the others we'd interviewed. Both his hairline and jawline had mostly stayed in place.

"But the circumstances being what they are..." He smiled. His charm was a good fit for his profession. I kind of wanted to donate to whatever legislation he was pushing at the state capital. Even if it caused cancer in chimps or whatever.

"Good memories here," Padget continued, "But it was only two, three years of my life. Dad was a lawyer for the paint factory, which is what brought us down this way. Lived outside Kansas City before that, which is where we returned after Heartland pulled stakes and everyone got laid off."

Decades ago, Heartlands Coating had employed a strong workforce in Mariston on the east side of town. They supplied industrial coatings and solvents, but eventually sold out to new ownership. The plant shut down two years later and relocated to Kansas, leaving an economic vacuum in Mariston. I was probably in preschool at the time, but I know it took years for the town to recover.

"Tried out for Thunder the summer before my seventh-grade year." Brett pulled the picture of the team closer and looked it over. Tapped himself, one of the boys kneeling in the front row. "Played with those guys for two years and then caught for the JV team in high school until we moved back to KC."

Padgett's jersey number was 19. I had a sudden, horrible vision of his mutilated body with a 1 and 9 number carved into his back.

"Get along with the team okay?" Shaw asked.

"Yeah, we had fun. Good times traveling, hanging out in the hotels on weekends. Our parents drank while we swam." He smiled, showing us his perfect teeth.

"Stay in touch with anyone from this photo?"

We all paused as a skinny teen girl brought our sandwiches.

"No, not really," Padget continued. "Not most of them. Winters is connected politically, so we cross paths. And Wiley …" he looked at the photo and nodded. "He was probably my best buddy on the team back then. Even after we moved, he'd come stay with us some during summers for the next couple of years."

Then, a smile again, but this one with closed lips and a cocked cheekbone. Padget looked from us to the picture and back again.

"He's not doing great, is he?" It was a question he didn't need an answer to.

Casey had been with me when we'd interviewed Wiley late yesterday. He was a wreck, chain smoking while we chatted on his deck.

Given the look of his rancher—warping deck boards, sagging gutters—Nick Wiley didn't have a lot of coins in his pocket right now.

As we chatted, one of his little girls pressed against the screen door to the kitchen to watch her dad and the detectives. She wore oversized red-framed glasses and what I thought was a red barrette. I later realized it was a Jolly Rancher tangled in her hair.

"You heard from Nick?" Shaw asked, refocusing the conversation.

"On and off," Brett continued. "He's messaged me some in the last two weeks. This thing's scared the hell out of him. All of us, of course, but I'm worried the ole' boy's going to have a breakdown."

"Anything in the messages?" I asked. "Or … can we have copies?"

"Nothing, and no, sorry. Not without a warrant. But, I'm sure he's already told you what he told me." Padget sipped his coffee and scanned around the coffeehouse. He spotted someone he knew and gave a wink and a wave.

"I'm not sure what you're talking about." With a subtle shrug of my hands, I invited him to keep talking.

"Right, of course. Nick thinks he's next."

"What do you mean?"

"He thinks he's the star of your next crime scene. I don't know what's got him more worked up, imagining the kind of pain the other guys went through or having his family see his body after some nutjob finishes with it."

It seemed we would need to have another conversation with Nick Wiley, this time at the station.

I asked Padget if he'd received any suspicious mail.

"I don't think so. Not at home, and my secretary would have alerted me to anything at the office. What kind of mail? A threat letter or something?"

"We were hoping you could answer that. Or anyone. It might be nothing."

"Yeah, no. Just junk mail and bills."

"Anything happen on that team that was out of the ordinary? Coaches behave? Any bullying?"

None of us had touched our sandwiches. Shaw and I had only ordered because Padget insisted on treating us.

"We could all be assholes—we were, what, eleven? Twelve? Thought we were hot stuff. But find a team of middle school boys that's any different. And the coaches? No, nothing there. They kept their hands to themselves, if that's what you're asking?"

"Not necessarily. Just trying to jog your brain."

"Yeah, I get it, and I appreciate everything you and your team are doing. You don't have an easy job, and I want to help if I can."

We worked through the four deceased men, giving him an open-ended opportunity to each of the names. Russell was a hotshot, Padget recalled. Acted like he carried the team.

"Jimmy was a quiet guy," he said of Woodhouse. Reliable. Loyal." Then, with a chuckle, "and J. T. was a smartass. Quick-witted. Fun to have around."

"What about Todd?"

"Found him at a church?"

"Yeah."

"What a deal." He played with his empty cup, tapping it twice on the table. "I mean, he was kind of a lug. I honestly didn't care for the guy."

As the conversation wrapped up, Padget told us he was going to check into his hotel and then grab a beer with a few friends. He'd be in town the rest of the week if we needed him. He hadn't hedged on our questions, but he also knew that his alibi was solid. His calendar for the last few weeks accounted for his time in Kansas City while someone was carving up middle-aged men here in Mariston.

Winters's intuition had been correct. These men and some other minor players in this drama were potential victims and witnesses. But, yes, they were also suspects, as were the former coaches. That included Padget's and Russell's dads, both now deceased, as well as Coach Wiley and Coach Todd, who each still lived in town.

The coaches were our Friday interviews. And while I'd led conversations with Winters and Padget, Casey and Witt had connected with the two remaining members of the team.

Rod Holtzer and Ted Dabrowski were the two local men from Thunder that I had yet to meet. I'm sure I'd get my chance eventually, but it didn't look like either had much to contribute to the investigation.

Shaw grabbed us to-go boxes for our untouched sandwiches, and we headed to the door. I couldn't tell, as we passed, if it was my imagination or if a couple of the patrons had watched us leave. Maybe a conversation at the coffee house hadn't been a good idea after all. Without any clear identity for our killer, my prominent role in the investigation had put me as the public face for Mariston's recent violence.

The local community has generally been supportive of our department, even during the rough years of national political battles over police funding.

But in situations like this, many people struggled to consider the nuances.

And maybe they were right?

The killer seemed to be delivering us bodies on a weekly basis. Each day brought us closer to the next body.

To use an analogy that would resonate with the men from Thunder, it felt like we were at the top of the 9th. And the score wasn't great for the home team.

CHAPTER 23

By the time I finally arrived home, Henry and Ed had finished supper, and Ed was cleaning the kitchen. A plate of lasagna and a bowl of salad waited for me in the fridge.

Henry was in the living room, wearing only athletic shorts and VR goggles. His arms flailed wildly as he gorilla-tagged somebody or sabered some beats.

"Another rough one?" Ed asked, looking over his shoulder as he scrubbed a pan in soapy water.

In case my slumped shoulders weren't enough, I let out a quick, audible sigh before giving him a hug from behind. His hair had grown even scruffier, if that was possible in just a couple of days.

I was into it.

"Thank you for fixing supper," I said, wanting to kiss the back of his neck. Wanting to, but refraining. I didn't feel like I could make the rules since I'm not the one who moved into a townhouse with a pool.

"You know what goes well with lasagna and shitty days?" Ed asked. He grabbed a towel and wiped soap bubbles from his hands. There weren't as many wine bottles left in the rack as there had been when he moved out—guilty as charged—but he grabbed a merlot and two glasses while I nuked the lasagna.

As we ate, we talked about my week. Or, I talked while Ed sipped his wine and listened. Yes, he'd seen Southern's special report, he told me. No, he didn't think Witt's theory was totally ridiculous. A stretch, maybe. But not quite batshit on the crazy meter.

Even rewarmed, the lasagna was delicious. Ed is horrible at a grill, but he nails it with pasta.

I mentioned the interview with Brett Padget and my concern that the interviewing would probably get tougher moving forward. We'd had our first and—unless new leads developed—our best chance with these men.

Dabrowski has been in a wheelchair after falling from a deer stand a decade ago. According to Casey's quick debriefing, he didn't get out much and stayed off social media.

Holtzer, like Padget, was cooperative and extremely concerned. He'd installed an alarm system, bought a gun, and just this morning sent his wife and kids to stay with his in-laws in Illinois until things were resolved.

"I designed Padget's house, you know," Ed said.

"He doesn't live in Mariston."

"Right, but someone connected us. It was really just a remodel and addition, but a substantial one." He seemed to be considering his former client for a moment. "Seems like a nice guy. Affable."

"He certainly is affable." I made a mental note to look up *affable.*

The light outside the kitchen window warmed and took a pinkish undertone. The forecast called for more heavy rain, but so far only a few wispy clouds drifted overhead.

We sat in silence for a few moments, with only the sound of the television in the other room.

Ed sipped his wine. He was always more comfortable with silence than I was.

"Look, if you need to head out …" I said, peaking at him through a curtain of hair blocking the left side of my face.

"I'm fine. Need me to stay here tonight?"

"No, it's okay … but maybe a little longer. I need things to be normal for a bit."

"I'm as normal as they come." Softness in his voice communicated his understanding that I needed him to continue taping me back together after a long and fruitless day.

"And maybe … another glass of wine." Hopefully, he hadn't seen the discarded empty bottle from Shaw's visit. Probably he did, but he went to retrieve Merlot anyway and topped off my glass.

In the living room, Henry wove his hands wildly above him, as if his last chance of desert-island rescue was flying overhead. He would stay immersed in that virtual world for hours if I didn't intervene.

"Okay, Player One," I said, patting him on the rear, "Are you *ready* for bed?"

"Hashtag mom joke," Ed said behind me.

"Wait, wait, okay." Henry swatted at something in front of him. "No, not you, my mom. I have to go."

I'd tried the VR goggles once—a roller coaster game that also involved shooting giant, anthropomorphic pieces of food. I nearly vomited.

Finally, Henry pulled off his headset and assaulted me and Ed with hugs before jogging up to his room to brush.

A minute later—way too soon for me to feel confident about our next dental visit—he darted back down the stairs to tell us both good night again.

I suspect he was enjoying the moment of normalcy, too.

I felt a tinge of guilt that I'd come home to sip wine and lament instead of asking about his day.

"Hey," I said, grabbing his hand before he could dart back upstairs. I pulled him next to me on the couch. "How was camp?"

"Good! We shot arrows!"

"At each other, I hope," I said.

"No, Mom, at targets."

"Darn. But that probably makes more sense."

"I want a bow and arrow."

"Got it. Bow and arrow. Maybe Christmas."

We all hugged again, and then Henry ran up the stairs.

"I'm glad he's having fun at the camp," I said, consoling myself with another sip and a self-promise that I'd be a better mother tomorrow.

Alone again, Ed and I sat near each other on the couch for minutes, both of us staring at the television. It was a rerun of *Two Broke Girls*, the episode where one of them makes slutty jokes and the other one acts appalled.

Thunder rolled in from the west and vibrated through our house. I leaned against Ed and the pillow between us. He lifted his arm inviting me against his side. The sky had begun darkening as the sun descended and thicker clouds approached. The storm was approaching quickly, and the heavy wind stirred up the trees in our backyard.

I had run out of things I wanted to share about my day, and I was debating whether foot rub requests were allowed during separation. Then, I noticed Ed hadn't shaved today, and I imagined the soft scratch of his cheeks against mine. His hand on my …

Wait, his hand!

I saw that the wedding band was back in place.

"Your ring," I said softly, taking the hand.

"Oh, uh …" he smiled and laughed. "Sara, I didn't realize you'd noticed."

"Of course, I noticed."

"I'd taken it off for a few days, but not because of …"

I sat up straight, trying to understand.

"I was on medication. My fingers were swelling."

I was relieved, but startled. Rain began a pitter-patter on the patio table.

"It's nothing," he said. "Inflammation stuff."

I pushed.

"It's okay." He took my hands. "Look, I'm just trying to avoid a conversation involving the words *bowels* and *rectal.* Autoimmune stuff. But I'm fine. Everything's fine."

I took his hand, my thumb feeling the curve of his ring. His knuckles.

Then I kissed him. My hand went to his scratchy cheek, drawing his face toward me, and I put my lips against his, hoping he wouldn't pull away.

He didn't pull away.

As the TV flickered, Henry lay in bed, and dishes sat dirty in the sink, my husband and I made out. Our tongues played together, and my fingers messed up his already messy hair.

Minutes later, my hand was under his shirt as he unbuttoned mine.

He kissed my neck. I sucked on his pinkie.

His hand unhooked my bra. Mine found his zipper.

He whispered sweet words into my ear. I whispered nasty ones into his.

The separation, the investigation, the guilt … all of that was happening somewhere else at this moment.

We made out for a while longer as our hands worked to liberate our hidden parts.

And then Ed stood and took my hand.

I held him back for a moment, grabbed my glass, and swallowed the rest of my wine.

Then, I let Ed lead me. To *our* bedroom.

Away from the case. Away from my guilt.

Outside of my problems.

Outside of time.

CHAPTER 24

Fifteen people had shown up, but only four of them, all high school kids, were under thirty. Disappointing, but Fr. Wes tried not to take it personally. Two years ago, both numbers would have been lower.

In addition to the nightmare in Mariston, the week's evening news had included coverage of a heat wave baking the southwest part of the country and the heightened conflict between Israel and Iran. Wes and a group of parishioners were planning a fall trip to the Holy Land, so he was particularly in tune to the latest struggles there.

Wes had hoped the Thursday night event would bring the parish together and engage the younger adults. Following adoration, he had pizzas and board games available in the parish hospitality room.

Besides the fellowship, he needed the company to keep his mind off his sister. Sara was older than him and carried a gun, but Wes still worried more about her than he let her or his parishioners know.

While he didn't want to put too much focus on the deaths in Mariston, he hoped the evening's collective prayers would send Sara the strength and wisdom she needed to stay safe and bring justice for the victims and their families.

But ever since being assigned to St. George parish, it had been one of Wes's goals to increase the participation of young people in parish life. Though the parish budget was tight, especially with insurance premium increases and the church in desperate need of tuckpointing, he'd budgeted a meager salary for a new youth minister.

But with no applicants—at least none that could pass the background check—he'd been trying on his own to invigorate ministry for younger parishioners.

But it was summer. Many of the parish families were on vacation, and Sunday attendance had dropped considerably.

After tucking away a few slices of the pizza for tomorrow's lunch, Wes had sent the rest of the food home with the four high school kids who'd come to Adoration and stayed to play *Catan.* Now, with everyone departed, he straightened tables and picked up a few bits of trash that remained after he and the youth had cleaned.

As he worked, he could hear, first, a gentle tapping. And then a heavier drone of rain as a storm cell moved in. The eminent thunderstorm likely kept some families at home this evening, he rationalized

Flipping off the lights, Wes double-checked to make sure he'd locked the entrance from the alley between the church and the rectory. With the school and parish office also on the same property, the grounds were a tight network of driving paths, buildings, and parking.

The door was secure

But from that angle, he could see headlights in the lot behind the parish.

Had someone returned?

Taking a quick scan around the room, Wes didn't see that anything had been left.

His living quarters were easily accessible from the stairs next to the hospitality space, so he otherwise didn't have to get out in the rain. But he remained at the door for a few moments, watching to see if the vehicle would leave.

Maybe one of the teens was having car problems and was waiting on a parent to come.

The headlights went dark.

Then, another light, this time inside the vehicle. Whoever was in the car must have opened the door, triggering the dome light. Through the glass and rain, Wes couldn't clearly make out the driver, though he saw movement as someone exited the vehicle.

The figure that emerged from the car and began up the alley was larger than the three kids who'd stuck around to build roads and trade sheep on the island of Catan.

Though Wes felt an impulse to simply call the police to drive by the property, he was safely behind the locked door, where he could see if the figure was a parishioner.

When the individual—a man with a raincoat and hood—passed, Wes cracked open the door and leaned out, still protected from the rain by the overhang.

He hesitated to turn away anyone who was in need, but he was wary of late-night drunks or even, as happened in another rural parish last spring, a possible vandalism attempt.

"Excuse me, can I help you?" he shouted over the increasing patter of the storm.

The man started and stumbled back a step or two toward the church exterior.

"Ah . . ." he said, putting his hand over his heart. "You scared me, Father."

Wes didn't recognize the man. He had a scruffy beard and wore glasses that were spotted with rain.

"Are you a parishioner?" Wes asked. "Nothing is open here right now."

"Oh, I …" the man said, looking up the last few yards of the alley in appeal. "I thought …" He shrugged and nodded. "I thought there might be … In my parish back home, they have the host displayed for perpetual Adoration."

"I'm sorry, but no, that's not available here."

While some parishes allowed 24-hour access for adoration, St. George didn't have enough takers to fill the slots or a secure location for evening access.

"Okay," the man said. The tremor in his voice was subtle. "I apologize for bothering you, Father."

The night visitor turned and started back toward his car.

"Okay, sorry," Wes said. "Safe driving in this storm." He stepped back and began to pull the door shut.

The man stopped and turned.

"Father," he said.

"Yes?"

"Can I bother you for a blessing? For my girl?"

Lightning lit up the town of Regensburg, and both men paused as the thunder answered.

"Sure, of course. But, are you a parishioner here? I'm sorry that I don't …"

"No, sir. From Arkansas. My wife and I came up to help out this week because my …" His voice broke and he appeared to be holding back emotion. "Because my little girl—she don't go to church no more—but my girl …"

The man pressed at the bridge of his nose.

More lightning flashed to the east.

Wes pushed the door open and held it for the man. "Step in for a moment, out of the rain."

The visitor accepted the invitation, following the priest into the basement and pulling the door shut behind him.

With the noise of the storm growing, Fr. Wes didn't hear the sound of the door's lock ticking into place behind him.

CHAPTER 25

"Can of corn … maybe because corn tortillas?" Casey cocked an eyebrow and looked at the group.

"Can of corn?" This was Witt.

"Means a pop fly. Like, 'There's a can of corn out to left.'"

"It's a stretch." Hollis waved him off with a flip of his hand.

"Okay, what about *bush league*?" Witt shouted. "Were there any bushes close by?"

"No bushes." Hollis said. He was looking around, annoyed, ready for food.

We'd gathered at El Rincón Friday afternoon. The killer had picked the dump spots deliberately, so we needed to continue immersing ourselves in his storyline of suffering and death. Hollis had tagged along with me, Casey, and Witt. I'd invited Shaw, as well, but she insisted on finishing her deep dive into some additional photos and other keepsakes that the Todd family had handed over from Brody's childhood bedroom.

El Rincón was one of several Midwest-style Mexican restaurants, all from the same family, that had popped up throughout town. They were efficiency machines, with waiters buzzing among tables, refilling salsa and fishbowl margarita glasses. Everything around us was red or green or brown. Or covered with queso.

We were brainstorming on Witt's theory that the killer was using baseball symbolism to communicate a message.

We were also tipsy.

"Got it!" Wick said, throwing his hands in the air in a gesture of inspiration. "Bean. You sling a pitch at a guy's head, it's called a bean, right?"

He dipped a spoon into the lumpy brown glob on his plate and held it up as evidence for the court. "*Bean*," he said again for the emphasis none of us needed.

I'd wanted us to gather at one of the sites as a team, and the late lunch at El Rincón doubled as a chance to get together away from the station. Sometimes a different context resets the brain.

The conversation had started as serious, with each of us looking deeply at the notes from the four scenes and scrutinizing the details. We pushed back on one another's contributions with a skepticism designed to stress test Witt's theory.

We needed some insight into who the next victim was or where the next body would be dumped. My hope, before our conversation deteriorated, was that Witt's theory had legs.

Unlike Russell's body.

Our discussion had started out somber and focused.

And then the drinks arrived.

By the second round, our brainstorming had deteriorated into a silliness.

"What about *walk off*… like a walk-off homerun. There's the walking trail near where we found the body?" This was Hollis, speaking louder than he needed to. He was competing with the Norteño playlist, his voice further amplified by the Dos Equis.

Riedel, who'd spent a lot of time in the key outfield position as a boy, had been dumped at the community *center*.

The drill holes in his body? Casey proposed fielding *drills.* Witt suggested being *drilled* with a line drive?

Hollis insisted the wounds represented *holes* in the fielding. "Maybe he's telling us we've got holes in our investigation," Hollis added. "Taunting us."

The conversation paused for a moment as our waiter arrived, with our steaming plates stacked like fallen dominos down the length of his left arm.

As we ate, we brainstormed other locations in or around Mariston the killer might use symbolically. Where would he leave a pitcher's body? Or the guy who played right?

We also considered the staging, such as how Todd's corpse had maybe been posed to look like a baserunner. Or how Russell's severed legs might have been a nod to his job as the *cut off* guy for left field. Or, from Witt, to make him truly a *short* stop.

I'd stopped taking any of this seriously a half hour ago and decided that we were all officially off duty, now.

Though the alcohol was cheap here, I'd ordered a Dr. Pepper. My headache from last night's wine had just recently faded, and I've given up alcohol for life.

After waking up three times during the night, I'd finally conceded defeat at just past four in the morning. My body literally dripped off the side of the mattress, and I got ready as quietly as I could. At just before six, I gave Ed a peck on the cheek and slipped out the door.

After weeks of trial separation, last night had been filled with the same electricity as our first time together.

Ed's body had felt *new* to me somehow.

Around nine this morning, Ed texted that he'd gotten Henry fed and off to camp and that he'd be on a video chat with a client for the next hour.

I'd hoped for something more.

Last night was awesome, maybe. Or, *Can I move back in?*

I'd have settled for an eggplant emoji.

When Shaw finally arrived, she found our table in perfect timing with the arrival of our food. She'd brought her own lunch—blueberries, chicken cubes, and quinoa. Such a party girl.

"Agent Hale asked where you were," she said.

Hale had texted me earlier, but I ignored it.

"I … told him we were all out to grab lunch." Shaw knew it was a mistake.

"You told him the Thai place downtown, right? Or, better yet, the Thai place in Thailand?"

"Sorry." She began poking at her chicken cubes. "But I don't think he was interested, anyway. Just said he wants to talk to you."

I noticed that, while Hollis surely overheard Shaw, he was avoiding my glance.

Maybe I'm back off the wagon, after all. I suddenly needed a margarita. "Muy grande, por favor," I told the passing waiter, pointing at Witt's half-empty glass.

We caught Shaw up on the quiz show that our lunch had become. She threw out a few guesses that sounded as silly as any we'd come up with before she arrived.

"I should know this after three years of Spanish," she said, "but what does *El Rincón* mean?"

"The Corner," Casey said.

"Like a street corner?" Witt asked.

"No, like a nook. Or a hidden place."

We all sat in silence for a moment, considering the information. The murders happened in hidden places? The killer hid in the dark corners?

"Hot corner," Shaw said before popping a blueberry in her mouth.

"Hot corner?" Witt again, probably remembering that Woodhouse had been tortured with some sort of a brand.

"Yeah." Shaw looked at the four of us with incredulity, realizing that she'd just spat out some trivia that nobody else at the table knew. "Woodhouse played third, right?"

"Most of the time," I said.

"Third base is called the hot corner because of all the action there." She realized that none of us had heard the slang before. "My dad's a baseball nut. He has an entire room devoted to his cards, signed balls, and all of that."

"The burn marks!" Casey pointed the fork at Shaw, who shrugged.

The symbolism still felt too silly to be legit. We were forcing the connections.

Or, I realized, the connections were intentional, but just another way the killer was playing with us by misdirecting our energy so we'd spend our time on puns instead of clues.

But *what if* the killer was drawing attention to their positions to emphasize that his motivation, whatever it was, was directly connected to that baseball team? Something that happened among the players, maybe. Some grudge that the killer has carried through all of these years.

"Salsa here is excelente, by the way," Casey said, dipping a tortilla. "Just the right amount of kick. Not runny."

I glanced at Witt. His eyes widened, eyebrows arched—a non-verbal *I told you so.*

"Anything worth chasing down from the Todd family?" I asked Shaw.

"Maybe." Shaw put down her fork and opened the accordion file organizer she'd brought with her. She pulled out a team roster and put it on the table between me and Hollis. It was a picture of the boys who had played on Thunder.

While the name of the team wasn't displayed anywhere in the photo, I recognized three of the coaches. The players looked familiar, but younger.

"That's the summer before sixth grade for these boys," she said. "They weren't called Thunder then, but the Bulldogs."

Shaw pulled out copies she'd made of the team photo and handed one each to Witt and Casey.

"Who is this?" Casey asked, pointing at an unfamiliar coach.

"I don't know," Shaw said. "One of the dads, I guess. Maybe *his* dad." She pointed to a boy in the front row.

The group shot made the details tricky to spot, so I used my phone to magnify the photo and look more closely at the face Shaw had indicated.

The boy had some distinct features that didn't seem to match any of the faces we'd scrutinized in the other photos. His ears stuck out, and there was a clear break in his left eyebrow, possibly a scar.

"I asked the Todds about him." Shaw paused as the waiter stopped by the table and refilled our waters. He pointed at Casey's nearly-finished beer, but Casey waved him off.

This new photo might mean nothing, but the tone of our lunch had changed. Had Shaw found another lead?

At the very least, this was one more interview worth chasing down.

"They can't remember the kid's name," Shaw continued, "and they offered to dig some more. *But* Mom Todd is pretty sure that the mystery coach is that boy's dad."

"One of these guys'll remember him," Casey added. "Let's make some calls."

My phone buzzed, and I glanced at it under the table. It was the number I'd saved for Nick Wiley. I stood and took the call.

"Detective Wren." I pushed back from the table. "Give me a sec."

Holding the phone against my thigh to mute my voice, I quickly reminded the group that Padget had only played with the team the last two years after replacing a kid who'd been cut.

"That's the kid," Hollis said as I stood and found the door to the patio to escape the noise inside.

"Sorry about that," I said, pushing open the door and stepping into the sun. "Nick?"

"Yeah, this is N-Nick Wiley."

"Nick, what's up?"

"You asked me about something I might have gotten in the mail."

"That's right. One of the other players got something in a small white envelope."

Brody Todd's wife never found the envelope she'd mentioned in our first conversation. After our last round of interviews, I'd all but given up on that thread.

"Yeah, I-I-I got something."

I didn't remember Wiley having a stutter. He wasn't doing well right now.

"You got something in the mail? Today?"

"Weeks ago." He sighed. "I know I shhhould have told you earlier, but …"

Hollis leaned out the door. He pointed at me and mouthed, *Everything okay?*

I nodded and gestured for him to hang tight.

"Nick, what did you get? What was in that envelope?"

"It's … it's something I have to show you, but not here …" A pause and forced exhale. He was nervous and, as with last time, was probably trying to smoke away his anxieties.

"Can you meet me at the station in twenty minutes?"

Nick agreed.

Back at the table, I interrupted Casey's theory of how Todd's staging in a parking space looked like a batter's box.

"Wiley got one of the envelopes," I told the group. Before anyone could ask, I continued, "Wouldn't tell me what was in it. We're meeting at the station."

"Need me there?" Casey asked. He'd been with me for the visit to Wiley's house. But his words were slurring, and I didn't need Wiley to feel ganged up on.

"I got the interview covered."

With a quick stop at the register to cover the tab, I was out the door and on the road, hopeful for the first time in days.

We'd gone out for drinks to let off steam, and two new leads had fallen into our laps.

Maybe margaritas were the key, after all.

CHAPTER 26

When Wiley arrived at just past three, he had the envelope in hand, but kept it in his grip as I led him to the interview room.

In jeans and a Bert Kreischer merch shirt, Wiley didn't look like he'd put much thought into impressing us. He wore a ballcap down low on his forehead, and with a bit of squinting and some imagination, I could picture him as an 8th grader dressed for practice.

Hale spotted me letting Wiley in from the lobby. He stood from his desk as we passed on the way to the interview room.

"Nick, this is Agent Hale," I said, trying to show as much hospitality as I could to put Nick at ease. "He's helping us with this case so we can keep you and your family safe."

Wiley nodded.

"Agent Hale, this is Nick, the *Wiley Coyote*, as the coaches called him."

In my head, I think I expected chuckles, handshakes, and some yuk, yuk baseball banter.

But Nick just nodded and cleared his throat.

I realized that, in my attempt to lighten the mood with the Road Runner comment, I'd stupidly implied that Nick was crafty while he stood in a police station with a cop and a federal agent.

Great start, Sara.

"Crazy-fast curve ball, right Nick?" I was trying to reset. "Some of the other guys said you were a terror on the mound."

Nick nodded, this time with a wry smile. "Yeah, I was all right," he said. "'Till my elbow got all ripped up."

His breath …

"Nick," Hale said, offering a genial smile. "I played a little ball in my salad days."

Only Hale would say *salad days*.

Wiley didn't answer, but instead glanced around the station, probably wondering why he'd agreed to come in. He was done shooting the shit and knew we were just trying to loosen him up.

"Nick, let's find someplace private to finish our conversation. If you'll excuse us, Agent Hale," I said, ushering Nick toward the interview room.

"Wren," Hale said behind me.

I stopped and turned.

"Can we chat for a moment after you and Mr. Wiley finish up?"

"It's *Detective* Wren, by the way, but sure."

Hale smiled and nodded. I did neither and instead guided Nick in the room and shut the door.

"Nick, you've got something in your hand that we probably need to take a look at, right?" I asked after we both were seated. I took a sip of coffee and gave him a moment to produce the envelope, which he didn't do. "Whatever this is, you got it a week or two ago?"

Wiley shook his head. "No, no, it was before … before that. Somewhere just after M-memorial Day."

The envelope remained hidden. I shifted gears.

"Nick, when we talked to Brett Padget, he said you think you're next. Is that right?"

Nick looked from me to the table and back again, shrugging. A furrow appeared on his cheek as he considered my question.

"Nick, you are not here under suspicion. But you have a family at home—three girls, right? All three of them cuter than should be allowed by law."

Wiley looked up. The mention of his daughters unlocked the next stage in our conversation.

"Bella, Regina, and …" I actually remembered the third—had reviewed our notes before buzzing Nick in from the lobby—but I wanted words to start coming out of his mouth.

"Gretta," Nick said. He glanced at the two-way mirror. There was nobody behind it, but it was probably disconcerting nonetheless.

"So, Nick, my job right now is to keep you safe." I leaned in. "To keep those girls safe and make sure nothing's going to happen to their dad."

Nick lifted the envelope into view and placed it on the table, his hand resting on top.

"G-got this, like I said, a few weeks ago. Don't know who it c-came from. Thought it was a prank, but I think different now."

He pushed the envelope forward and pulled his hand back.

"Nick, I'm going to put some gloves on and open this." I pulled two wads of latex from my pocket. "You've touched this envelope. We can expect your prints to be on it, but has anyone else touched it?"

"Well, the mailman, I guess," he said. "But not L-Lottie. Not nobody else."

"Okay." I opened the envelope and pulled out the one item from inside.

It was a baseball card.

The card was obviously homemade—two sides had been printed on copy paper and laminated with strips of clear packing tape.

Someone with low to medium photo edit skills had pasted a grainy picture of Wiley over a stock image of a ball player. Nick's name ran in white font across the top of the card. The word THUNDER had been imposed in blue letters over the jersey. Other than selecting italics and tilting the text slightly to match with the angle of the shirt, the creator of the image had made little attempt at realism.

Silly looking, but not alarming. Not until I flipped it to the back.

The bold-lettered heading "STATS" was followed by the following text:

Elbow surgeries–1
Douchebag activities–2,872
Children molested–4
Affairs–2
Jobs in one year–3

I refrained on commenting that it was an impressive number of douchebag activities.

"W-what it says about the children … that's a damned lie," Wiley said, leaning forward.

"And the rest of it?" I put the card on the table with the statistics facing up.

He looked at one of the cameras in the corner of the room, as if considering whether his wife Lottie was right now dialed into it. Maybe watching it with his girls.

"Lottie knows about one time," he said. I assumed he was referring to the affairs. "But not the other one. That was a m-mistake."

He rubbed the back of his neck. The gesture made him look smaller, cornered.

"But the kids? Never. I swear to God, never. I got three girls of my own, for Chrissake."

I kept my mouth shut, not pointing out that having kids of their own never stopped a lot of pedos. But besides not wanting to upset him further, I believed Wiley.

It didn't help him that some of the other information on the card was accurate. Blackmailers often exploit indiscretions to bolster exaggerated claims.

Though Wiley didn't comment on the three jobs, I suspected that was accurate, too. But it was irrelevant, and we could verify that later.

But while not as scandalous as the accusation of affairs and molestation, it was still a jab that probably cut to the core of the man across the table from me, who I knew was struggling to keep up with his bills.

"You didn't tell anyone about this card because at least some of it is on track," I said. "You worried that people would believe the part about the molestation, right?"

Wiley nodded. We let the moment linger, hoping he might say more, but he just looked at the table, his thumb rubbing over a gouge along the edge.

The rest of our conversation retreaded the earlier conversation on Wiley's deck. He finally shared that there were any number of people who knew about one of the affairs.

"I thought it was blackmail, at first," he said, chuckling. "Didn't know what they thought they were gonna get out of me. Blood from a stone, right?"

"Anyone got a score to settle? Financial or otherwise?" I tipped the carafe over Wiley's cup, pouring a cup of caffeine and good will now that Wiley seemed to be opening up.

Wiley gave over some names with the promise that we wouldn't tell Lottie or anyone else about the card. They were all small debts, and I doubted any of the leads would propel the case.

"But it d-don't make sense," he said.

"What do you mean, Nick?" There'd been a bit of grit in his voice. I just wanted to keep him talking.

"What about the other guys? Did they get something like I got?"

"Maybe." I said, shrugging. "Don't know about the victims, but if anyone else on the team got something like this, you're the only one brave enough to talk about it. Doing so might have saved your life, you know? Might get others to open up."

Nick nodded. He hadn't touched his coffee. His thumb still rubbed the corner of the table. He either wanted a smoke or there was something more on his mind.

"Nick." I leaned in. "Is there something else? Something that might help us here? Help us keep your family safe?"

Finally, he looked up, but with just his eyes, his head still tilted toward the table. I've been in a lot of interrogations and interviews. That wasn't the posture of a man who was about to open up his soul to us.

"That's all I got, detective," he said softly. Then, he looked up with more resolve. "I'll give a shout if anything else comes up."

I tried to prompt him a couple more times, but Wiley let me know by his short answers and stiff posture that we were done for the day.

As we were wrapping up, Wiley agreed to let a patrol car sit outside his house in the evenings for a while. While it would draw attention to him, he was worried about his wife and three girls, and they had nowhere else to stay.

We'd need to circle back with the other guys from the team, this time to ask very specifically about whether they had received something like Wiley had handed over. And while I hoped that Samantha Todd came across a white envelope hidden away somewhere in the house, I hated to think what she would find out about her husband when she opened it.

Had all of the murders been preceded with the baseball card taunt?

And if so, how long had the killer been studying these men? What other secrets did he have on them?

But, as Wiley had pointed out, there were no signs of attempted blackmail.

It's possible the killer wanted to make sure that these men spent their last few days living in fear of scandal and ruin.

After walking Wiley out of the station, I saw that Hollis had returned to the office. We chatted for a bit about the conversation with Wiley, and then I cornered him about Shaw's earlier comment.

"What's Hale want to talk about?"

Hollis sighed and avoided eye contact, staring straight down the hallway, like he was trying to teleport himself away from this conversation.

"He's pushing to bring in some additional support from the feds. He thinks we're losing control over this."

"Bullshit," I said flatly.

"That's what I told him," Hollis said. "But maybe not so diplomatically."

"Next time you see him," I said, standing up. "Please quote me directly."

I paused at the door.

"Roy, you put me in charge of this case. I'm not going to let you down."

CHAPTER 27

Shaw did a bit more digging and learned the name and some background on the boy in the Bulldogs team photo. Calvin Feltrop still lived in Mariston and worked at a local hardware store. Witt jumped in to help with a deep dive background search. But so far, all we knew was that Feltrop was divorced with one adult son who now lived in Colorado. We needed to pay him a visit soon.

Saturday morning, Casey and I tracked him down.

Nobody had been home when we went to his house, a cracker box rancher on the north side of town. Despite the summer heat and drought, the yard was green and mostly free of clover and crab grass. A tidy border of dark rock and tidy bushes lined the front and sides of the house. Feltrop's was easily the most well-maintained home on the street.

Our next stop was the home goods store where he worked. Feltrop's manager verified that he was on the clock and currently working in the lumberyard behind the store. We asked for a private room and were led to the manager's office, where he radioed for Feltrop to meet him.

"Go Chiefs," Casey said when the manager finally stepped out. The office was red and yellow with Kansas City Chiefs gear, including an autographed football in a glass box in the bookshelf.

When the door opened again, the manager stepped aside and gestured for Calvin Feltrop to step in.

"Do you want—" the manager began, stepping in after Feltrop.

"We're good, thank you. But pull that shut on your way out.

Feltrop paused for a moment at the door, looking from us to his manager, as if in appeal.

He was obviously the boy from the photo. If a giant had taken that kid by the head and feet and stretched him, it would be the man who stood before us now. The ears. The scar dividing his eyebrow in two.

"Calvin Feltrop," I said, standing up and offering my hand. My badge hung from a cord around my neck. My blazer was back in the car, my holstered gun exposed. "I'm Sergeant Sara Wren, a detective with the Mariston police department."

"I seen you on the news," he said, ignoring my hand.

Great. He'd no doubt caught Southern's report.

"This is my partner, Detective Pete Casey."

"Hey, bro," Casey said, giving Feltrop a casual salute wave from where he sat. Casey adapts well to just about any context, whether he's working a drug bust undercover or at a fundraiser ball. But Calvin Feltrop, with his comb-over, adult acne, and store apron—Casey didn't have a setting for that.

The manager's office was a cramped space for a conversation, but we made it work with three chairs arranged in a tight triangle near the door.

Having a table between us, as we sometimes do in the station, gives the person we're interviewing or interrogating the perception of a psychological barrier.

But sitting as we were—with me and Casey just feet away from Feltrop and nothing in between us—it put him in a vulnerable position.

Feltrop kept his hands on his lap, fiddling with the strap of his work apron. The tight arrangement wasn't an intentional decision on our part, but I was aware that it could have one of two possible effects on his participation. It's possible he could clam up, but it's also possible he might ramble, especially if he knew something useful. People tend to overshare in these situations when they're trying to control the conversation.

We started with some general questions—*yes questions*, I called them. Softball tosses with comfortable answers. It helped set a tone of cooperation.

Worked here for a while? Staying cool outside?

Before moving into the case, I took notes as Casey probed Feltrop a bit on his personal life. He told us that he kept in touch with his ex-wife and had only been out of town once in the last couple months when he visited his son in Denver late May.

When we finally guided the conversation to the junior high team, Feltrop gave us a breakdown of his association with the victims. He'd been homeschooled through fifth grade, but most of the boys were in his class when he started formal schooling. But he didn't know the rest of the team until his parents had signed him up for baseball later that year.

The Bulldogs was a non-competitive team, he'd mentioned. I remembered that he'd supposedly been cut from the team, which didn't make sense in that context, but I had him talking and didn't want to break the momentum.

Though he'd gone on to high school with most of the boys, Feltrop said he'd dropped out his junior year, gotten his G.E.D., and then headed west to Pendleton to join the Marines. He said he was medically discharged after two years due to a heart murmur.

When we showed him the team picture, he was able to name most of the boys in the picture.

"Yeah, that's Dad," he said when we asked about the fourth coach. "He helped with the team for the two years I played."

"Eli Feltrop, right?"

"Elijah, yeah."

"And he quit when you didn't make the team in 7th grade?"

"Didn't make it?" Feltrop sat up straight and looked at me directly, his fidgety hands repositioned on his thighs. His scarred eyebrow twitched twice.

"When we interviewed the other men, they mentioned that you didn't get selected at try-outs. Brett Padget took the spot, right?"

"Well, that's …" He acted as if he was going to stand, but then leaned back against the chair and then forward again, rubbing his nose and then shaking his head. "Well, that's just not true. That's just not true at all."

Casey glanced at me and then Feltrop.

"We *quit* that team," Feltrop said.

"We?" Casey asked.

"Dad had enough of that team. Had enough of Coach Wiley."

We knew from earlier that, in addition to Feltrop's father, the other coaches were the dads of Brody Todd, J. T. Russell, and Nick Wiley. Padget's dad started helping after Brett made the team going into 7th grade.

Feltrop explained that his dad and Coach Wiley didn't get along and that they'd had a big argument in front of the team late in the season. He didn't remember what they were arguing about, but he remembered being scared that the two men were going to start throwing punches.

"My dad would have hurt him bad," he said.

Feltrop's dad had passed away from a heart attack in his early fifties, so we wouldn't be able to contact him. But while we'd had a brief early conversation with Coach Wiley, it seemed we needed to circle back around. The coach hadn't offered much beyond two- or three-word responses to our questions. "Don't know about any of that," had been his answer at least twice.

Most of the rest of our conversation with Feltrop was a rundown of what we'd asked the rest of the team alum.

No, he's had no contact with any of the other men. No, he hadn't received anything strange in the mail. When we prompted him by mentioning the possibility of a homemade baseball card, he looked at Casey, as if to verify that he'd heard right. Then he laughed out loud.

"Well, that sounds stupid as shit," he'd said.

But then …

"I had dreams about them, though," Feltrop volunteered.

Neither Casey nor I had asked him about his dreams. When we have an interview or interrogation, I sometimes mentally rate the subject on an honesty scale. Feltrop was already at a 5 or 6 in my mind with the oversharing and excessive gestures. This nugget about his dream dropped him to a 4.

"Dreamed about Russell," Feltrop continued, even though nobody asked him to. J. T. Russell had been the body we found at Wagner Creek.

"'I'm on that bridge," Feltrop continued, "and he's crawling toward me on those stump legs. Ain't that the damndest thing?"

Now he's a 3 on the scale.

"That's creepy as shit, bro," Casey said.

"Then he turns to me," Feltrop continued, "and I know he wants my legs." Feltrop laughed a little as he thought of it.

I'd never gone in the negatives with my scale, but I was tempted. This was beyond bizarre.

"Don't know what that means," he continued. "Just got in my head when I seen the news, and it come to me while I's asleep."

After the conversation with Feltrop, Casey and I connected in the parking lot.

"We need to keep an eye on this guy. Can you give Coach Wiley a call? See if he can tell you anything about that argument?"

"I'll give him a shout on the way home." Casey held copies of Feltrop's work schedule from the last two weeks. Before we'd left, he'd volunteered to provide them. Given the store hours, I doubted that he had any shifts that would rule him out as a suspect.

He'd also been out of state the last three days to visit a friend and, he assured us, could provide documentation. I accepted the offer and handed him my card even though there was nothing from Wednesday until now that suggested the killer had been active.

Feltrop was firmly on my radar, but, it had been a long and frustrating week. I planned to be back at the station early tomorrow. For now, though, I just wanted to get home to be with Ed and Henry.

Then I caught it.

My hand on the door handle, I paused at my Durango.

"Casey," I shouted as he reached his own car.

"What's up, boss?" He leaned on the hood of the car between ours.

"Russell's legs … did we release that detail? Was it in any of the coverage?"

He considered it for a moment. "Don't know that we did." Casey watched me consider that for a bit. "Word gets out, though, but … the news? I don't think so. Maybe I missed it."

"You're probably right," I said, remembering an earlier leak that ended up in Southern's report. "Like you said, word gets out. I need you and Witt to dig into this guy a little deeper for me."

"You got it, Mamma." He drummed three quick beats on the car between us and then slid into his car.

Driving home, I replayed the conversation in my head. Feltrop couldn't remember what his dad and the coach had argued about, but he said they'd have come to blows if the other coaches hadn't stepped in.

I refused to believe this case was as simple as an unresolved argument between a couple of baseball dads, but something about that team continued to fester three decades later.

Something had been rotting in Mariston since when these men were boys.

CHAPTER 28

Ed was sitting on the back patio working on his laptop when I arrived home. Henry had a friend over from down the street. Both in their swim trunks, they were on the trampoline with the sprinkler attachment to keep them cool.

Other than to compete with Ed's pool, I'm not sure how Henry talked me into buying a trampoline water sprinkler. The wet surface, two bouncing boys, all those teeth … what could go wrong?

I'd grabbed a beer from the fridge en route from the garage. Twisting off the cap, I half-emptied it on the first tip. Gulp, gulp, gulp.

Ed and I chatted for a bit about my day and his. He and Henry had gone for a bike ride early in the morning before the heat settled in. Then, Henry cut the grass while Ed logged some hours on a current project.

For several minutes, we just sat and watched the boys bounce and bump heads. Henry attempted a backflip and landed on his face, chest, and knees.

Eventually, Ed tucked his laptop into its canvas case and pushed back the patio chair.

"I should go," he said.

"You don't have to." I smiled slyly and played with my empty beer bottle. Maybe played with it a bit suggestively.

Then …

"Hey, um …" He looked at the boys, still splashing and defying gravity. "Can we … can we talk for a moment inside?"

My stomach lurched. I suddenly wished for Henry or the other boy to knock out a tooth, just to keep whatever was about to be said from being said.

Ed nudged the patio door shut after I followed him inside the living room.

The boys continued their feral behavior.

"So, the other night was … nice." He smiled and put his hand on my arm for a moment. Squeezed my shoulder like he was offering condolences. "I've missed that. Missed *us*."

I nodded, but the tone wasn't right. Whatever this was, it was going to hurt.

"I missed *us*, too. But?"

Ed's free hand was trembling, his eyes moist, but he kept talking.

And I listened.

Ed told me that he *felt* he needed to get back to his townhouse. Maybe, he said, Thursday night had obscured the truth of our marriage right now.

obscured

and

The truth of

What were those words?

"When I married you," he said, "I knew what I was signing up for. My love for you—the love I still feel—meant that I would put up with the long days. The stress. The worry that you might not come home."

Ed does a very slight twitch with the right side of his mouth when he's nervous. I watched it as he spoke what he'd obviously rehearsed before I'd come home, conditioning himself to say it with conviction. He'd packed in cushion words to protect me.

The love I still feel.

Then he paused. And here it comes.

But …

I knew what I was signing up for, he'd said, *but …*

"But," Ed pursed his lips before saying the hard part. "Even when you come home, you don't really *come home.* When we're together, your mind is still pouring over evidence. Perseverating. Rethinking leads."

He'd wanted the separation to be a wake-up call, he told me as we stood by a patio door while our son laughed outside.

Particles of dust floated in the shower of light filtering through the blinds. The decorative clock above our couch ticked the seconds as Ed waited for me to respond.

"Sara," he continued when I remained silent, looking at the reflection of us in the patio door glass. The woman there looked like a ghost of me. "You aren't able to compartmentalize the two big things in your life anymore."

You need forgiveness, Wes had told me. *From yourself.*

Ed proposed that the two of us just accept that this case would demand more bandwidth than the two of us had at the moment.

"When this guy is locked up on death row somewhere," he said, "then maybe we can see if there's a path forward for us."

My lips tightened. My heart raced. My eyes watered.

I suddenly wanted a table between us.

But I stood and listened and nodded.

I held back tears. Then I cried a little anyway.

And then I accepted his hug.

And then …

Ed left.

CHAPTER 29

"Forgive me, Father, for I have sinned."

Fr. Wes grunted. The tape over his mouth restricted him from doing more than that.

He thrashed and arched his back against a tight cord, pushing to free himself from the chair. With duct tape securing his head to a support beam, he could not assess the knots and loops that held him in place.

Light seeped from the door at the top of the stairs. It was all that Wes had to see the man perched on the stool before him. He knew, from when he was alone earlier in the day, that there were two narrow windows at the top of the wall to his right. Then, sunlight had been shining through and illuminating more of the room. He'd seen the bare concrete walls and pallets with taped boxes stacked atop them.

Now, though, the windows were dark. Either they were covered or it was nighttime. He had no way of telling.

"I've killed four of them … recently, at least." The man said. "There will be more soon, but it doesn't work that way with forgiveness, does it? No accounting for future sins?" He sat in a chair opposite Wes. Next to him was a small table with various instruments on it.

A utility knife. Garden shears. A pair of pliers.

The implications of these instruments were not lost on Wes, and he understood that this man was the one that his sister pursued.

"You've heard the stories, Father, of mafia priests? They get a call in the middle of the night. 'Father, meet us under the bridge.' The priest drives to the bridge, where he finds a car, and men standing around the car. And they open a door for him to get in."

Wes's heart pounded as the man continued. The sweat stung his eyes.

"The next day, the priest reads about a body that washed up on the banks of the Calumet."

The HVAC system kicked on. It was the only sound besides their breaths for a moment. Wes noticed the scar that split one of the man's eyebrows. He had to remember this if he escaped.

When he escaped.

"Isn't that interesting," the man continued, "that these mobsters respected the man enough to offer a chance for a last confession before his death."

The man leaned in and, with his thumb, traced a cross on Wes's forehead.

"So, my question to you, Father—because I respect you—is whether *you* have had a chance for confession lately?"

Since he'd first woken up in the basement, Wes had kept his sanity with a litany of whispered prayers and Scripture. The mice and the cockroaches were his congregation.

And after you have suffered for a little while, Wes remembered from Peter's first epistle, *the God of all grace, who called you to his eternal glory in Christ, will himself restore you and make you strong, firm, and steadfast.*

"There were some men I know who needed *your* absolution," The man continued. "But four of them will have to hope for mercy without it. They've gone on to account for their lives."

Since Wes first woke up here after the attack in the parish community room, the man had visited him twice a day, providing food and water.

At first, he had tried to refuse the food but the man gave him the choice of eating or receiving an intravenous feed. It was important that Wes retain his energy, his host explained, and remain alert.

The man told him that he had plans for their time together.

That things were accelerating.

That the songbird was getting too close.

"I don't think she suspects me, yet," the man said. "But she came to my workplace today, if you can imagine that. And I was thrilled to see her."

He picked up the box knife and began playing with it, extending and retracting the blade.

"She wants to protect these boys. She wants to sub in, I think." Then, his voice heightened. "'Put me in, Coach, I'm ready to play.'"

The man stood.

"So," he continued, "let's put her on the roster."

The man now took a couple steps back and posed as if he were at home plate, loaded up for a pitch.

"They never trusted me to hit. The boys called me Captain Strikeout. The Wiley Coyote called me 'the walker.'"

"'Look, the walker is up,' he'd whisper as I grabbed my bat. Coach Wiley always gave me the take sign. Every time." He tilted his head, voice light. "You know how it works, Father? When a third base coach gives signs?"

Wes didn't answer.

He grunted—more breath than sound—as he strained against the cords.

"There are different signs," the man explained.

He thumbed the switch to extract the blade again. He then returned to his chair and scooted it closer, his knees nearly touching Wes's.

We rejoice in our sufferings, Wes recited in his head.

"If Coach wants you to swing, he runs his hand down his forearm."

K*nowing that suffering produces endurance, and endurance produces . . .*

It was a quick action, what the man did with the blade.

Wes strained against the cords, his cry of pain muffled by the gag. A red line bloomed along Wes's forearm, blood pushing through where his captor had unzipped the skin.

"But I always got the take sign. Every time I was up to bat. He'd run his hand across his chest, like this—" He cut again, across the chest this time. Wes tried to suppress a response this time but couldn't suppress a grunt, followed by several coughy sobs. "He was telling me to just stand there. Take the pitch. Hope for a walk."

The black shirt sagged where the cut had been made. It grew dark and heavy with the blood spill. Wes struggled noisily for breath through his nose, sucking in tears.

"I wasn't supposed to swing. Just stand there and watch. Hope for four balls and shuffle down to first. My job was to get out of the way so we'd circle back to the top of the lineup."

Wes's face had gone pale and slick with sweat, but his eyes were locked on his captor.

Tears welled. His breath came in short, shallow huffs. His body screamed with pain.

"Nothing to say, priest?" The man leaned closer. "Not even your prayers now?"

He smiled.

"If we were supposed to steal, Coach had a real funny sign—grabbing his crotch!"

He raised the blade and slashed downward fast and brutal, stopping just shy of Wes's zipper.

Wes lurched against the restraints, anticipating a pain that never came.

The Walker giggled. "Just kidding. That would be creepy, right?"

He leaned in, voice lower now, more intimate.

"But who knows? Given how his son and a few of the others acted when the grownups weren't around… maybe Coach Wiley was just a big old creep. A pecker-fiddler."

He set the utility knife back on the table and stood, performing now. He looked into the dark, toward an imagined batter and mimed the signs, hand brushing arm, chest, cap.

He chuckled, then, and returned to the table, picking up the shears, and stepping behind Wes's chair.

"Of course, Coach couldn't let the other team figure out the signs. That's why he had an indicator—something to show when the signs were real."

He placed a hand on Wes's left shoulder, giving it a gentle squeeze.

"The signs mean nothing, Coach told us, if you don't see the indicator first."

Then, delicately, he pinched the lob of Wes's left ear, pulling down on it.

"This was Coach Wiley's indicator," he whispered. "A tug on the ear."

He slid the open blades around the top of the earlobe. Wes clinched his eyes shut.

… *that you should follow in his steps*, Wes thought.

"So even if he told you to swing, or bunt, or take the pitch…"

He closed the blades slowly. Wes, his head bound to the beam, could not pull away from the pain.

Finally, the man stepped around, pinching the severed lobe between his finger and thumb.

"…it didn't mean a thing without a little tug on this right here."

CHAPTER 30

I needed the shooting range.

This case was consuming me, but Henry was in bed, asleep within minutes. The trampoline and sun had emptied him. I couldn't go into the range, as much as I wanted to take my Glock and feel the violence in my hands.

To inhale combustion and exhale frustration.

Catharsis through carnage.

The house was quiet. Too quiet.

After Ed left, I stood for a moment in the living room, listening to the laughter and yells of Henry and his friend in some parallel universe where everything was just fine.

I could picture myself and Ed, standing where we did by the patio door, as if I had witnessed the conversation in third person. A silent observer to the end of things.

Nothing had changed.

What happened between us on Thursday night—the wine, the kisses, the bedroom—had it all been the flicker of a dying light?

Meanwhile, the case stretched on endlessly. Casey's deep dive into Feltrop failed to expand our lead base. Eli Feltrop, now deceased, left his wife Margaret when their son Calvin was a baby.

He never remarried, though there is a trace of evidence in Mariston public records that he might have lived on and off with various women.

Other than traffic violations and an outstanding debt, Calvin's criminal history was clean, but his dad's record was not. Eli Feltrop was a thief and a thug.

Around the time Calvin would have been a freshman, his dad went to prison for the better part of two years after dragging a man from his car and assaulting him in front of the guy's wife and kids.

Feltrop was homeschooled for most of his childhood and jumped around jobs as an adult. He'd been wearing the home improvement store apron for the last five years. During that time, he lived alone in a small house in south Mariston. He kept to himself and paid his taxes on time.

That was all we had. Feltrop's dad was a better suspect than he was, but the old man died years ago.

In an effort to keep myself from sulking about my marriage or the case, I tidied the house after Henry went to bed. The towels Henry and his friend had used were both draped over the rod of his bathroom curtain. I dropped them in the washer. A pile of clean laundry rested on the dresser. I hung shirts and stuffed socks into drawers.

Ducking my head into Henry's room, I listened for his sleeping breath. Saw the hints of his face lit by moonlight through the tilted blinds.

"Mom," he said. His voice in the dark like a soft tap on a minor key.

I answered with my presence, finding his bed and crouching next to it.

"Did you catch the serial killer?" he asked, the question jarring me.

Serial killer … How was that even something he knew to say?

"We will," I whispered, combing back his hair with my fingernails. "Henry, are you worried about this? About me?"

"Not here," he said, pulling back his pillow to show me the kitchen knife he had tucked underneath. "I'll help if he gets in."

My heart accelerated as I moved my hand slowly to the knife, trying not to let Henry see my alarm.

"You don't need this, Monkey," I whispered.

I placed the knife on the floor next to me and laid my head on his shoulder, scratching his back through his t-shirt. "I'm safe. The house is safe. Henry, *you're* safe."

"That's what I told them," he whispered.

"Told who, Henry?"

"My friends. They keep asking me about the killer and saying he'll come find us. Sometimes we pretend we're hunting him in the …"

He didn't finish. I knew why. These were friends from his online games, and he didn't want me to take those away from him.

With a couple of deep breaths, I assured him again, but I kept my head pressed against his chest, listening to his heart.

I lay there until he fell asleep again

As I left Henry's room, kitchen knife in hand, I snagged his baseball bag from where it was slumped on the floor and lugged it down the stairs and to the garage.

I hung the bag on its hook and noticed my own glove on a shelf beside it. I'd used it in high school, pulling it out a time or two for playing catch with Henry in the backyard.

My fingers slid into the leather. It became an extension of me.

A bucket of Henry's practice balls sat at my feet, and I smacked one into the palm of the glove.

Maybe, I thought, I didn't need the shooting range after all.

I went to my room and changed into a t-shirt. Skipping the socks, I slipped my feet into tennis shoes.

Though the sun had gone down, our patio lamps and the moon gave plenty of light to see by as I pulled cushions from the patio chairs and arranged them as a backdrop against our house.

As a teen athlete, I'd been used to a bigger ball. But my fingers found the stitching naturally where I stood, several feet away from the house, near raised garden beds that wouldn't get planted this year.

The first throw went wild, bouncing off the brick of the house and off to my right.

The second was closer, but still missed the cushions.

A neighbor's dog heard the two thuds and began barking. Someone yelled at him to shut up, but the barking continued for a while longer.

Unlike the windmill underhand throw of a softball pitcher, my throws from the short stop had often been over-the-shoulder rockets to home plate as a runner charged in to score.

Another throw. This one hit the cushions in the top, right corner.

When I wore a softball uniform as a teenager, I didn't *think* about how to throw or bat or dive for a low line drive.

Not during the game. Then, I was just in the zone. My body took over. Muscle memory and adrenaline automated me.

The same as in the gun range.

Deep inhale and squeeze, squeeze, squeeze.

I threw three more balls. Two hit the cushion.

When I'd emptied the bucket, I gathered them up and started again.

Inhale and throw. Inhale and throw. Inhale and throw.

When I was in that zone—out there on the high school field—I'd learned to shut everything else out. Upcoming tests.

My boyfriend. Whatever drama was stirring within my circle of friends.

The balls bounced and rolled wildly.

Whop. The ball deflected toward the fire pit.

Whop. This one hit the corner of the cushion and sprung toward the privacy fence.

Whop. This one was dead center and bounced back toward me through the grass.

I am Sara. I am Ed's wife.

Four balls in quick progression, each hitting the cushion.

I am Henry's Mom.

More throws, and the bucket is near empty again.

But for right now, until this ends …

Until I find the person who killed these four men …

I am *Detective* Sara Wren.

Cushion and bounce.

I have …

Cushion and bounce.

to solve …

Cushion and bounce.

this case.

My last throw hit with such force that the cushion recoiled and fell.

I dropped to my knees, my chest heaving, my breath hard and quick. Baseballs were scattered throughout the yard like bulbous mushrooms.

A fox wailed somewhere deep in the conservation forest. The wind rustled the leaves of our sugar maple. The cicadas sang.

I remained on my knees in the grass, my eyes closed and my hands at rest on my thighs, one still tucked into the glove.

Finally, my breath calmed. I stood and began collecting the balls again.

And that's when my phone buzzed. An unknown number. A familiar area code.

"Sara Wren?" the woman said when I answered.

"Yes." The bucket dangled from my left hand.

"I'm sorry to bother you this late—it's Mary Claire, the secretary at St. George. Fr. Wes … he didn't show for the 6:00 Mass. We've tried his cell, his rectory line. I drove to the rectory, but nobody answered. You're listed as his emergency contact."

I pulled my phone back and took a quick glance. It was 9:37.

The world narrowed to the space between my feet and the patio.

"Mary Claire, 6:00 was over three hours ago."

"I'm sorry, I know. Deacon Paul left me a voicemail, and I just saw it."

"That's all the deacon did? He left a voicemail?" I made a mental note to strangle Deacon Paul. "When did you last hear from Wes?"

"Thursday."

For the love of God, could this possibly be more of a clusterfuck?

"Father texted me something about heading out of town," Mary Claire continued. "His car is here, but no one's seen him since. We didn't think too much about it when he didn't come in on—"

"I'm on my way."

The bucket fell, the balls spilling into the grass as I ran toward the house.

CHAPTER 31

The night was hell.

Armed and dressed, I waited by my car for Ed to arrive, watching down our street, willing his headlights to appear. Henry's window remained dark. What kind of morning would he wake to?

My mind, desperate to make contact with Wes, pulled me back into the past.

My brother was one when our mom died. I was six, the big sister. Dad had just removed the training wheels from my pink Power Ranger bike the summer before.

Our mother had been out for her regular morning jog. It wasn't a hot day. She hadn't gone far. She was less than three miles from our house when her heart overloaded.

I know her death spot. Could drive there now …

When we found Jimmy Woodhouse, I'd had a momentary recall of the memorial bench my dad secured with his donation to the park program. The bench where we found Jimmy's body also bore a plaque dedicating it to someone's memory.

Mom's heart defect was congenital, though not hereditary. But my dad had both me and Wes checked out anyway after Mom's death.

We were both healthy. Dad's heart was fine, too.

But after Mom's death, we learned about the broken part of Dad that our mom had been holding together.

I didn't even know the word *hoarder* at the time. When I was a kid, there were no reality TV shows sensationalizing the condition.

Things just began accumulating slowly. And then not so slowly.

Stacks of magazines.

Broken appliances.

He might read those magazines again, he told me.

The microwave is fine—just needs a new fuse.

I didn't think much of it.

I was a girl and he was a dad. There was a sense to the world that only adults understood.

Then, like a fungus, the piles grew and spread.

Boxes of paperwork in the hallway that connected our bedrooms.

Empty detergent bottles lining the shelves in our basement until there weren't enough shelves any longer.

Eventually, the garage piles forced him to park outside through the sludgy Missouri winters.

Even though I had friends in that neighborhood, I stopped inviting them over when Maggie Turnbull told me that our home smelled like her uncle's pig farm.

Stuffed and tied trash bags piled up in the laundry room. Getting to the machines became an obstacle course. A pile of egg cartons reached almost to my belly and then grew even taller in the pantry.

Though lost in the memories of those early days of my family's unraveling, I was pulled back into the present by the glow of headlights approaching our road. Ed neared and pulled into the drive to the right of my car, and I shot Hollis a quick text to let him know I was on my way.

Ed got out of his car.

"Thanks for coming so quickly," I said, opening the car door as he circled behind his car and approached me. "Henry is asleep and doesn't know I'm …"

Ed grabbed me and pulled me tight against him and held me there for longer than I had time. I cried against his shoulder.

"Go find your brother," he whispered. I nodded, but remained in his embrace a moment longer.

Pulling back, I wiped my eyes and met Ed's. I didn't know what to say, so I didn't say anything. I got in the SUV, pulled the door shut, and backed into the street.

In my rearview mirror, I watched Ed standing there, watching me drive away.

The rest of the team had already arrived at the station by the time I got there. Hale was on his way back to town. While he maintained a motel room in town, he often commuted to his home near the field office in St. Louis on weekends. But he'd driven in without question and put himself at my service.

This was not just about circling the wagons around me and my missing brother. This was the freshest lead we'd had since finding Riedel's body. If the parish had good surveillance, we could maybe get a video of the killer. Or of his car.

This was assuming that Wes had been abducted by the man we pursued. I really had no solid reason to believe that is what happened. For all we knew, he left with a buddy, and their car took a curve too quickly on those snaky rural roads, tumbling his car down an embankment and out of sight from passing traffic.

But my gut knew differently. This had something to do with the Mariston murders.

Momentum deteriorates when the clock ticks on an investigation—witness recollection blurs, the search geography widens, the chance of harm increases.

With this thought, I had flashbacks of the victims. Woodhouse's burns, the beating that Todd had endured. Miller in pieces and Riedel full of holes.

Witt had taken the lead on the BOLO, looping in state patrol and sheriff's departments in a fifty-mile radius. He's good under pressure. Before I'd reached the station, he'd already mapped out key back roads and gas stations.

Casey and Shaw were working with the Brenn County badges to canvas Regensburg and neighboring communities, especially those that lie along the highway between the town and Mariston.

Unfortunately, the rural towns and the highways between them were not outfitted with the expensive LPR camera system. But if we could catch a glimpse of those plates, we could scan for Thursday night action in Mariston.

We would also have trouble getting business owners to answer phones at this time of night or to cooperate with our late Saturday requests. We'd need warrants, and I could probably get them on rush delivery given the circumstance. I had county judge Bolden's home number in my contacts, and he'd be responsive to the circumstances.

But from the request for a warrant to its execution—even if done in hours instead of days—is still *hours* that we didn't have. That Wes might not have.

Hale did what he does best and got access. On his drive to the station, he had already been in touch with the phone carriers, pushing for a tower dump around the parish. We were trying to track a ghost. But every ping, every shadow, might be the one that leads us to the door behind which I could find Wes.

Unfortunately, I'd worked cases with tower dumps before. They never came quickly. First, the carrier has to pull raw data from every phone that pinged off a given tower during a given window. And then IT analysts comb through thousands of numbers to find a thread that might matter. Even with Hale leaning on them, it could take hours or days.

After the team dispersed, Shaw rode with Hollis to Regensburg, trailing me through a light sprinkle of rain. The long highway drive and the hypnotic swoop of my wipers allowed my memories to haunt me again.

My mind drifted back in time to when the cockroaches eventually established their kingdom in my childhood home. I would see them scatter sometimes in the bathroom when I flipped on the light during the night. My dad had purchased bait traps, which he placed throughout the house.

The hallway to our bedrooms became narrower as my dad's mental health deteriorated. Piles of trash and memories grew like artery plaque, and it became increasingly difficult just to leave my room.

One night, as I lay in bed, unable to sleep, I spotted the first mouse. I knew already that the creatures lived within the changing topography of our house. I'd caught glimpses of movement. The mouse had heard me stir, and it sat for a moment, perched on its rear legs and staring at me. Then it scurried back into the mountains and valleys of accumulated junk.

The next night, I left out a piece of bread near my bedroom door. It wasn't that I was trying to lure it to my room. I was just trying to keep the night visitor away from where Wes slept.

Looking back, I realize now that Mom's death may have only exacerbated my dad's mental health struggle, but it probably didn't cause it.

When I was old enough to do research into his decline, I learned that, in addition to environmental and psychological causes, an inclination to hoard could be linked to a genetic disposition.

Possibly a hereditary one, unlike Mom's bad heart.

Wes accumulates books, and I've yet to donate Henry's old clothes and toys. But Dad had a bathroom floor littered with empty shampoo bottles and bags full of cardboard toilet paper cores.

I'm sure there's a difference.

Now, as a cop, I know that children are very seldomly removed from the home of a hoarder, and that's not what happened with us.

Outside our home, unless Maggie Turnbull happened to tell you our secrets, you wouldn't have known about the way we lived. Dad dressed nicely for his job. He kept our lawn mowed and our gutters clean.

When Aunts Patty and Terri stepped in. I wasn't part of the intervention. Dad resisted, but Aunt Patty out-stubborned him.

The house got cleaned, mostly, but Dad kept hoarding piles of yesterday.

Every year, my aunts would come over to help us clean out the house again. I still remember Terri coming from the garage, a cigarette dangling from her mouth. She was carrying my pink Power Rangers bike.

I almost ran and pulled it away from her, but my aunts were trying to make dad healthy again.

The bike I'd outgrown was part of his sickness, so I only watched as she tossed it into a rented dumpster and returned to the house.

Even though Patty eventually got Dad to donate our mom's clothes, he insisted on keeping a yellow dress. It was his favorite thing that she wore. After he passed away four years ago, Wes and I found that dress still in his closet.

It's in mine, now.

When Wes was still a toddler and found a box of old lightbulbs in the dining room. I heard the *pop, pop, pop* as my brother tossed the bulbs from where he sat on the table, laughing as they exploded on the hardwood floor.

Wes was careless and risk-prone as a child. As I hurried to clean the mess, he climbed down from the table and sliced the sole of his bare foot on the glass.

I wrapped a towel around the bleeding foot and tried to call my dad at work. When he didn't answer, I dialed 911. I still remember the look on the first responder's face when I let him in the front door and he saw the condition of our house.

But all that mattered to me was that he fix my brother.

Despite the trauma we'd experience as children, both with Mom's death and Dad's decline, I'd like to think the two of us turned out mostly okay.

Though we'd both escaped the clutter and pests of our dad's house, the experience of living with a hoarder colored our view of the world.

Sin and crime accumulated around us and nasty things crawled within it. Wes had chosen to respond with prayers and holy water. Me? Handcuffs and a gun.

As a big sister, I still feared that the jagged edges of life waited to cut him. Even in our adulthood, I felt it was my job to protect him, though as a cop, I usually live on the other side of the 911 call.

Hollis and I turned into St. George parish at just before midnight. As I pulled in among the cluster of sheriff's vehicles, I wondered …

Would I be able to protect him now?

CHAPTER 32

The county team had already secured the scene when we arrived. Hollis stayed down among the deputies in the community room while Shaw and I hunted down the incompetent Mary Claire.

Shaw quickly located the parish office, where a female deputy was helping Mary Claire download the video onto a portable drive. The secretary seemed to have had no idea that the camera system was capable of anything but live feeds.

Deputy Martin, a straight-faced woman in her early 30s, indicated that they'd make me a copy as well. In addition to giving us more information to track the killer, the video footage was the last I'd seen of my brother. While the Mariston PD and the county team sometimes butted heads over jurisdiction, Martin assured me that everyone with a badge had come together to help find my brother.

With the videos copied onto an external hard drive, we thanked Mary Claire for her help and reset the search parameters to take us back in time.

It wasn't hard to follow Wes's evening as recorded by the parish surveillance system. Knowing about the youth activities in the community room, we started with a camera perched in the corner opposite the exterior door.

The timestamp read 9:52:12 as I watched Wes move around the room, stacking up the empty pizza boxes and dumping them in a trash barrel, along with plates, napkins, and soda cans.

Wes packaged up the board game spread out over the table. Typical of Wes, he meticulously organized the small pieces into individual storage bags before packing everything systematically into the box.

"He's not very priest-like when it comes to board games," I said. "I thought I'd have to get my kid therapy after their last game of Battleship."

For several minutes, nothing happened of any significance.

"Hold up," I said, putting my hand on Martin's shoulder as she prepared to slip ahead. "I need to see everything."

Eventually, at time stamp 10:07:23, Wes flipped off the lights and secured the door to the alley. He remained there for over two minutes, staring out through the door's window.

"What's he looking at?"

"Right. Let me find that one back." As Martin navigated the security system's menu to find another angle, I took in my surroundings. Near a crucifix on the wall, there were photos of the pope and the local bishop. Next to these was a print of the Sacred Heart, and a picture of my brother with a large group of teens. They were on a mission trip somewhere. Wes wore shorts, a t-shirt, and a bandana headband.

"Seems like they like him here," Shaw said, following my glance, her hand on my back.

The deputy found the right exterior footage.

"It's hard to make out anything," Shaw leaned close to the screen.

"Rain and dark don't help." I was growing frustrated.

"Nor does this old surveillance system," Martin added. "The software is out of date and the camera domes are foggy."

At 10:08:11, the footage in the parking lot captured the car, the parking lot lights reflecting off the dark, wet paintjob. Unfortunately, the resolution wasn't clear enough for us to read the plates. The vehicle was most likely stolen and would turn up abandoned within days.

"Is that the SUV?" Shaw asked.

"From the Community Center?" I said. "I think so. Similar, at least."

We watched for several seconds before the driver's door opened and a man stepped out. He surveyed the area around him and began walking toward the parish office building.

Martin switched to another camera, this one with a view of the alley between the parish office and the church. She backed up a few seconds so we can see the visitor round the corner. Wes popped his head out the door, and the two men interacted.

There was, of course, no audio. I *needed* audio right now. Not just to know what they said, but to hear my brother's voice.

The visitor was taller than Wes, but the loose-hanging jacket and hood made it difficult to discern much besides his height.

It seemed, for a moment, as if the man was leaving, but then he paused and turned.

"Wes ..." I whispered, trying to will him to shut and lock the door.

But they talked for a few moments. Finally, Wes nodded and gestured for the visitor to follow him inside.

Martin returned to the view inside the community room.

10:14:52

The video was noisy and grainy for a moment until Wes flipped the light switches by the door.

The cameras don't give a good view of the stranger at that point, but there was quick movement behind Wes as he turned on the lights, and something was in the other man's hand when it appeared above my brother's shoulder.

"A syringe." Shaw paused the video and tapped the screen. She's probably right, though zooming in only pixelated the object.

As the video continued, Wes's hand grabbed at his neck as he turned, but his abductor appeared to kick him into the room. Wes stumbled back, falling to the linoleum floor. The stranger reached inside the pockets of his jacket, tucking away the syringe he held in one hand and pulling out a handgun with the other.

I couldn't see Wes's face as he scooted back.

The man was careful to keep his head down and shrouded under the hood. I'm confident that, were he to look at the camera, I would see Calvin Feltrop staring at me.

But even if we had caught a glimpse of his face, I suspect he would have disguised himself in some way. This was not a random act of violence. My brother's abduction had been planned. Just as it had been with the four men whose bodies we'd found around town.

With that thought, I considered the grieving families of those men and our visits to their houses for those painful conversations.

Our parents were dead, and Wes lived a celibate life. He had no wife or next of kin to receive a police officer's condolences.

I am the one for whom the doorbell would ring.

The stranger held my brother at gunpoint until the contents of that syringe did its work. Wes's arms gave out from under him. He shifted on the floor and tried to lift a shoulder. And then he was still.

10:28:09

Several minutes passed as the man searched for and found Wes's keys, and with Deputy Martin navigating from one camera to another, we followed him to the parish office, very near to where we huddled now. He found a wheelchair tucked near the breezeway over the alley to the church.

I felt a hand on my arm and wanted to shake away Shaw's attempt to comfort me, but I also didn't. She stepped closer and her hand held tighter.

Wes is a big guy, so it took a few minutes for the man to wrestle him up from the floor and into the chair. His body wanted to slump over and tumble out, so his abductor pulled out a loop of cord and secured my brother to the back of the chair.

Switching back to the exterior cameras, we watched the stranger push my brother toward the car. He struggled to heft Wes's limp body from the chair, but eventually managed to fold him into the opened hatch of the small SUV.

The hooded man then collapsed the chair and slid it into the back seat.

We were able to track the car until it exited the parish property and turned south.

10:57:44

That main road through Regensburg feeds into the highway back to Mariston. By now, they would have arrived wherever the killer did his work.

"Wren, there's something I found earlier that I need to tell you," Shaw said as she and I tracked down Hollis in a downstairs annex. The sheriff's team had set up a command post there, utilizing the whiteboard and conference table to organize their investigation.

But before I could answer, Hollis approached us.

"One of the deputies chased down a crossover at a gas station down the road," Hollis said. He stood back, watching the county team work. "Just some guy driving home from his night shift. Story checked out. Plates didn't match. Car was the wrong color."

"Right," I said. "Too bad jack shit can't be put in an evidence bag."

Shaw and I combed the grounds again, walking the alley and the parking lot with flashlights, every puddle and scrap of litter a potential clue. Yellow evidence tents littered the path from the lot to the community room.

The brief rain had moved on, leaving an earthy smell. The wet pavement reflected the floodlights and exterior lamps.

"Unit three-niner," I heard over one of the vehicle radios, "Ran the loop twice now—Main, County Road 14. Nothing but deer and armadillos. Returning to the patrol position."

A deputy crouched to photograph a saturated parish bulletin plastered against the asphalt where the abductor's car had parked.

Inside the community room, a detective from the county team dusted the door handles and light switches. But how many dozens of people had touched those surfaces in the last few days alone?

Every little motion around me—the shuffle of boots, the low murmur of voices, the whine of radios—blurred into the same dull rhythm of futility. We were chasing shadows. The trail was already cold. But I could have walked the scene a dozen more times, and I would have still felt we'd missed something.

Then I received the text.

My phone buzzed at 12:03 a.m.

I almost ignored it for the moment.

It seemed that many of the officers were mulling around, trying to appear busy. The sheriff's team would remain on site a bit longer, but we'd most likely found all there was to find here.

Hollis stood outside the door to the community room, coffee in hand. He cocked his head and raised his eyebrows. *Nothing?* His expression asked.

Shaw exited the command post area and stood next to me. Whatever happened next was my call.

I turned from the two of them and lifted my phone, swiping my thumb over the lock screen.

One message from my brother's number. The preview line read simply, *Wes: Image.*

My heart began racing. This wasn't good.

The picture of my brother showed him from the shoulders up. The side of his face was stained, and despite the poor resolution, it was clearly blood stuck to his skin and matting his beard.

His slitted eyes looked into the camera, his mouth agape.

I stumbled back and braced against the walls of the church.

"Sara!" Shaw shouted, running toward me. Maybe others raced to help, too, but I was dizzy and on the verge of fainting.

The phone buzzed again as Shaw helped me slide down into a sitting position. And then it buzzed a third time.

Pictures of the long, deep cuts.

I allowed myself just a moment to be Wes's sister. Only his sister.

Hollis tried to get me to respond, but I could only hand him my phone as I inhaled deeply and held my breath, trying to calm my nerves with controlled breathing.

This was so much more than anything I've dealt with emotionally in the past, but if I didn't pull it together, Wes would die. The killer might come after Ed or Henry next. I couldn't let that happen to me, and I couldn't let it happen to another of the men from Thunder.

Wes is only involved because the killer was trying to get to me. This was my fault.

You have to forgive yourself, he'd told me.

"This is …?" Hollis asked, looking at the pictures.

I nodded and started to stand, accepting help from Hollis and Shaw.

"Yeah, it's Wes. And if I just got these photos, maybe the killer is with him now. And if he's part of this team …"

"We can isolate those men and confirm their whereabouts," Shaw finished.

I looked around at the sheriff's team. While we spun our wheels here, the score had just changed back in Mariston.

Not only did the killer's latest move threaten to entangle me emotionally, but he had effectively shifted our efforts thirty miles east of where he probably had my brother now.

"One of those men has my brother." I pushed away from Hollis and ran to my car.

CHAPTER 33

My lights flashing, I sped from the parish lot. Shaw rode shotgun. She'd followed me to the car, and I'd reluctantly agreed to let her be my emotional support animal for the ride home.

"Call Casey," I told her as I merged onto the highway. "Have him get the team to the station. We need everyone we can drag out of bed."

The return drive to Mariston gave me a chance to push back my emotional investment in this case.

I kept glancing at my phone, which I'd tossed into the passenger seat. I hadn't responded to the texted pictures, but I would have to eventually. It might give us an indication of if the phone was traceable. If I could get the killer engaged in a conversation, no matter how painful it was, we might be able to ping the phone and determine its location.

More than likely, though, the killer kept the phone shut off or even removed the battery to keep it untraceable. He'd shown incredible caution with the previous victims.

His motive might be nothing more than to taunt me, the lead investigator into his violence. But it was communication, nonetheless.

But what would I type?

Any response felt either antagonistic or desperate. And the killer no doubt wanted a reaction from me. He wanted to strip away the instinct and training of my several years as a cop and break my resolve.

"Hey, Google," I said as I crested a hill. My phone beeped through the Bluetooth sync. "Call … Hot Sauce." I cringed saying my phone nickname for Ed out loud.

Shaw paused whatever she was tapping into her phone and gave me a look.

"Calling Hot Sauce," the voice assistant responded, far too cheerful for the context.

"Worcestershire was taken," I muttered.

The phone rang until voicemail picked up. I ended the call without leaving a message and fired off a quick text instead.

Stay inside, I dictated to my phone's system. *Lock the doors. Call me when you wake up.*

Two minutes later, my phone buzzed.

"Sara?" His voice was thick.

"Everything's fine." I was lying, and he'd know it. "Just keep Henry close. Don't let him out of your sight until I get home."

"Sara—" he started, but I cut him off.

"I'll explain later. Just … just do it."

I tapped the end-call button and lowered my foot another fraction of an inch on the pedal. I'm pretty sure we caught air for a second or two on the last hill. Shaw white-knuckled her door handle.

"Shaw," I asked her as we neared the Mariston city limits. "You had something you wanted to tell me earlier, at the parish."

"Feltrop," she said. "Before you called everyone in, I was going over my notes from the interviews. Witt was helping me cross reference with anything we could find online."

"What did you find, Shaw?"

"Feltrop said he was honorably discharged from the Marines."

"Okay." I only vaguely remembered that detail, but if Shaw recalled it, then it happened. She'd meticulously coded all of the conversations we'd had during the investigation.

"Dishonorably discharged, Wren. For assault."

"Maybe we misheard him?" I glanced at Shaw as we passed near downtown Mariston, nearing the station.

"I don't think so. Casey said he remembered the same as was in the notes."

I wanted to believe it was Feltrop. There was so much weighing against his innocence. His association with the team, and later his abrupt departure from it. His strange interview and, now, this lie about his military service. The nightmare about J. T. Russell and his severed legs …

Had we released those details?

More and more, I was having difficulty granting the killer anonymity. My imagination continued to plug the adult faces of the Thunder roster onto the shadowy killer's face.

But Feltrop's seemed to fit the best.

We needed to talk with Coach Wiley tonight and learn about why the Feltrops had left the team, but I also needed someone I could depend on to track Calvin Feltrop down and find a way to detain him until we could locate Wes.

Casey and Witt were already at the station when I arrived. Hollis trailed me by five minutes. I'd also called in a few uniforms who'd been instrumental in earlier investigations. Many had already made it in. Hale took his usual spot in a back corner.

The room was a stark contrast to our nighttime investigation outside St. George. I needed the fluorescents inside the station. It was like turning on the bedroom lights to shake loose a nightmare. I cut between the columns of chairs and stepped up and behind the podium.

"Tonight, we track down anyone even remotely connected with that ball team." The faces before me were marked with puffy eyes and finger-combed hair, but everyone was tuned in. Almost nobody was sitting in a room full of chairs. They were ready for action.

"We wake these guys up and determine their whereabouts for the last three days. Each of them gets a shadow until we figure out who's missing."

Any anxiety that might have leaked into my voice burned off during the drive back. I was pissed. The killer was trying to play a game, so I was suited up. Bat in hand and black grease under my eyes.

Metaphorically, of course. Given my last eight hours, I probably looked like a mess and had never changed from the clothes I'd come home in from this afternoon.

Shaw had pulled up the roster from our earlier briefing. I gestured to names on the displays. "Shaw, these are your guys. Witt can handle the out-of-towners. See if they'll consent to a phone interview for now.

"Wiley is low priority," I continued. "He's high risk, so we've had a car outside his house each evening since the last time we chatted. But everyone else gets interviewed."

"We won't get cooperation from most of them," Hale interjected. He'd put on his suit for the meeting and stood in the back of the room. "If they haven't already lawyered up, they will as soon as a cop shows up at the front door at one in the morning and wants to give the fifth degree."

I caught Casey giving Hale the stink eye.

"Then tell them to call their lawyer. But at least we'll know where they are right now."

"Do we have reasonable suspicion of any of these men?" Hale asked again. "Anything at all that will justify a warrant."

My lips pursed in frustration. Hale was right, and I'd wrestled with this on the drive back to town. I had nothing to justify an arrest or search on any of these men. Nothing to detain them if they simply got in their cars and drove away. I had consoled myself with the hope that most of the men would want to prove their innocence and assist the investigation.

"Agent Hale, if they refuse to talk, we park a patrol car outside and monitor the house for the next twenty-four hours for their safety. And, if we need to, we'll start knocking on the neighbors' doors and asking them about what sort of activity they've observed in the neighborhood over the last two days."

"You don't think …" He looked around the room. "This is going to come across as police harassment?"

Never in my history with the Mariston PD had I ever seen audacity like Hale was modeling now. Not in a high-stakes context like this. Even when disagreements occurred, they were resolved elsewhere, often behind a closed office door.

But I met Hale's challenge and stepped forward.

"No. We monitor for their safety and we interview the neighbors because, whether they cooperate or not, I'd rather be an ass with a badge tonight than the lead investigator on their murder in a week." I scanned the room to reinforce my message to the group. "Whatever is going on here is connected to this team. These men. Our responsibility to protect them isn't limited to their comfort zone."

Hale maintained his smug smile, but didn't say anything further.

"If you need, Agent Hale, I can clarify the nature of your advisory role." I noticed Hollis locate himself closer to Hale. "Otherwise, do you have any other questions?"

Every eye was on Hale now. He met my gaze for a moment before answering.

"No further questions on the matter, Detective Wren. Thank you."

"Casey," I continued to the group without even a non-verbal acknowledgement of Hale's response. "I want you on Calvin Feltrop. We know he was at work this ... *yesterday* morning."

I realized we were just a few hours from sunrise, when the parishioners at St. George church would wake to learn that mass had been cancelled for the weekend at their home parish. "But you do *not* let that man out of your sights."

"You got it."

I wanted Feltrop for myself, but we had to connect with Coach Wiley to see what information he had. We needed everything we could find if we hoped to bring Feltrop in tonight.

"Hale," I said. He looked up, surprised or startled to hear me addressing him again.

"You're coming with me to talk with Coach Wiley."

To the team, I concluded the meeting. "I need to know immediately if you find anything that smells suspicious, including unaccounted for chunks of time, especially on Thursday evening from eight to midnight. If anyone is missing or evasive, I want to know."

Everyone departed the briefing room except for Shaw and Hale. Shaw approached me at the front of the room, where I was snapping pictures of my whiteboard notes.

"Wren, are you okay?" She said it low enough that Hale wouldn't hear us from the back of the room.

I glanced at her and then Hale.

"Get to work, Shaw. We're running out of time."

As Shaw hurried out the door, Hale approached me.

"We're partners now, Detective Wren?"

"I'm trying to make up from all the times you got picked last a lot in PE class."

He'd tried to project some of his earlier boldness, but we both knew the score, here. Everyone who was in the briefing room moments ago did.

Grabbing my bag, I walked past him, pausing at the door.

"Two things. First, I don't know what your game is, but don't you ever try to challenge me like that again. Are we clear, there?"

"We're clear."

"Second, we disagree on a lot, Agent Hale, which is why I want you along. I can separate myself emotionally from this, but I don't have time for confirmation bias to get in the way."

My peripheral vision caught Hollis standing in the hall monitoring the situation.

"I want you to call bullshit if I'm reading too much into things," I continued. "But I think there's something deeper that Coach Wiley, Calvin Feltrop, and some of the other men aren't sharing."

He stared at me a moment, glanced at the whiteboard, and then nodded.

"I don't think you're … *totally* off base here," Hale said. "Let's find your brother."

CHAPTER 34

With Hale riding shotgun, I drove for fifteen minutes through sleeping Mariston to Coach Dean Wiley's house on the west side of town. His was one of several two-story brick structures lining the street, most of them built midway through the last century.

"Coach is neglecting his lawn care," Hale said after we exited my car and stood at the curb. The grass wasn't out of control, but it was well past time for a mow. Four newspapers lay in a loose cluster on the driveway.

The carriage-style garage doors had windows along the top panel. On tiptoe, I could see a car parked inside, but it was difficult to determine the make and model, other than that it was some kind of blue coupe.

The sidewalk needed to be jackhammered and replaced, and as we approached the front door, I almost snorted when Hale's toe snagged on the uneven surface and he stumbled forward.

The porchlight was on, as if Coach Wiley was expecting us. I'd attempted to call him from the car before knocking, but nobody answered. I doubted he'd flipped on the light to welcome us. The rest of the house was dark except the flicker of a television from another room.

I knocked. Waited. Rang the doorbell.

Somewhere in the house, dogs began going batshit. Other than that, nothing.

The knob was secure.

"Probable cause, Wr– … *Detective* Wren. Let's do this clean."

Ignoring Hale, I stepped off the porch and tried to peer into a window that possibly opened to a bedroom. Something smacked against the glass, and I fell back, tripping over my own steps and landing in the grass.

Thankfully, Hale also repressed *his* snort.

"Dog," he said.

"Is that what the paws against the glass tell you?" I asked, accepting his assistance to stand again. "Or was it the loud woof, woof sound?"

We rounded the corner and found another window. There was no response from my tap on the window this time, other than the now distant sound of our canine friends. They had to be confined to that first room. I tried to force this window, but it was locked tight.

"Just checking security," I told Hale. "I'd never actually crawl in through here if you weren't looking."

With my phone as a flashlight, I led the way around the side of the house

A chain link fence enclosed the backyard, which was also in need of a mow. As we approached, I felt my phone buzz twice, each time sending a jolt through my nerves. Both were benign updates on the men we were tracking.

In the backyard, a warping gazebo and a firepit hinted at Dean Wiley's life before his wife passed away from a stroke three years ago. A flat, pink inflatable pool lay in the yard, folded by the wind. Nick Wiley's three cute girls had probably splashed around in that pool this summer.

The gate was unlocked. I didn't have my Glock drawn as we stepped through and started toward the patio, but my hand rested on the butt of it. Nothing felt right about this.

Through the French doors, I could see that the ceiling fan lights were on in the living room. Though the television was out of our line of sight, the flicker of it reflected off the wall above an olive couch.

"Living room lights are on," he said.

"How can you tell?"

"Because I can see …" he sighed. "You're hard to tolerate, you know?"

I walked past Hale, stepped up onto the porch, and tried the main door. It unlatched easily, and I pulled the door open several inches.

"Wren."

"The door was ajar," I said. "Probable cause."

Hale looked around and then back at me and nodded. "That door was ajar. We should probably check things out."

I considered my new investigation partner for a moment. "Yeah, right on. Good call, Hale."

Taking a moment before entering, I scanned as much of the house as I could from outside. There were a couple chairs, the couch, and a coffee table where someone had left a dinner place and glass. Both were empty except for crumbs.

A large family picture above the couch included Wiley's now-deceased wife, Nick and his brother, daughters-in-law, and children. A waist-high giraffe sculpture filled up some corner space next to what appeared to be the entrance to the kitchen. The room smelled like cigarettes and dogs.

"Mr. Wiley? Dean?" I yelled into the house, holding the door open just enough to poke my head in. The only response was barking from somewhere down the hall. "Mr. Wiley, this is Detective Sara Wren, and I'm with Agent Victor Hale."

No response. I glanced at Hale, who shrugged and gestured for us to continue in.

Pulling my gun, I called out one final time. “Mr. Wiley, we have reason to be worried about your safety. Agent Hale and I are entering the house now.”

The television was set to a news channel. At nearly 2:00 in the morning, it was probably repeat airings of the Saturday’s programs.

I called out our presence again.

“Bedroom, first.” I led the way down a hallway to the left of the living room. The older home had a traditional floor plan, with a bathroom and bedrooms all lining the hall. More family pictures dotted the walls, including a younger photo of the coach and his wife. The man in the picture looked a lot like his son, Nick, but with more facial hair.

The barking came from the second door to our right, the first being a bathroom.

I knuckle-tapped the door. The dogs answered, barking and scratching against the wood. I gripped the knob and turned.

“Mr. Wiley?” I edged the door open an inch and a muzzle pressed against the gap. The room smelled like dog shit.

“They’ve been in there a while.” Using my leg to block an escape, I pushed the door open a bit more, enough to stick my head in. Two emaciated beagle-looking mutts hopped against my leg as I scanned the room. I kicked them back, and they barked at me, panting. There was no source of food or water in the room.

The old furniture sat atop a gray carpet ruined by feces, vomit, and urine.

I pulled the door shut.

My phone buzzed again, and I hoped that Hale hadn’t seen me start.

The next room was empty and appeared to be used mostly for storage. Several boxes were stacked on the bed and around the room. A Christmas tree and outdoor lawn decorations for the same season were stacked near a closet.

At the end of the hall, the master bedroom was ajar, the lights off.

"Dean Wiley, this is Detective Wren from the Mariston police department. We've entered your house out of concern for your safety, and we are approaching your bedroom."

Nothing.

And when I reached the door and flipped on the lights, we found no sign of Wiley other than the unmade bed and a CPAP machine on the nightstand.

With a quick check of the master bathroom, we returned to the living room and did a walkthrough of the kitchen, dining room, and a family room near the front door. No sign of Wiley anywhere.

Taking a moment to check my notifications, I saw that the text from earlier was Casey

"Feltrop isn't home," I told Hale.

"At one in the morning," he answered. "What the hell is going on?"

I texted Casey back and told him to wake the neighbors and see if they had doorbell footage. Two of our prime suspects were missing in the middle of a weekend night. The team I'd dispersed across Mariston suddenly felt much too small.

Slipping the phone back in my pocket, I lifted my gun at the ready as we continued our search.

Remembering the layout of the house from the outside, I passed through a small laundry nook adjacent to the kitchen and opened the door to the garage.

The car I'd seen from the outside was a sporty Honda Civic occupying the one spot inside. Many of the older homes in this area, if they had garages at all, weren't designed for multiple vehicles. Aside from the car, the walls were lined with gardening equipment and a few shelves with plastic storage boxes.

"The basement," I said.

When out in front of the house, I'd seen that the topography sloped down on the west side of the house, suggesting a lower level and probably a garage access. We found the door leading downstairs off the kitchen. I'd walked past it just moments ago, assuming it to be a pantry or closet—neither of them places we'd expect to find Coach.

Nor would we expect him to be in the basement, unless it was finished and he had dozed off there the night before. Or unless …

The basement door hinges needed to be oiled. Anyone downstairs would have heard me pull it open. The weight of my body on the first bare-wood step continued the symphony of unhelpful noises.

"Dean Wiley?" I shouted, aiming into the dark. "Anyone down here?"

No response, so I flipped the light switch, which only lit up the stairs. Hale's flashlight over my shoulder only cut a few feet into the dark below.

In many of the older homes in this area, it was rare to see the downstairs turned into a living space, and this house was no different. The smell of must and dust suggested the moisture that inevitably permeates the cracks in the several-decade-old foundation. The floor beneath us was aged concrete.

As we descended, we could only see stacks of boxed storage on shelves along the opposite wall.

My gun and eyes scanning in sync as I reached the basement floor, I reached behind me and found the light switch.

A single exposed bulb in the center of the basement brought the scene to life.

I lowered my weapon.

"Dear God," Hale said.

Coach Dean Wiley was strapped to a chair. There was no chance he was still alive.

CHAPTER 35

Cause of death: pesticide.

A gray-blue tint clouded the man's face and arms. Beneath it, faint marbling traced the veins of settled blood. His hands and feet were swollen, the fingers tinged purple.

His head held over the back support of the chair by a thick loop of duct tape, Wiley's sunken eyes stared at the floor joists above him. His mouth, forced open as wide as it would probably go, was stuffed with rags, which surrounded a plastic tube. The visible end of that tubing connected to a funnel. The other end of it was somewhere down his throat.

The bottle of pesticide lay on the ground next to him, the spill of it dried on the concrete.

"He's been dead for well over a day," I said quietly, though Hale didn't need me to tell him.

As Hale shined his light throughout the rest of the basement, I examined the body closer. Dean Wiley had drowned on either the chemicals or his own vomit. I'd read once that victims of water drownings sometimes encountered euphoria in their final moments. I doubted that this method had produced the same experience.

"Detective Wren," Hale said.

I didn't answer. For just a moment, I felt overwhelmed. Helpless. This couldn't be happening now. Soon, we'd have an emergency response team here, further exhausting our resources.

"Sara," Hale said. Hearing my first name from his voice broke me from my emotional paralysis.

"With your permission," Hale said, his voice softening to a tone I hadn't heard from him before. "I'll take care of securing this crime scene."

I nodded. Hale knew that I needed to focus on the search for Wes.

In a short span of time, the guy was growing on me, and I wondered if I'd only assumed some of the antagonism I'd sensed since he joined the team.

The barking continued from upstairs, probably carried to the basement through the HVAC.

"Call for a response team and start documenting the scene," I told Hale. "I need to see who all's been blowing up my phone."

As I climbed the stairs, I caught up on my calls and messages. Then I paused.

"Hale." He looked up at me. "Before anything else, find some food and water for those dogs."

As I continued upstairs, I saw I'd missed two calls, one from Shaw and one from Casey, but they'd both followed up by text. Feltrop's neighbors weren't helpful, Casey had written. One had a doorbell cam, but the angle and distance were both wrong for it to have caught movement outside Feltrop's house. Another held a gun when he answered and slammed the door in Casey's face when he identified himself.

I thumbed through the queue of messages as I climbed back upstairs. Behind me, Hale was on the phone with dispatch.

My phone buzzed again. This was Hale in a group text, informing them of the situation here. Casey responded soon after that he would head this way to assist.

Several other messages were just updates as the team checked on the men from the Thunder roster.

Then my phone buzzed again with another response to the thread that Hale had started. With this one, again from Casey, I froze in the kitchen at the top of the stairs.

Officer Lachance has gone silent. Casey wrote. *Backups sent.*

While it was hard to keep track of all the worker bees in the increasingly messy case, I remembered that Officer Jaycee Lachance was one of the rookies on rotation outside Wiley's house.

Last point of contact? Hollis asked.

Four hours ago, Shaw responded.

Though they'd probably heard updates through dispatch by now, I updated the group on what we'd found in Coach Wiley's basement and then dialed Shaw and did another pass through the house as the phone rang.

"Wren," she said, answering after the first ring. "What's going on? Everything's blowing up."

As I filled her in on the bedroom scene, I returned to Coach Wiley's bedroom, scanning to see if there was anything out of the ordinary, trying to spot some evidence of his last actions before walking down the basement steps for the final time. A quilt and sheets had been tossed off to the side. The surfaces and walls were filled with family and religious pictures.

My phone buzzed. I pulled it away from my ear and saw that Casey was trying to reach me again.

The closet door in the coach's bedroom was open. It was single-man messy, with shoes spilling out past the threshold.

"Shaw, Feltrop's disappeared from our radar. Call Casey and see how he needs your help there. I gotta go."

Ending the call, I sat on the edge of Wiley's bed and looked at the pile of clippings on his nightstand. They were articles about the murders, and they hadn't just been clipped. Key details from the stories had been highlighted.

Pulling open the drawer, I exposed the contents more fully.

Inside the drawer were folded maps of Mariston with red ink marking each dump site. Candid photos of the victims, clearly pulled from social media posts, had been printed on cheap paper. I quickly snapped pictures of everything.

The second page of a small spiral notebook had a handwritten list of the *Thunder* roster. It was the 8th-grade version, which didn't include Feltrop as a player or his dad as a coach. The names of the deceased had been crossed through.

If I hadn't just seen the man's body downstairs, I'd take these items as evidence of Wiley's involvement in the murders. But I suspected he was tracking the murders, either out of grief or worry that his time might be approaching.

I needed to think. This couldn't be where the evening led.

Hale was in the living room when I left the bedroom. He put his hand up to stop me. He had his phone pressed to his ear.

"Hold on a moment," he said, pressing the phone against his side to update me. "It's Casey. Lachance is dead."

The look on his face suggested the news would get worse.

"And Nick Wiley is missing."

"What about the girls? His wife?"

"They're all fine," he said. "Wiley's wife didn't realize he'd gone missing. Said she felt him get up and that he was going outside for a cigarette, but she fell back asleep. The officers who arrived to check on Lachance woke Mrs. Wiley when they knocked."

Wiley's nicotine addiction, heightened by his stress, probably saved his wife's life. Maybe his daughters', as well, as Hale said there were signs of the abduction on the deck. A tipped chair. A pack of cigarettes and a lighter on the wrought-iron table.

Would the killer have gained access to the house or had he observed Wiley enough to know his nocturnal habits? I suspected the latter.

Two missing men and two new dead bodies. Within hours, the case had doubled in intensity.

Whether or not I found Wes, the killer intended to bring things to a climax tonight. This told me we were close, but it also suggested that the timeline was tighter than I imagined.

Officer Lachance had been found slumped over in her patrol car, Hale continued. Her doors had been locked, her windows closed. There was no sign of forced entry, gun shots, or struggle. The responding officers thought, at first, that she'd just fallen asleep.

I stepped onto the patio and began pacing. The reflection of police lights against a neighbor's brick wall told me that the first of our reinforcements had arrived out front. Doors opened and slammed shut from that direction.

Feltrop and Nick Wiley were both missing.

Feltrop was our guy. I knew it.

But knowing he was the killer didn't do us any good if we had no idea where the hell he'd gone.

My phone buzzed again, and I scooped it out of my pocket. The queue of unread messages included some from Casey, Witt, and Hollis. But it was the third line down that caught my attention. It was from Wes's number.

The new message indicated another image file.

My thumb trembled as I brought it over the message.

But it wasn't a photo of Wes.

The picture I found when I clicked open the thread was of Henry.

Taken from a distance, the somewhat pixelated zoom showed my son in at the summer camp he had attended this week. He and some other boys were lugging kayaks into the lake.

In the photo below it, Henry was balancing his way across a rope bridge.

Another captured him sitting at a picnic table, eating the lunch that Ed had no doubt packed for him.

I took a deep breath and forced the inhale through pursed lips, processing the two messages. The damage done to my brother. The threat made against my son.

Then I scrolled the thread upward and saw the message that the killer had sent.

Come alone, he had typed. *Our secret. No singing, songbird.*

Ten minutes had passed since that message.

Reply YES if you value his life, the killer had written minutes later, probably frustrated that I had not responded.

Yrs, I quickly typed, my unsteady thumb and raw nerves uncooperative with the text keyboard. *Yes*, I corrected and sent.

Another deep breath, and then I more carefully typed a second message.

Where? When? No answer.

Hale stepped outside. Over his shoulder, I could see the uniformed cops entering through the foyer and spreading throughout the house.

"The car in the garage," he said. "Do you have a picture of the tire tread from Wagner Creek?"

He could no doubt see from my face that I'd been rattled.

"What's wrong, Wren?" he said.

My thumbs hovered over the phone. I pressed them to the phone case so Hale wouldn't see the tremble. Each second I waited to respond might be the last second Wes knew.

No singing, the message had warned. I wanted to tell Hale about the messages, but the killer had stayed one step ahead of us since the first body. The paranoia kept me from trusting him with my new crisis.

"Texts from Shaw about Lachance," I said. "We should have partnered her up."

The words sounded as unconvincing to me as they surely did to Hale.

"Detective Wren," he said, looking at me a moment longer. "There's something else?"

I needed someone inside this moment with me. Someone to help carry the weight of it.

"Hale …"

A cop stood at the door, waiting for one of us to return to direct the response.

"Wren, what is it?"

No singing.

"Casey's in charge when he gets here, Hale." I brushed past him and into the house. "Keep me updated."

CHAPTER 36

Hale followed me out the front door. Outside, two more black and whites arrived. First responders from the fire station were rounding the corner. Lights popped on at houses around us as we woke the neighborhood.

An older man supported by a cane and railing watched me jog to my car from his front steps across the street. He wore a robe tied loosely around whatever he slept in.

Two houses down on Coach Wiley's side of the street, a younger couple stood together at the edge of their property, the man with his arm around the woman, holding her tight. His glasses reflected the glow of a streetlight.

Hale studied me for a moment. "You know something, don't you?" He glanced at the phone, still in my hand. "Something about your brother."

"This is a distraction," I insisted. "We have three missing men to find. One of them is our guy."

"You're holding something back,"

"I'm going to wake up Judge Bolden and get a warrant to search Feltrop's house," I lied, though it wasn't convincing.

Hale's eyes narrowed on my phone. "If something's changed, I need to know."

"What's changed," I said, turning away, "is my brother's still missing while we're standing here arguing. I'm going to find him."

Inside the Durango, I slammed the door shut, and glanced at the house. Hale stood watching me, but he had his phone pressed against his ear. He wasn't going to let me go rogue. I had to move quickly. If I met the killer with an obvious tail, it was bad news for Wes.

I'm coming, I typed back to the man who had Wes's phone. *Just me.*

"Hey, Google," I said as I pulled away from Dean Wiley's neighborhood, putting distance between me and the chaos left behind. My phone beeped through the Bluetooth sync, and I once again requested a connection with Hot Sauce.

I had to change that name.

Ed picked up after three rings. I had no concept of how much time had passed since Mary Claire's call from St. George. The dashboard clock insisted it was only 3:13 a.m.—just over an hour before sunrise—but it felt like the whole world should be awake by now.

"Hello?" Ed's voice was raspy. He cleared his throat. "Sara?"

It wasn't until he answered that I realized my fear that he wouldn't.

"Is Henry with you?"

"Of course. Sara, what's –"

"*With* you, right now."

"He's asleep in his room. What's wrong?"

"Get Henry and leave the house. Go somewhere safe and wait there until I call you again. Not your place, either."

"Sara …"

"Now, Ed." I hung up the phone, which immediately began buzzing. It was Casey. No doubt Hale had told him about my exit, and he was trying to track me down.

Letting the call go to voicemail, I pulled over into the lot of an apartment complex and opened my texts. There were several new messages, but none of them from Wes's number.

I opened the thread from the killer again. There'd been no new messages since he'd sent me the pictures of Henry.

My fingers trembled over the screen.

Where? I texted again.

Nothing for several seconds.

"Come on ..."

Had I waited too long?

Was Wes already dead?

Then, three bouncing response dots appeared at the bottom of the screen.

The dots disappeared for a moment and then started again.

A street address I didn't recognize appeared next in our conversation.

Was this where I would find Wes? Or where the killer waited to end my life.

Where *Feltrop* waited to end my life.

After a short stretch on the highway through town, I exited near a retail area, which included a Walmart and the types of businesses that gravitate to the hypermarket's orbit. Except for street lights and security lamps, the area was dark. This Walmart hadn't stayed open all night since before the pandemic. The city never fully slept, of course, but I only passed one other car in this area. Most likely, it was someone finishing a shift.

My phone buzzed and Casey's ID flashed. I rejected the call. I didn't want to lie to him, but I couldn't afford to sabotage my attempt to meet Feltrop on his terms.

Once I had a better understanding of the situation, maybe I would be able to guide Casey and the others to back me up. Until then, I had to assume that Feltrop would somehow know I had tipped them off.

The inability to trust my team was crippling, but the photos of Henry had disarmed me.

I was kidding myself to think I had any control here.

Why didn't I send someone to my house to protect Ed and Henry?

Casey tried calling me again, as did Hollis. Then Shaw again. By now, everyone knew I'd gone solo. Previews of the messages appeared on my dash screen, but I ignored them all. They'd be on my tail soon enough, as the Durango, like most of the precinct vehicles, had a tracking device.

Surely, Feltrop realized that I wouldn't be able to sneak away so easily.

What if Dean Wiley's suicide and these texts from Wes's phone were just attempts to occupy and divide Mariston's law enforcement?

What if Wes was already dead and I was just walking into a trap?

My navigation system informed me that my destination waited just ahead. *Overtime Athletic Gear*, a used sporting goods store, was only open on weekends. My passing headlights reflected off a display window, obscuring the golf clubs and bags showcased inside.

Of course, he'd led me to a sports store. The theme continued. I wouldn't be surprised to be assaulted with a pitching machine when I arrived.

While the parking lot appeared empty, I cruised past at regular speed, surveying the area.

A small, black SUV was parked along the side of the building, near the dumpster. It had the same body style and dark black exterior as the one the cameras picked up driving from the community center.

Continuing past the store, I pulled into another lot a block down the road and parked, letting the engine run as I thought through my next move. I *was* walking into a trap, and the monster who had abducted Wes had no intention of either my brother or me surviving until daybreak.

My Glock was already tucked into my shoulder holster, but unlocking my center console, I pulled out my loaded P365 and the extra magazine I kept there as a backup. In addition to the gun, I spotted a jackknife in the console.

With a quick contortion, I tucked the Sig and its holster against the small of my back and slipped the jackknife and the extra clip into my front pockets.

Back on the road, I entered the *Overtime* lot again, pulling up so that the nose of my vehicle faced the waiting SUV. A pair of headlights passed on the boulevard above me, but otherwise, the roads were empty.

For a few moments, I remained in my driver's seat, scanning the dark. The area behind *Overtime* was mostly wooded and dropped down to a drainage path that snaked behind the cluster of businesses. Feltrop could be hiding in the foliage or behind any number of walls or structures. He could be on top of a roof, his crosshairs tracking me.

But I don't think this is how the story ends for me. It didn't match the nature of his previous kills. Wes was the bait for a trap more elaborate than a shot to the head in a vacant lot.

Stepping slowly out of my car, gun in hand, I continued scanning around me. A heavy wind rustled through the June-lush trees. A fast food wrapper danced past the back of my waiting Durango.

Across the street, several delivery trucks were parked in the lot of a bottling plant. While I could see security cameras mounted on the exterior of that building, nothing seemed to be pointed directly at where I had parked. Nor did the sports shop have an exterior security system in place. Even if there had been one, Feltrop would have sabotaged the cameras as he'd done in other locations.

Cameras wouldn't do any good now, anyway. Whatever was going to happen tonight wasn't going to happen here.

This was a vehicle swap.

CHAPTER 37

Though the rear windows were tinted, I was able to see the vehicle was empty as I began circling it, my Glock in a teacup grip. An old paperback had been tossed in the front seat. An umbrella lay on the rear floorboard.

The vehicle was pulled up against the side of the building. As I passed the driver-side door, I spotted the white envelope resting on the seat.

Songbird, it said in block letters across the front.

I tugged the handle and felt the latch disengage.

Before opening the door, I remembered I had recently texted Hale a picture of the tire tracks from Wagner bridge. While it was of little consequence to whatever happened next, I crouched next to a rear tire and retrieved the photo.

As well as I could tell, the prints were a match.

Tomorrow or soon after, regardless of how this ended, a forensics team would be completing the same analysis.

Returning to the driver's door, I opened it, leaned in, and grabbed the envelope. As I did, I spotted the trail camera strapped to the headrest of the passenger seat. When else had he been surveilling me this evening? Had we missed cameras inside Dean Wiley's house? Were they hidden outside my own?

Inside the unsealed envelope was a folded letter, an ignition key, and a piece of my brother's ear.

I knew what the bloody flap of skin was without pulling it from the envelope. The severed lobe was supposed to further disarm me psychologically, but I was well beyond that.

Done crying. Done with palpitations.

I pulled out the key, put it on the hood of the car, and removed the letter. I tossed the envelope back onto the passenger seat of the car. After I put a bullet in Feltrop's head, Wes will want the earlobe back as a souvenir of survival. He's that kind of strange.

The letter was typed, the text centered both ways on the paper in a near-haiku syllable count.

```
You're in a pickle now!
Toss the phone and the handgun.
Meet me at first base.
```

What did that mean? Just days ago at El Rincón, the team's margarita-soaked conversation had almost seemed to be a parlor game as we brainstormed connections between the dumpsites and baseball terms.

Had we been on to something then?

I typed a quick response, asking what he meant by *first base?*

The response: a kiss emoji. First base on a date. Feltrop was toying with me.

I pushed away an image of the pimple-faced man we'd met at the home improvement store, I focused on solving the puzzle. *First base* could be anywhere. First National Bank? First Street in downtown Mariston? First base was also called the *gateway* base.

Was I supposed to drive an hour to St. Louis, the Gateway city?

The *bag*. The *sack*.

Nothing was connecting.

Who'd been the regular first baseman for Thunder? Of the players still alive, I couldn't remember what we'd learned in our interviews. Other than the conversation at El Rincón, their defensive positioning seemed irrelevant to the investigation.

But Feltrop was playing games, so I had to reject regular logic.

What do you mean? Tell me where I go?

But there was no response. Not immediately or after I stared at the screen for nearly a minute.

Would it jar him into a response if I called him out by name? If I taunted him?

Or would it trigger his anger and my brother's death.

But then I remembered the photos of Henry. Wes was first, he was telling me. And then the rest of my family.

This could get much worse.

Wes was depending on my survival, as were Henry and Ed.

I had to end this man and his violence tonight.

If I could just figure out what he meant by his cryptic messages.

Wait …

I opened my gallery app and began thumbing through the photos I'd taken of the contents of Dean Wiley's drawer. In one of the pictures, I'd captured the rough map that the former coach had drawn of Mariston, with X marks where the bodies had been found.

We had a similar but more accurate diagram on a city map posted at the station, and I thumbed through the images to find it.

Why hadn't we seen this before?

As much as we'd studied that map, trying to identify a pattern or triangulate a prediction for the next location, we'd missed it.

On our larger map back at the station, Woodhouse's body is marked by a pin near the left side of the city map. Todd's was slightly higher and far to the right, and Russell's was between them. Todd had played 2nd, Woodhouse was 3rd, and Russell was a regular at short.

Riedel, who played outfield, had been found at the Community Center, north of the city. A pin marked it near the top of the map.

If I imagined the map of the city to be a ball field, the location of the bodies roughly corresponded to the positions the men had played as boys. The placement wasn't perfect, but it was close enough to seem intentional.

Now that I'd seen the corresponding page in the notebook, I couldn't unsee it. Coach Wiley's sketch removed the distraction of the overly detailed city map.

Meet me at first base, the killer had written.

I zoomed in on the station map, sliding the image to zero in on the right side of the photo.

First base. Spreading my index finger and thumb wider on the screen, I tried to enlarge the details for the streets and landmarks in that general area. With the imprecise placement of the other bodies, I was working with a few miles of possible locations.

Street names blurred as I maxed the zoom.

But that didn't matter.

I knew where the killer wanted me to meet him.

On the Mariston map, I immediately recognized the location I had visited days before with Witt. It was the neglected Eagles field where the boys from *Thunder* had played their home games.

If I alerted Casey or Shaw, the woods behind that field could provide cover for my team to arrive from the back end to support me. Phone still in hand, I quickly typed a message to let Casey know my plans and to warn him that the killer would be expecting me to arrive alone.

But then my thumb paused above the send button.

I couldn't click it.

Paranoia was paralyzing my ability to act with prudence.

Would the killer somehow know I'd alerted them?

Or was it possible that this *was* all a distraction? What if the killer *wanted* me to ignore his instructions? And while Casey and a backup team rushed to the ballfield, however discreetly, our antagonist was enjoying his time with a new victim somewhere else?

Or he was tracking Ed and Henry.

The idea seemed far-fetched, but already Dean Wiley's death had drawn attention away from the hunt. And just three weeks ago, I wouldn't have imagined dealing with a series of murders the magnitude of what had occurred in sleepy Mariston.

I submitted myself to the game and pulled out my Glock and my phone. Sliding into the driver's seat, I showed both items to the camera and then tossed them into the weeds alongside the lot. I then showed my empty hands to the camera like a child proving he'd eaten all his food.

The Sig and knife tucked behind me would have to be enough for me to handle Feltrop's trap on my own. With the key I'd found in the envelope, I started the engine, I exited the lot and drove east to the ball diamond.

CHAPTER 38

The Eagles hall and the club's baseball field sat just outside city limits.

Both were along a strip of desperation, including a motel that had been converted into economy apartments. We've found both drugs and corpses in past visits there.

As I drove, I passed a payday loan office, a dollar store, and a drive-thru for cigarettes and vapes.

To call it the armpit of Mariston would be an insult to armpits.

At just past four in the morning, I pulled the crossover into a lot several yards down from the fraternal hall. There was little chance any other vehicles would pass where I had parked or where I was heading.

I'd shut off my lights before cresting the hill above the last stretch of road, but I held little hope of catching the killer off guard. For all I knew, he'd placed his own tracking device in *this* car. Or he was watching me from the shadows.

Would a gunshot break the evening's silence as I stepped out of the vehicle, dropping me alongside it?

Possibly.

Probably.

I stepped out, banking on the killer's mind games and ready to play them, at least until I found Wes and understood the situation. Streetlights ran the length of the road as far as I could see. Somewhere up ahead, an intersection light blinked red.

When I was in my twenties, I ran a lot in the early mornings. Whether to wake myself up for a morning shift or to decompress after a late one, I found that the early summer mornings transported me from the world I knew. The genial pause to the summer heat. The lingering haze.

It was just me and my crepuscular friends in those fleeting hours before dawn.

Especially where Ed and I lived at the time—a small house outside the city limits—I could find miles of road with only moonlight to reveal the road ahead of me.

But the silence around me now was not the peace before daybreak. It was, instead, the world holding its breath.

As I approached the fraternal hall and the ballfield behind it, I realized I'd unconsciously tucked both hands into my pockets. They otherwise felt like pointless appendages dangling at my side without the familiar grip of my gun.

I'd stepped into some other place outside of my life. But it wasn't the place I remembered from those morning runs.

Somewhere ahead of me was a man who wanted me dead.

Somewhere ahead of me was Calvin Feltrop. And my brother.

Even as I approached, I was conscious of the possibility that Feltrop was tracking me. Yet, I had to demonstrate resolve. He wanted to break me.

The lot in front of the hall was paved for several yards, with packed gravel beyond that. I walked across both and alongside a storage shed toward the field. From where I approached, a two-story structure blocked my view of the field. The narrow building allowed for a concession booth on the lower level and an announcer's booth up top.

There were bleachers in front of the narrow building and a tall backdrop fence behind home plate. The lights surrounding the complex were dark and probably hadn't been maintained any better than the rest of the field. But even with the electricity shut off, the moon was full over the woods behind the outfield.

In the pale light, as the field opened up with my approach, I saw Wes.

I recognized his frame and his thick beard, even if his back was to the moon and his face a shadow. He was in a chair in the infield where first base would be if the bags were placed for a game. I resisted the urge to reach for the gun tucked behind me as I neared the field, scanning for Feltrop.

That's when I spotted another man strapped to a chair at the second base location. Though I couldn't make out his identity, I knew it had to be Nick Wiley.

"I'm here," I shouted into the dark, my hands in the air to show I wasn't carrying a weapon. "I came alone."

Wes moved at the sound of my voice, lifting his head from where it had been resting against his chest.

Still alive.

I saw movement on the other chair, too, but my attention was split between Wes and the surrounding darkness. So many shadows and obstructions. The killer could be anywhere. In the concession area or the woods surrounding us. Behind me.

"Calvin Feltrop," I yelled into the night. "I've done my part. Stop being a chickenshit."

Slowly, I approached the first base dugout, through which the field could be accessed.

In the dugout, a beer can had rolled under the bench, and another one lay half-crushed just through the door. Both were probably from late night teen mischief at the field.

Unfortunately for me, we were unlikely to be interrupted by a high school party during our early morning business here.

The field had been marked, as if for a game. But, it wasn't with the straight lines a chalking machine would have left. In preparation for my arrival, the killer had poured a trail of the white powder from home plate and around the diamond of bases.

"Wes," I stage-whispered as I stepped onto the field, still scanning around me. "Where is he, Wes?"

Wes shook his head and grunted again. The side of his face was still covered in dried blood.

"Here I am," I yelled again.

With a few more steps, I was behind Wes, where I could see more closely how he was bound. His hands were strapped with zip ties, and his arms were secured to the back of the chair with tightly-looped cords.

I could free him in seconds with the knife in my pocket, but I knew better than to attempt it now.

"I'm getting you out of this, Wes." I edged past him, now seeing the figure on second more closely. It was definitely Nick Wiley. The glow of the moon reflected off his balding head and his body sagged against the ropes.

When I made eye contact with Wiley, he turned his head slowly toward the spectator section, back to me, and then to the fencing behind home plate again.

The bleachers on the third-base side of the concession booth had been constructed up the slope of a hill. The building had been fitted into an excavated section of that hill, which crested level at the base of the announcer's booth in the second level.

Though the concession counter was covered with cardboard, the wide window in the upper room was half opened, the glass window slid to the left.

The canopy extending from the building blocked most of the moonlight. But within that dark room, I thought I could make out a shape. Maybe a shoulder. Maybe.

I could reach for the Sig and attempt a shot through the opened half of the window, but Feltrop had the advantage here. I'm a quick draw when properly holstered, but he'd drop me as soon as he saw my hand move toward my back.

Looking back at Wes and then Wiley, I was at a loss as to what I was expected to do.

This didn't make sense.

Maybe Feltrop expected me to rush to Wes. Another game. He'd probably shoot my brother as I crouched next to him and worked at the ropes.

Wiley grunted again. He was trying to communicate.

I edged toward him, my hands still high and visible, my eyes on the announcer's booth.

At the halfway mark, I paused and glanced at Wiley. He watched me with hope.

Another side step. Then another. What was the game here?

Another step.

Then the gun shot and a flash from the announcer's window. The shot was loud, but muffled. It was the sharp crack of a bullet fired through a suppressor.

My brother lurched against his restraints, his cry checked by the tape over his mouth. Blood dripped from his chair.

"Wes!" I darted toward him.

With a sharp clack, another shot came from the upper window. The sound I made wasn't a cry or a word, but the audible release of the shock that spread through my chest from inside my gut.

Behind me, I heard Wiley howl through his gag, thrashing his body so forcefully that his chair tipped toward me and then toppled. Still strapped to his chair, he lay on his side in the infield dirt. A pool of blood spread from his leg, edging toward the baseline. His body thrashed and his legs slamming against the toppled chair.

I froze, paralyzed by confusion and panic.

Wes hunched over as far as his restraints would allow, rocking against the tension. I couldn't see where the bullet had entered.

The silence following the last shot wrapped itself around me, holding me in place. My brain, trying to command a reaction, was responding to some Pavlovian instinct.

Each time I'd moved, the man in the box had fired a shot, but not at the man I'd attempted to help.

And never at me.

This felt familiar to me. I'd been here before.

Then I remembered the letter.

You're in a pickle now.

CHAPTER 39

Wes to my left. Wiley to my right. No good decision. The killer had me in a rundown. Or as baseball players often call it, a *pickle*.

As a short stop, I'd helped trap several baserunners between second base and either third or first. The runner pivoted and dashed, trying to find safety at one bag or the other.

I was the one caught in the trap now.

Whichever direction I ran meant another bullet for the victim I'd abandoned.

And, like a runner back in my softball days, just standing on the baseline between them both wasn't an option. If I stalled, he would come up with a way to accelerate the action. Most likely it would involve Wes bleeding through another hole.

In less than an hour, the sun would rise behind me, casting enough light to see the announcer's window clearly.

But for now, the booth remained a shadow within a shadow.

I saw hints of movement, which I imagined to be his shifting body as he pivoted to find me with his scope.

In a softball game, a runner caught in a rundown starts making mistakes when she panics, unsure of when to stop and turn and when to go for broke with one base or the other.

The best-case scenario is that one of the fielders loses momentum and drops or overthrows the ball.

I had to outguess Feltrop and jar his momentum.

Wes had received a non-lethal shot. The smooth blood spill didn't suggest a ruptured artery. I assumed the same for Wiley, who continued squirming and grunting on the ground.

But, the next shot might be different. It could be the lethal one for either man. Feltrop was running out of time, too. The sun would be up soon. The town would awaken.

I suspected he anticipated me rushing to Wes. Feltrop probably had his gun focused on Wiley now, ready to take a shot opposite of my next move.

Yes, he could switch his aim, but it would take a moment.

Maybe a long enough moment.

I darted three steps toward Wiley and dove, my hand reaching behind me for the Sig. I hit the ground, and a round cracked from above. Dirt puffed inches from my left foot.

Shifting into a firing posture, I squeezed the trigger once. The glass exploded next to the opened section. Adjusting left, I fired again and pushed into a crouch, delivering several more rounds in quick succession before racing from my open position on the field, hoping I'd created enough distraction to find cover.

I was abandoning my brother and Wiley, but there was no way to save them from the field.

As I darted through the dugout, my left foot caught the edge of the concrete pad. I fell against the bench, and my face slammed against the chain-link screen behind it. I pushed away and escaped the dugout.

Though I had put a difficult angle between me and the upper window, my brother remained in his direct line of sight. Any moment I expected to hear another loud snap from the opened window.

But there was no shot as I raced to the concession area, pressing myself against the white-painted block wall, trying to control my breath.

I listened for movement above me, though I worried that Feltrop had already escaped the booth. The rear entrance was nearly flush with the hill behind it, with only a small flight of stairs from door to dirt.

I'd spent seven shots. I think. There had been the two I fired from the baseline and then … *five* more as I raced from open exposure?

The magazine, designed for easy concealment, only held ten rounds, which left three.

Nothing above me. No noise. No gunshots.

Ejecting the nearly-empty magazine, I dug for the full one in my front pocket.

There were two ways to get to the rear door of the announcer's booth. The bleachers had been built into the natural slope of the hill, but if I edged back in the direction of the admissions gate, the retaining wall extending from the building offered some cover. I chose this direction, my gun trained on the back of the booth.

Feltrop had drawn blood on Wes and Nick Wiley. Fired through a suppressor, the shots would not have raised any alarms in the nearby trailer parks or apartments. But my gun might have woken someone nearby.

Without any other way of calling for reinforcements, I hoped the noise of gunfire would prompt a 911 call. So far, though, I heard no approaching sirens. Just a light crackle of gravel beneath my feet as I backed away, canvasing the area around the announcer's booth.

A few yards from the building, I could see where the rear door to the upper room was open. It had been shut when I arrived. I'm certain I would have noticed, otherwise.

Though there were concrete stairs leading up the slope to the booth, they were in a more exposed area. So, I used the capstones on the retaining wall, instead, balancing on the narrow steps to climb the hill, my gun locked on the door.

The background of trees left Feltrop too many places to hide, but I continued to scan them, watching for movement and hoping my shot had been fatal.

Drops of blood marked Feltrop's exit from the booth. The trail led down the small set of access steps and into the grass.

He could have gone in several directions. Continuing straight would take him down the other side of the hill, where he could have disappeared behind a storage shed. The woods were just yards away.

As I crossed the doorway, I took a glance inside the announcer's booth. A scoped rifle lay on the floor where Feltrop dropped or ditched it as he fled. I had to assume that he had a back-up.

But if he was too injured to use a two-handed weapon, he had much less control over this situation.

This was my chance to free Wes and Wiley.

With one more scan of the trees, I descended from the hill again, this time by way of the bleachers. This allowed me to keep an eye on the areas where Feltrop might have disappeared.

A gunshot exploded from within the trees, missing me by inches. The bullet chipped the concrete on the building behind me. Wherever he hid among those shadows, Feltrop had a clean view of me.

The bleacher seats weren't designed to be a stairway, and I misjudged my first step as I raced down them for cover.

The Sig flew from my right hand, and I hit the bottom rows hard. My left thigh and ribs absorbed impact on the metal benches. With my body tumbling over the remaining rows, the back of my head bounced against concrete where I landed. The bleachers and fencing around me wavered.

"Songbird," Feltrop called. I heard the voice, but I couldn't see him from where I had landed.

My gun had landed somewhere above me. My thigh and, on the same side, my lower ribs screamed as I struggled to pull myself into a crouch. Probably concussed, I felt as though the concrete beneath me was balanced on a ball.

The thigh didn't feel broken, but at least one of my ribs definitely was. Each breath was a blade into my side.

I couldn't spot my gun.

I was in trouble.

Pressing into a hunched stance, I shifted my weight to my right side and limped to look for the weapon. In my peripheral, I saw the outline of Wiley squirming in his toppled chair.

Behind him, the first glow of daybreak turned the treetops into embers.

Still no sirens. Either the neighbors didn't hear the gunshots or didn't care.

"And … the runner is out," I heard next.

Calvin Feltrop stepped from the shadows, his pistol aimed at my head.

CHAPTER 40

While the man standing on the hill above me was the same Calvin Feltrop that Casey and I had interviewed earlier in the week, the intensity of his dominance now made him seem larger.

He stood on the hill, just behind the top of the bleachers. He was dressed in black, his face darkened with paint to help him disappear in the shadows.

I still hadn't spotted my gun, and even if I found it, the chances of grabbing it and firing off even one shot were less than the chances that a rogue meteorite would hit Calvin Feltrop in the head right now.

He smiled and took a careful first few steps onto the top bleachers, keeping the gun aimed at me.

In a brief and painful flashback to my mother's death, I pictured her memorial bench. Was *this* ballfield the place Henry would visit to remember me?

"You stepped off of the baseline," Feltrop said. Each of his steps was measured. He wasn't going to recreate my violent fall. "That's an automatic out."

I shuffled back, biting down at the pain in my left leg, which radiated upward through my body. "Is all this because you weren't good enough to make a baseball team, Calvin?"

He sneered and paused in his descent. His finger was on the trigger. Just one quick squeeze and I was through.

"Or maybe they were tired of your drunk, abusive dad helping coach."

Feltrop's combover whipped in the breeze. Even in the shadows under the canopy, I could see the fury in his eyes.

But I was trying to control the narrative. Placating Feltrop wouldn't help. He wanted me to be pleading right now, so maybe I could stall him long enough to figure out some way to reverse the advantage he had over me now.

But it didn't work.

"I was really looking forward to killing the priest-brother while you watched," he said. "But I promise you he and I will have plenty of time together after you and I finish here."

"All those men we interviewed, Calvin, they resented you. They were embarrassed that you were on the team."

Feltrop's arm tensed as he prepared to end my life. He looked as if he wanted to say something in response. Then his resolve hardened. He shook his head and smiled, dismissing my taunt.

"Goodbye, Songbird," he said.

I tried to run for cover but stumbled against the fence with my weakened leg.

Gunfire exploded behind me.

Drops of blood splattered my arm as I turned my body toward him.

Somehow, I was still alive.

Feltrop's body remained standing for a second before he collapsed onto the bleachers and tumbled halfway down.

CHAPTER 41

Though exhausted and stunned, I recognized Casey as the first of the two men who appeared over the top of the hill behind the bleachers, gun in hand. He jogged down with ease, pausing briefly to verify Feltrop's death, which wasn't difficult since the left side of the killer's forehead was now missing.

Hale appeared next, a rifle still held at the ready.

I collapsed onto the lowest bench and took the deepest breath I could without passing out from the pain in my chest.

"You okay, Wren?" Casey crouched next to me, his hand taking mine.

"Yeah," I said. The word came out as a hoarse whisper. I considered the man they had taken down. Feltrop's body looked small and insignificant to me again.

Casey smiled and winked and nodded at Hale. "There's your sharp-shooter."

Hale shrugged. "I was a sniper in another life."

On top of his clean shot, the FBI stiff was capable of pulling off a joke. I was doubly-impressed by him.

"My brother," I said. "And Nick Wiley." I struggled to stand, and Casey scooped me up, offering his shoulder as my crutch.

Together, with Hale trailing, we left Feltrop's body behind. I limped against Casey as we returned to the infield to free my brother and Wiley.

Wes tracked us, his eyes widening as we approached. The first thing I needed to do was get the gag out of his mouth so he would quit grunting at me.

"You two can take care of Wiley," I said, fishing the jackknife from my pocket and releasing Casey's shoulder.

As I limped toward Wes, he watched Casey and Hale walk away. His grunts grew louder, as he looked from me to them.

Something was wrong. I turned back to the men.

"Wait, how did you two find me?" I asked, the knife still in my hand.

"You texted Casey your location, Wren," Hale said. He held the rifle in one hand as he lifted his phone to his ear with the other. "I'm calling for—"

"Hale!"

I realized the truth and denied it at the same time as Casey lifted his own gun and put his bullet through Hale's phone.

The shot exploded throughout the cleared field. The agent fell onto the ground next to where Nick Wiley remained bound.

Casey pointed the gun in my direction now. I stepped away from Wes, distancing him from what was about to happen to me.

The sky to the east glowed orange now above the trees, but whatever Casey intended would happen before the sun broke the horizon.

"Relax, *Traviesa*." The name was no longer a causal flirtation. "This turned out messier than it was supposed to, but we'll make it work."

I reached for my gun. Except I didn't have a gun.

"You left it on the bleachers," Casey said. "Throw that over here." He pointed his gun at the knife in my hand. I hesitated a second before tossing it in his direction.

"Now get on the ground, over there, away from him."

"Someone heard the gunshots."

Casey arched an eyebrow and looked around, considering the isolation of the area. "Maybe yes," he said. "Someone in the trailer village down the road, you think? Or one of the bums in the motel de cucarachas?"

"Why?" I looked at Hale's body. His right arm stretched just over the baseline.

"I couldn't let him call for help, right, Traviesa? Besides," he said, "el payasso just killed my brother."

Brother?

I realized what he was saying but couldn't process it. Feltrop couldn't be his brother. Besides the different last names, if you put Casey in an opposite machine and hit the go button, Calvin Feltrop would come scuttling out the other side.

Casey lowered his gun to his thigh and regarded Wes for a moment. As he walked the baseline toward my brother, I edged closer to Hale's body. His rifle lay beside him, and his pistol was in the shoulder holster.

But, as Casey reached Wes, I was still several feet away from where Hale lay.

Casey used the tip of his gun to nudge where the earlobe had been removed.

"Thank you for your hospitality that night in the rain," Casey said to Wes, his voice soft, as if he was attempting a quiet confession.

As I tried to make sense of this impossible reality, I realized how easily Casey had eluded us. His camera awareness cloaked him in anonymity during the abductions. His role in the investigation allowed him to filter much of the information that came to me.

"Our father taught us about justice." Casey continued to stare at my brother as he spoke, but the change in tone told me he was now speaking to me. "Justice is always vigilant, but sometimes patient."

Casey walked over to Hale's body, tucking his pistol back into the holster as he did. As he picked up the agent's dropped rifle, I glanced around, looking for options on a night without options.

Casey pressed the muzzle of the weapon against Nick Wiley's cheek as the bound man shook and cried.

"The Wiley Coyote," Casey said. "See, the way this was supposed to work was we'd frame you for these murders, Nick. You'd still die, right, but I'd be the hero and your little girls would only know you as the monster you are."

I slowly scooted back inches as Casey taunted Wiley. My fingers felt for what I'd spotted laying in the dirt behind me.

"You remember what you and your friends did to my brother, don't you?" Casey asked the bound man.

Wiley grunted through his gag and tried to pull back from the metal tip pressing into his face. Somewhere in the hills, a rooster announced the new day.

Casey reconsidered the gun's placement and moved the tip of the weapon, pressing it against Wiley's stomach. "Did you know what Eli Feltrop did to Cal when he found out? Or what he did to my mamma when she tried to stop him?"

He fired a shot into Wiley's gut. The bound man's body began twitching and jerking.

A heavy vehicle passed on the street alongside the Eagle's lodge. Morning had come to Mariston. Whatever was going to happen here would happen soon.

I inched back further, my fingers searching behind me.

Casey moved the rifle's tip to Wiley's head and pulled the trigger again.

For the first time, I was seeing Casey as he truly was.

Casey, who'd once posed undercover as a mid-level dealer, had a gift. Often during interrogations, I'd seen him mirror personalities and gain trust. Disengaged teenage boys. Distressed housewives (of course). Boomers or Millennials. Rich or poor. Suspect or victim.

A shape-shifter stood before me. Both in personality and in appearance.

The only time I recall him seeming out of step was during our interview with a gawky Calvin Feltrop.

Hey, bro.

He'd been playing *me* then.

"It's done now," I said. "Whatever they did to Calvin has nothing to do with me or Wes."

Casey smiled. "Sometimes justice is sevenfold."

I edged farther away from him, as if afraid for my life. Which I was. But as I scooted, my splayed hands continued searching.

"I want you to know that you weren't supposed to die, Traviesa. I even thought I might get a round or two with you after your husband checked out. But big brother got carried away and mucked the whole thing." He crouched in front of me. "I think Calvin had some serious issues," he said, his tone level as if he was trying to reason with me.

"Cal got carried away in that basement. What he did with that drill. That was hard to watch." He took a few steps back from me and regarded Wes. "I'll hand it to our team, though. That afternoon at El Rincón. They actually figured out some of Calvin's riddles."

"So, you kill me now, and then the rest of the men from the team?"

"Oh … no." Casey looked genuinely confused that I'd suggested anything beyond the men who'd already died. "This one finishes it off," he said, gesturing at Wiley's body. "He and the other four. They were the ones."

"And Dean Wiley?"

"You're stalling, Wren, but I'll tell you," he said. "Mostly, I just helped with the heavy lifting on the other guys, but Coach Wiley was mine. For Cal, it was about revenge, but for me, it was justice. A coach has to own the behavior of his team."

Sirens.

They were faint, but I heard them. And Casey heard them.

"I'm sorry it ends this way, Wren." He stepped back and took the rifle in ready grip. The sirens were too far. "Calvin fixated on you. And he got sloppy. And here we are."

He lifted the rifle and pointed it at my chest. My heart was pounding. I thought of Henry. Wanted to plead to Casey not to take me out of my son's life.

The sirens grew louder.

"No, this isn't right." Casey pulled back the rifles and glanced briefly at where Feltrop's body lay on the bleachers. "Brothers go first."

He turned and pointed the gun toward Wes.

CHAPTER 42

I didn't think. I didn't aim. I just acted.

My searching fingers had scratched across stiffened leather just as Casey put a bullet into Wiley's head. Of the half-dozen water-logged balls littering the field, I'd spotted one in the center of the diamond, as if dropped there by a pitcher who'd just left the mound.

As Casey lifted the gun toward Wes's head, an explosive mix of anger and sibling love flooded my body, coursed through my arm, and exploded out my fingertips.

I became, for a moment, the girl at shortstop. The team's only chance. My body a machine, I launched that bloated, leaden ball.

Casey must have heard me grunt, or he caught the movement of my catapult arm. His finger still on the trigger, he turned and swung the rifle in my direction.

The ball cracked against his nose, just under his left eye.

The rifle fell, and his hand flew to his face, the blood seeped over his fingers.

At that moment, I scrambled into a crouch and dove toward Hale's body, pulling the agent's gun from the shoulder holster a pain seared through me.

Casey stumbled backward and reached a bloodied hand for his pistol.

But I fired first, grazing his shoulder.

My adrenaline-driven accuracy was gone, and I struggled to shift to a more stable position for a second shot.

I'd further disoriented Casey and he stumbled into the outfield grass, almost falling before a half-crawl recovery allowed him to recover his footing and put distance between him and my gun.

As the emergency vehicles swerved onto the gravel drive, Casey took several steps back, looking at his arm and then to me. His expression was incredulity, as if he couldn't believe I had torn his shirt.

Then he turned and raced into the outfield and toward the left field foul line.

My side, already searing with pain, exploded to a level I'd never felt before as I pushed into a crouch and ran after him. Behind me, doors slammed shut and officers yelled.

But by the time Casey reached the fence, he'd put several yards of distance between us. Knowing I couldn't catch him, I fired again, missing him completely. But the shots disoriented him. He cleared the fence, but landed poorly, tumbling into the undergrowth.

Somewhere past the acres of trees, a train approached Mariston, sounding its horn as it neared the city limits.

I was in no shape to parkour after Casey. Besides my injured side and thigh, he was bigger and faster than me and had already disappeared from view. Instead of following him over the fence, I cut left and exited through the third base dugout.

As I ran toward the trees, I heard a yell from behind me.

"Wren," Shaw shouted, but I didn't turn. I had to end this.

Under the trees, it was practically night again. The sun had not yet risen high enough to seep through the leafy branches above me. I crouched next to a large trunk and tried to listen over my own harsh breath. The woods smelled of wet leaves and old earth.

My pulse was frantic, but my head was clearing.

I would never catch Casey with a direct chase. But softball and cop work are both about anticipating the opponent's next move. Working the angles.

If I were Casey right now, I'd cut right and circle toward the service road. That was his only escape and most likely where he and Hale had left the car that brought them here.

The intensity of pain in my side brought sweat, and my heart was in overdrive. I hugged against a thick trunk and watched for movement. Something stirred the leaves overtop me, but the woods were still for as far as I could see in any direction.

The train continued past, following the tracks just west of a distant tree line.

Using the sound of the passing train as my cover, I darted to the left, slipping through scrub. Thorns tore at my clothes and my exposed arms. The canvas of limbs and leaves above us blocked out most of the pink-orange morning light.

Ducking under branches, I stepped carefully to keep from broadcasting my position as the train passed and the morning softened. It seemed there was movement everywhere and nowhere. Something in my peripheral would startle me, but I'd turn and see nothing but more brush and trees.

Casey could be a quarter-mile away by now, possibly already in his car. He could be in the shadows, his bead centered on my chest.

I was certain he wanted me dead more than he wanted to escape. At some point, Casey may have planned to frame the murders on Nick Wiley, but his quest for justice had driven him to follow Feltrop down a path from which there was no return.

The men from Thunder were now dead, their punishment for whatever they had done to Calvin as a boy. I was the last remaining symbol for whatever injustice their family had experienced.

Pulling my collar up to wipe at my forehead sweat, I continued down a steep hill, moving from tree to tree for support.

Somewhere behind me, officers yelled as they entered the woods, probably spreading out to find me and Casey.

Exhausted and experiencing a pain that rivaled childbirth, I was tempted to collapse onto the blanket of leaves and let the team resume the hunt for Casey.

But I pressed on. Having come to the bottom of one hill, I leveraged saplings and branches to pull myself up another.

Then, I spotted him.

Casey was crouched in the brush several yards ahead of me, looking back in the direction from which he'd come. He'd expected me to have followed him. The sun was mostly above the horizon now, and with the light that spilled under the cover of trees, I could see his face covered with blood.

Lowering myself to a kneeling position, I brought Casey into my gun's sight. The gun felt twice its normal weight in my hands, and I didn't feel confident I could make the shot.

He was too far. I was too exhausted and in too much pain.

The window of exposure was too tight.

Moving slowly to the right, I sought exposed rock and patches of dirt to muffle my steps.

Casey's profile was now sharply in view in the pale spill of dawn that had broken through the canopy of foliage.

I almost had the shot I needed.

Another step to the left.

And then another.

The branch that snapped under my foot was enough.

Casey turned. Both of us fired.

My shot pierced his side, but his found my arm. The round entered just above my elbow. It wasn't pain, but a jolt, as if someone behind me had just yanked a rope that had been tied around the arm.

The Glock fell from my grip, tumbling a few feet down the hill.

Someone yelled from far behind me. More shouts followed.

Casey stumbled and cursed, steadying himself against one of the trees. As I stooped to grab the dropped gun, the surge of pain was so great that I felt light headed momentarily, nearly fainting.

"Casey!" My voice cracked through the stillness as I struggled to take aim. "It doesn't have to happen like this."

But, of course it did.

"Traviesa!" he yelled, clutching his side and leaning against a trunk. It was no longer Casey's voice. The child that Casey had once been still lived deep within him. He'd grown into some kind of creature, driven by a fury that would no longer be contained.

Casey was pale beneath the mask of blood. He swayed and coughed. The fight in him was almost gone.

So was mine.

"Your good arm is not so good anymore, is it, Wren?"

He knew I now clutched Hale's Glock in my left hand, though I barely had strength to clutch it.

It was with my right hand that I'd thrown out runners from short.

I wrote with my right and favored it at the range.

But my right shoulder was now useless. It was a nucleus of pain and a fountain of blood.

The yells behind us were louder. Cops would swarm this area any minute.

"Game over, Wren," Casey said, lifting his arm.

Then, we both heard it. "Casey!" someone called from a small ridge above us.

I spotted Shaw, trained her gun in Casey's location. But she didn't have a shot. I could see her stepping to the side, trying to find a better angle.

"Drop your weapon," she shouted.

Casey pivoted and fell against the tree trunk, using it as cover as he swung his gun in Shaw's direction.

This was all I needed.

Casey was correct about my right arm.

But he'd forgotten from our time at the range—my left isn't bad either.

With one last squeeze of the trigger, I spent the last bit of energy I had, missing his chest but ripping through the side of his neck. I stepped toward Casey and tried to clench my finger on the trigger a second time, but my legs were giving out.

Dropping the gun, I hugged the nearest tree in slow collapse.

Casey took two stilted steps backward, clutching at where my shot had opened a hole in his neck. The blood pumped out from between his fingers.

His gun fell from the other hand.

Then he collapsed into a dried creek bed.

His head bounced twice against sandstone.

His body was still.

CHAPTER 43

The exhaustion, the blood loss, and the pain. It was all too much.

The woods swam around me as my vision narrowed.

Sunlight pierced the leaves.

Then the light and the trees blended. A luminescent green and brown fog filled my world.

And then everything went dark.

At some point later—seconds? minutes? hours?—I woke again.

Shaw crouched next to me, pulling at my arm. I didn't understand why she was pulling my arm.

"Shaw, stop pulling my …"

I woke again as they carried me like a casket. Radio chatter and heavy footsteps marked our journey up the hill and out of the woods. My body shifted on the gurney.

The sun had risen. I was out of the woods. I tried to shield my eyes, but my arms wouldn't move.

Shaw was near. I couldn't see her, but her voice said it was okay. Everything was okay now. I would be fine.

But I wasn't fine. It was cold. I'd never been so cold.

The voices around me—some of them were shouting. Was that Hollis? Was that Casey?

Then I remembered what Casey was.
And that I'd left my brother to chase him.
Wes …
My eyes closed again.

CHAPTER 44

"Mariston, Missouri, a town where Friday nights mean high school football, and Sunday means church bells." Stacey Southern's voice overlaid drone footage through the historic section of town along the Missouri.

When the footage cut to the reporter, she stood in the gravel lot outside the ballfield where Calvin Feltrop, Nick Wiley, and Agent Victor Hale had died.

It is the ballfield where my brother Wes and I almost died and where the mask fell from my partner's face.

"Yet," Southern continued, "new details continue to emerge following yesterday's dramatic conclusion to a multi-week homicide investigation that has shaken the Mariston community and raised questions about law enforcement oversight and trust."

Southern's expression was grave and her hair caught the early light. A graphic at the bottom of the screen read, ***SHADOWS OVER MARISTON***. The report had first aired yesterday evening, but I'd slept through it.

With my phone propped on the overbed table of my hospital room, I sipped from a small box of grape juice. I was saving the chocolate chip cookie as a treat for later.

"Authorities have confirmed that Mariston police detective Peter Casey was killed here, in the woods you see beyond this field. Detective Casey's death came during an armed confrontation with local officers early yesterday morning."

As Southern continued, the screen cut to a headshot of Casey that looked like it came from his Instagram profile. He's smiling and wearing a casual polo shirt, the open blue sky behind him.

"Detective Casey, who had been embedded with the Mariston Police Department for several years, is now believed to have been directly involved in the recent homicides."

The report continued over footage of Feltrop's house as Southern explained that Casey may not have acted alone. I hadn't been informed of everything that the team had learned in the last couple of days, but I did know they've since accessed the inside of Feltrop's house.

While the upstairs reflected the same obsessive neatness as the exterior, the basement revealed what we already knew. Instruments of pain had been neatly arranged on a workbench. Two chairs and concrete were stained with the blood of the men who had suffered there.

Hollis had stopped by to visit me earlier, but he'd left over an hour ago. Officer Ken Schwarze remained in the hallway nearby, posted to my room during the immediate aftermath of yesterday's violence.

Wes had his own room down the hall. He'd been stitched up, pumped full of medicine, and treated for an emerging infection. Feltrop's shot had entered and exited his body just west of his kidney.

In addition to my brother's severed earlobe, I'd learned that Feltrop had extracted one of Wes's teeth. He'd probably need to hunt down a good oral surgeon before it came time for the parish directory photos.

"Sources close to the department indicate that Detective Casey may have used his law-enforcement credentials—"

I swiped the feed off, laying my phone face-down on the bed cart. The story was too raw to process.

As for my own injuries, I had broken two lower ribs on my left side. My thigh was not broken, but the bruise was roughly the size and shape of Guam. Casey's bullet had grazed an artery in my arm, leaving a perforating wound.

Without Shaw's timely arrival, I might have bled out into the dirt. Using her shirt as a tourniquet, she'd stayed with me until additional help arrived. A trauma team took over for my ride to the hospital. I remember none of this.

Shaw had also taken shifts to relieve Ed, who'd insisted on staying with me through Sunday night. After passing out in the woods, I'd slept an almost unbroken sleep throughout the rest of Sunday and throughout most of Monday.

I don't remember dreaming during that time, but in the intermittent moments of medicated alertness, I had waking nightmares of Casey. One moment, I expected him to peek his head into the room, visiting to sit with Shaw or Hollis. And then I would have flashbacks of him looming over me, the barrel of his gun trained on my face.

Traviesa …

I was in the denial stages of a trauma-induced grief, my brain trying to reconcile that the two men were the same man.

How long would his ghost linger?

Following a quick three knocks, my door opened slowly. Dr. Lamothe peaked in. I hadn't met him in person, yet, but I found his picture on LinkedIn after I learned he'd sewn my arm back together.

"Good morning," he said, opening the door wider and stepping in. "Got your breakfast in and you look bright-eyed and bushy-tailed on a sunny Tuesday."

I looked around the room in fake confusion. "Oh, wait, you're talking to me? I'm the bright-eyed and bushy-tailed one?"

My left side flashed with pain when I spoke. Nothing but whispers for a bit.

"There's the funny girl this morning. That's a good sign."

The doctor's tie was a bit too wide and ended a bit too far above his belt. But that fit his overall look and personality, which was that of a high school principal from an '90s sitcom.

"So, everything's fine up here," he said, watching my vitals on a screen somewhere behind me and to my right. "Blood pressure is back up." Lamothe pulled back the sleeve of my hospital gown. "Suturing looks good. You're keeping this arm still, right?"

Both Lamothe and I heard three light taps and glanced back at the door. Ed pushed it open a few inches and peaked in.

"Oh, um, sorry. We can wait out here," Ed said, always deferential. Henry pushed his head into the gap between his dad and the door frame.

"Oh, no," Lamothe said, stepping aside so I'd be visible to my visitors. "That's not necessary. Mom?"

"Get in here," I said, my voice softer this time.

Ed took a seat in the recliner by the window, and Henry pulled up a smaller chair up next to my bed. Behind them, sunlight came in slices through the blinds.

Both of my men wore shorts and t-shirts. I should have warned them that the thermostat seems to be stuck on arctic in my room.

Henry's hand snaked under the sheet and found my left hand, holding it as Lamothe continued.

"I was about to explain to Mom that she'll be in here for at least a couple more days. The injury to her arm barely grazed the brachial artery, which is good news. Vascular spasm slowed the blood flow until someone secured a tourniquet."

Lamothe explained to Henry how arteries will sometimes constrict under trauma.

"Arteries take the blood away from the heart," Henry added. Ed patted him on the shoulder and gave me a wink.

"The bad news is you'll have some scarring and you're going to be in rough shape for quite a while." He gave a practiced grimace to Henry. "Mom's probably going to hang out with us for another couple days. Nothing strenuous for a good while after that."

"Mr. Muscles, here, can do the strenuous stuff." Ed squeezed Henry's shoulder.

"The ribs, unfortunately, are going to take at least two months. Nothing was displaced—some more good news—but you'll need to move slowly and as little as possible for a while."

Lamothe stayed with us a few minutes more, fielding questions, mostly from precocious Henry. Before leaving, he said he'd check on me a couple more times, but a general hospitalist would probably take over for the rest of my stay here.

Ed and Henry remained for a couple of hours while I drifted in and out of sleep. Their quiet chatter was a lifeline.

When they left, Ed paused at the door and then returned to my bed.

His eyes traced my bandaged body.

"I'd hug you right now, if I could."

"I would damage you if you tried."

He smiled. "I'll be back up later."

Then Ed bent over, and kissed me on the forehead, letting his lips linger. It was the way I'd check Henry's temperature when he was younger and ill.

"I'm proud of you," he whispered.

CHAPTER 45

During my time in the hospital, I worked on healing and binge-watching a reality show about Amish kids gone wild. When Shaw next visited, I'd just finished the episode where Urie and Jedediah went crazy one night and played a round of Overwatch while pounding Red Bulls.

I was glad to see her and wanted to hug her despite the pain it would cause.

She told me how great I looked, but I knew what she was here for.

While I slept through Monday, the survivors from Thunder had started talking.

"Winters opened up first." Shaw had pulled up a chair next to my bed, which I'd elevated as far as my ribs would tolerate. "He wasn't there when it happened," Shaw continued. "But he'd heard about it. He said all of the boys had."

I listened and sipped on the peanut-butter shake Shaw'd brought me. I can't comprehend being allergic to peanuts and lactose. I tried to convince her the shake was worth an EpiPen injection or two.

Winters had been on Shaw's list of men to check on Saturday night. When she'd arrived, he had been rattled and belligerent, at first. But when he realized the violence was coming to a head, he'd rambled his way into spilling the secret that the men from Thunder had kept for over three decades.

"None of the others from the team were there," Shaw said. "except the men who died."

It had taken place in the Wiley basement garage. Coach Dean wasn't home, and neither was Nick's mom. Woodhouse and Todd were there. So were Riedel and Russell.

Calvin Feltrop lived over two miles away and hadn't arrived when the rest of the boys had. He wouldn't even have been invited. Except Nick had an idea.

By way of alleyways and sidewalks, Feltrop made the trip in under twenty minutes.

"Winters said Feltrop was always trying to be part of the group," Shaw said.

By the time Feltrop dropped his bike in the front yard and rapped on the side door to the basement garage, the rest of the boys already had their shoulder tattoos finished.

Nick Wiley's older brother had an amateur tattoo kit that their dad didn't know about.

But Nick did. He'd shown it to the boys as they passed around the Pabst Blue Ribbon he'd sneaked from the basement fridge. His dad wouldn't notice just that one missing can.

Each of the boys showed Feltrop their tattoos, the word THUNDER with a small lightning bolt beneath it. This was the name coaches had chosen now that the Bulldogs were entering a competitive league.

Calvin should get a tattoo, too, the boys had told him.

What they didn't tell Calvin Feltrop, however, was that they'd used a fine-tip permanent marker for theirs.

"That's what I learned from Ted Dabrowski," she said. Ted had played for the team from its start. "He was more forthcoming than Winters after he realized I'd learned about the incident."

Dabrowski had informed Shaw that the boys had tried to persuade Calvin, even offering him some of the beer.

"Supposedly he agreed, at first."

"He wanted to be part of the group," I whispered.

"Yeah, but Dabrowski thinks he resisted when they started. That he tried to leave." Shaw explained that, from what the survivors heard, the other boys had held Calvin Feltrop down and finished the job.

Steve Winters had assured Shaw that he wasn't cool with what he heard they had done, as had the other surviving members of the team. But, yet, for fear of their reputations, they'd kept a secret that could have saved Hale and Nick and Dean Wiley.

He said that there were other things they'd done to harass Feltrop over those two seasons.

"But this was probably what broke him," Shaw said. "Especially after his dad found out."

After she learned about the incident in the garage, Shaw had the leverage she needed to coax more of the story from them.

When Nick finished injecting ink into Calvin's arm, one of the boys held Mrs. Wiley's handheld mirror so that Feltrop could see his shoulder.

But it wasn't the word THUNDER, and it wasn't a lightning bolt.

Of course, the word PENIS was reversed in the reflection, but Feltrop surely knew what they had written into his skin and what they had drawn underneath.

Winters and the others said that Feltrop kept the mark hidden for a long time. Even when the team had a swim party after one of the tournaments, he'd kept his shirt on.

'Did you know what Eli Feltrop did to Cal when he found out? Casey had said to Nick Wiley before putting two bullets in him. *Or what he did to my mamma when she tried to stop him?*

Winters and the others knew something awful happened when Feltrop's dad discovered the tattoo. Rod Holtzer, who mostly played outfield, claimed to have seen the large, indented scar tissue that we found just under Feltrop's shoulder after he was loaded onto an autopsy table.

"The worst part for me," Holtzer had told Shaw, "was that I heard the little brother was there, too. He'd followed Cal and watched through a window when they did that to his brother."

Did Coach Wiley know about what his son and the others had done? Probably not, but the men Shaw interviewed think that was what the argument was about when Eli Feltrop pulled his son from the team.

When I'd found the clippings and notes at Wiley's house that early Sunday morning, I hadn't had time to look thoroughly through everything. Among the items in the nightstand drawer, the investigators found a homemade baseball card like the one Dean's son Nick had received.

CHAPTER 46

The church was packed. I sat in the back pew.

A family with three kids sat to my right, and a woman in a wheelchair rolled into a handicapped space to my left.

I'd gotten a few glances from the parishioners around me. They knew the story. But I wasn't the one they were here to see.

This was Wes's first day back from sabbatical—two weeks away in retreat at a Benedictine monastery in Illinois. Not only did Wes come back renewed, he'd apparently written five chapters in a book about his experience. I know because his first phone call to me after returning was to run prospective titles past me.

Among them:

The Book of Lobe

The Tooth Shall Set You Free

And my personal favorite: *Ear Me, Oh Lord!*

His working subtitle: *How I Survived a Serial Killer and My Sister Kicked His Ass.*

The monks should dial back their program.

The Gospel reading, from the book of *Matthew*, included an exhortation to the apostles to proclaim the Kingdom of Heaven and heal the sick. Behind the lector, Wes sat with his head lowered as he listened.

Henry appeared at the end of the pew and stumbled over the family's knees to get to me.

"There wasn't any toilet paper," he whispered.

I sniffed. He was in the clear, but I didn't want to think about how he'd solved that problem.

The lector finished, bowed to the tabernacle, and returned to his pew.

As we stood for the *Alleluia*, I saw the family to my right shifting again as Ed squeezed past them, apologizing in whispers.

"Sorry I'm late," he whispered to me over Henry's head during the congregation's response. Then, sheepishly: "Got a ticket just inside city limits."

After pulling Henry against his side, he reached further with the same hand and gave me a quick scratch on the back.

We all sat as Wes approached the pulpit.

"Good morning, my friends," he said, "and welcome to my first mass back—proof that even a priest with a missing ear can still hear the call to serve!"

Wes paused for the polite chuckles from the pews.

"They're just laughing because he's a priest," I said to Ed. The man in front of me threw a glance over his shoulder. "I've always been the funny one," I whispered to the man. He shook his head and returned focus to the homily.

Even if I had found Wes hilarious, I refused to laugh. I was only three weeks out from my hospital stay. My ribs weren't completely cool with unpredictable lung action.

Luckily, Henry sat to my right. On that side, I could handle it when he nuzzled against me.

During that time, Henry also took my hand and Ed's, putting them together and holding them in his.

As the homily continued, Wes discussed the nature of evil and suffering in the world. He made only vague allusions to his time in a basement with Calvin Feltrop and Pete Casey.

Wes gestured to a mural of the parish namesake above us on the front of the choir loft. In it, St. George brandished a sword as a dragon leered over him.

"There were beasts among us, weren't there?" Wes said, near the end of his homily. "He slouched down the road to our community. To our parish. But St. George defeated *that* dragon, and …" Wes made eye contact with me across the heads of his parishioners. "And we defeated ours."

After church, Ed, Henry, and I waited off to the side as the parishioners swarmed their hero priest.

Then we went as a family to the Regensburg café.

I ordered the Patty Cline Melt and Henry got the Reba Mac-N-Cheese.

Suzette flirted big tips out of Wes and Ed, and for the first time since waking up in a hospital bed, I felt whole.

CHAPTER 47

Earlier in my career, I wondered if I should attend the funerals of those who died on our watch. But then I realized that our presence is a reminder of what the grieving survivors would just as soon forget.

I didn't attend the burials of James Woodhouse, Brody Todd, or J.T. Russell. I wasn't there to watch Curtis Riedel or Nick Wiley lowered into the ground.

Shaw and I did drive to Illinois for Hale's funeral. We sat in the back pew of the Presbyterian church where he'd attended. His brother gave an elegy before the service and then returned to the pew, sitting by his wife. Next to her was Hale's sister and her husband. All of this I inferred from the program, which also said that the agent was survived by his mother, Bessie, his daughter, Charlee, and his grand-daughter, Rose.

Charlee held the infant Rose throughout the service.

That night, I wrote Rose a letter, telling her about what kind of hero her grandfather was.

Officer Jaycee Lachance was buried in Mariston two days later, receiving military honors for service in the national guard.

Because she was just sitting in her car during a slow overnight watch, LaChance's body cam was not recording when she died.

Surely, she would have started it if she'd been threatened somehow.

The toxicology reports had not come back for her death outside Nick Wiley's house. But there had been a near-empty coffee cup in her console, even though she'd brought a thermos.

I imagined it to have happened this way:

Three raps on the window, and Lachance starts and then sighs with relief. There's a mechanical hum as the window lowers.

"Didn't mean to scare you, Muñequita," the voice says. It's some sort of flirty nickname like that. "Brought you some caffeine to help with the night duty."

They chat for a while. He makes her laugh. Eventually he leaves. She sips more coffee. Her eyes close and open slowly. Eventually, they close and don't open again.

Over these weeks, I've second-guessed every missed clue. And as I healed, I had time to reflect on Casey's role in the investigation.

He had been the gatekeeper between me and so many of our deep dives and interviews.

"Why do you think Casey recommended you for the case," I'd asked Shaw during one of her visits to my hospital room.

"I know exactly why." She looked at the window for a moment before answering. "He thought I was another thing he'd be able to control. Because of our …"

"He underestimated you," I told her, holding up my hand, which Shaw clasped. "So did Agent Hale. And so did I."

After my dismissal from the hospital, I'd begun retracing our notes. In the profile on Calvin Feltrop that Casey had supplied, he'd noted that Eli Feltrop had lived with various women after the early death of Calvin's mother.

But he lived with one of those women for much longer than any other. Isabella Verdugo. She and a man named Quinton Casey are listed on the birth certificate for their son, Peter.

During his time living undercover in the narcotics division, Casey had taken on the persona of a man named Pedro Verduga.

None of the men from Thunder recall knowing Isabella. Nor did they have any memory of what happened to her when she tried to stop Eli Feltrop from carving the family's shame from Calvin's shoulder.

Whatever Eli did to her, it was something very bad. And a little boy named Pete Casey had watched that, too.

We, all of us, are a product of our childhood.

Henry slept in his room now. Ed was probably doing the same at his condo. We've started working on things again during my leave. Tonight, we went as a family to watch a movie. Henry ordered Milk Duds, which he shared with me.

This evening felt good, but my leave ended in a few weeks. What then?

I tried to banish these thoughts as I walked toward the bedroom. Changing into my nightshirt, I pulled torn ticket stubs and a flattened candy box out of my jeans pocket.

In the back of our closet, I retrieved one of two shoeboxes stacked in the corner, under where my winter clothes hang. Placing the lid on the carpet next to me, I folded the candy carton flat, pressing it and the ticket into a pile of items already in the box.

A to-go bag from El Rincón.

A bulletin from St. George.

My hospital bracelet.

A feather from Wagner Creek …

ABOUT THE AUTHOR

Raymond Bruce is the pen name of Spencer Allen, who lives in the Midwest with his wife, kids, and his passive-aggressive dog. He can be reached by email at contactspencerallen@gmail.com

ACKNOWLEDGMENTS

I came up with the idea for this book while dipping back in the classroom to teach a couple of sessions of creative writing. Thank you to my students for inspiring me to get back to the keyboard.

Thank you to everyone who read all or part of this book and gave valuable feedback, including Sheri Wieberg, Erin Polson, Randy England, Mike Broker, Destiny Blume, Linda Gruchala, Elaine Hassemer, Leslie Patterson, Rebecca Cassmeyer, Stacy Gier, Sr. Jean Dietrich, Denise Noonan, and Sarah Kempker. My high school English teacher, Laramie Thompson not only encouraged me as a writer back in my teens, but she recently caught a few remaining errors in my late drafts, and she provided the voice of Sara Wren for an audio version at the Wolfner Library for individuals with vision impairments, blindness, or other disabilities that present challenges with print materials. Thank you especially to Det. Jason Ambler and author Richard McGonegal for early feedback and encouragement.

Finally, I want to show appreciation for my law enforcement friends back home. The PD where I live are all in for our community and have always had our back at my day job. I wanted Detective Wren to be someone they'd have on the team.

www.ingramcontent.com/pod-product-compliance
Lightning Source LLC
LaVergne TN
LVHW020702110826
845149LV00012B/2068

* 9 7 9 8 9 9 2 9 3 2 6 2 1 *